Rooted in Deceit

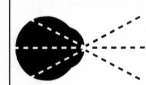

This Large Print Book carries the
Seal of Approval of N.A.V.H.

GREENHOUSE MYSTERIES

ROOTED IN DECEIT

WENDY TYSON

WHEELER PUBLISHING
A part of Gale, a Cengage Company

GALE
A Cengage Company

Farmington Hills, Mich • San Francisco • New York • Waterville, Maine
Meriden, Conn • Mason, Ohio • Chicago

Wheeler Publishing Large Print Cozy Mystery.
The text of this Large Print edition is unabridged.
Other aspects of the book may vary from the original edition.
Set in 16 pt. Plantin.

LIBRARY OF CONGRESS CIP DATA ON FILE.
CATALOGUING IN PUBLICATION FOR THIS BOOK
IS AVAILABLE FROM THE LIBRARY OF CONGRESS

ISBN-13: 978-1-4328-6352-4 (softcover)

Published in 2019 by arrangement with Henery Press, LLC

Printed in Mexico
1 2 3 4 5 6 7 23 22 21 20 19

For Angela.
I am very blessed to have you as my
mother and my friend.

ACKNOWLEDGMENTS

Special thanks to my fabulous agent, Frances Black, and everyone at Henery Press, especially Kendel Lynn and Art Molinares. You made this book possible.

A big thanks to Rowe Carenen, Larissa Ackerman, and Claire McKinney for your marketing and public relations expertise — and your inspiring love of books.

A warm thank you to my childhood friend Marnie Mai for going with me to all of those spas over the years. By the time I wrote this book, my vision of the fictional Center was firmly set. (There is no one I'd rather go to a real spa with, Marnie!)

Thanks to my husband, Ben Pickarski, for your gardening know-how and seemingly endless patience with the earth and my questions.

Thank you to my son Matthew for helping me with the logistics behind this fictional murder.

A big thank you to Mandy, Ian, and Jonathan for all of the support — online and offline.

And finally, thank you to my mother-in-law, Ann Marie Pickarski, for the food chats and vegetarian recipe shares. No matter what you make, it's always delicious.

ONE

Megan spread stain across the new barn's fascia with slow strokes, watching the thick Indian Summer red bleed into unprimed wood. The day was hot and humid, a soupy late August afternoon that teased a cooling rain but delivered little more than sweat and sunburn. Megan wiped her hand on her denim overalls. She wished her farm manager, Clay Hand, would hurry. She was impatient to see how the interior of the new barn looked.

According to Clay, Washington Acres Farm already had enough reservations for the next Saturday's wood-fired pizza event to pay for the pizza oven — an oversized stone monstrosity that Clay had built by hand in his spare time over the course of the spring and summer. Now Clay and his sister Clover, Megan's store manager, were putting the finishing touches on the serving area while Megan and her farmhand, Brian

Porter, completed the last of the exterior painting. Clay and Clover wanted to surprise her with the look of the new restaurant. Seemed it was a week for surprises.

"Ready!" Clover said a few minutes later. The twenty-something wore a pair of khaki cargo shorts and a sage green tank top. Her long, thick hair was imprisoned in a tortoiseshell clip and escaped strands clung to her face and neck. One thing the new pizza farm didn't have yet was air conditioning, which was being installed later that day, and it showed in Clover's red complexion and soaked shirt.

Megan quickly washed the brush with cold, soapy water using a bucket and the hose. She dried the brush and placed it next to the can on the lawn to dry, anxious to join Clover. Last she saw the interior, the new barn had still been cavernous and barren, a stark wooden structure with high ceilings, a bathroom at one end, the oven at the other, and a lot of empty space. Before that it contained unused horse stalls that doubled as storage units. The pizza farm had been Clay's vision for that section of the barn for a long time. It was finally coming to fruition.

"Close your eyes." Clover took Megan's arm and led her through the red entry door.

She positioned Megan gently. "Voila."

Megan opened her eyes. She let out a long, slow whistle. "Wow. Just wow."

The barn had been transformed. The space was filled with cedar picnic tables painted in primary colors: scarlet, lapis lazuli, turquois, and yellow. Atop each one was a Mason jar filled with blossoms — sunflowers, lavender, daylilies, and dahlias — from the farm's abundant flower gardens. The rafters overhead had been strung with tiny white lights, giving the place a cozy, festive feel. Two paintings, a landscape and a portrait both painted by Thana Moore — a local artist and long-ago friend — had been hung on the walls. While Megan had mixed feelings about the artist, she was happy to see Clover and Clay had found a use for the art, which until then had sat propped against a wall in her office. The stone hearth, on which sat the giant wood oven, rooted the eye, pulling it the length of the barn. A large dinner plate clock and wooden forks and spoons hung on the upper part of the hearth. "Washington Acres" was painted on the clock in red block letters.

"This looks amazing." Megan wandered around, touching everything.

A new hostess station sat near the barn

entrance. Clay had gone over a basic pine frame with milk-white paint. A chalkboard propped against the barn wall listed the pizza menu. A laptop computer sat alongside a Mason jar full of pens, a large bouquet of flowers, and an easel on which Clover had painted " 'Laughter is brightest where food is best.' –Irish Proverb."

"I can't believe it. You did it," Megan said, clapping. After months of suggestions, hints, and proposals, Megan had finally caved in to their insistence that the town needed a wood-fired pizza venue. She'd used the farm's meagre savings to fund the new pizza farm amidst promises from Clay that he, Clover, and Porter could build the main structure and oven for a pittance. It hadn't quite been a pittance — to her and her grandmother, Bonnie "Bibi" Birch, at least — but it *had* been an impressively low sum of money for something like this.

Megan hugged Clay, then Clover. "I absolutely love it."

"I told you," Clay said. "If you build it, they will come."

"You already have a full house coming next Saturday." Clover used a parchment paper menu to fan herself. "And you haven't even opened yet."

"Want to try out the oven?" Clay asked.

12

"Are you offering to make dinner?" Megan smiled.

"I am." Clay scrunched up his nose. "Do you want to invite . . . everyone?"

"That'll be a party," Clover's words dripped with sarcasm.

Megan sighed. "We should. Can't exactly exclude one person." Much as we might like to, she thought. She looked around the barn. It seemed large enough to house everyone's ego.

Clay wiped his hair back from his face with large, slender hands. Clay was a strikingly handsome man in his early twenties. He looked like a rugged Jake Gyllenhaal with long hair and a warm smile. "We can get streamers and balloons. A homecoming celebration."

"A homecoming, indeed." Only Megan wasn't thinking streamers and balloons. She was thinking ear plugs, Tylenol, and convenient hiding places.

"Megan." Sylvia Adriana Altamura air-kissed each of Megan's cheeks with perfectly rouged lips. "Darling, it's so lovely to be here, at your quaint homestead. This farm is gloriously antiquated. Charming, truly. One would never really know how close to bankruptcy it was." Sylvia kissed Clay, tak-

ing a little longer than seemed necessary. "Edward has said many kind things about you." She looked from Clay to Clover and back again. "About all of you."

"I'm sure," Bibi responded. Megan's grandmother's face was curled tight as a newly sprouted fiddlehead fern. "And we've heard so little about you."

Megan shot Bibi a look. While Sylvia was saying all the right things, her flat tone and constant blinking seemed to tell another story. *But maybe I'm biased,* Megan thought. Bibi certainly was. Megan's father's new wife — the woman her father had left Washington Acres and Bibi for — was not exactly the person they'd envisioned her father would choose. Not because of Sylvia's appearance, certainly. In her mid-fifties, she was tiny — barely breaking five-feet tall — with long, straightened, red hair in a shade nature had never intended, a prominent nose, thin, expertly painted lips, and hooded green eyes. Her look was sensuous, her personality . . . challenging. She had a way of standing tall, neck and head extended, eyes sharp, surveying everything around her with a judgmental gaze and a quick, biting comment. She exuded confidence and entitlement. So much so that Megan wondered what she saw in her father, Eddie Birch.

Eddie Birch — Megan had called him Eddie since she could remember — was known for many things. His casual good looks and easygoing personality. Being a dreamer. An infectious laugh. Not finishing anything he started. But he was *not* known for his good judgment or his wealth, so being the husband of a successful Milanese boutique owner seemed a stretch. And while Megan was trying hard to play nicely in the sandbox, Bibi had thrown the toys out with the sand. She and Sylvia seemed to take an instant dislike to one another. Maybe because Bibi still resented the way Eddie had left the farm on an impulse two-plus years ago to chase after Sylvia and Italy. Maybe because their personalities conflicted. Maybe a little of both. If Eddie noticed, he wasn't letting on.

"How was your flight?" Clover asked.

Eddie took the cue and regaled them with stories of multi-continental travel woes while Sylvia corrected him at every turn. They sat in the barn around two picnic tables that had been pulled together. Clay had prepared five pizzas, and he brought the first of them to the table. It looked and smelled amazing, a succulent mixture of rich tomato sauce, locally-made cheeses, and Washington Acres spinach, onions, and peppers on a chewy-crispy, smoky crust.

"So this is what all the fuss was about," Bibi said, digging in. "Now I get it."

"Amazing," Clover muttered. "So good."

"Americans are so enamored with a cheese-heavy version of pizza." Sylvia picked a pepper off her slice and pushed it to the side with sharp fingernails. "In Italy, the ingredients make the dish. No need for —"

"It's perfect, sweetheart," Eddie said to Megan. He glanced at Clay. "Delicious."

Sylvia pursed her lips, mirroring Bibi's inverted smile.

"A toast," Eddie said. He stood, his white linen shirt billowing in the light breeze from the new split-system air conditioner. "To family reunions and new endeavors." His gaze landed on Megan, and the warmth of his smile made her blush. "You took a failing farm and turned it into a treasure. I feel the love, pumpkin. I feel the Birch spirit. I'm so proud of you and all you've accomplished."

"Hear! Hear!" Bibi tapped her glass against Megan's.

Wine and beer were flowing and there were toasts all around. Only Sylvia sat quietly, observing, her hand cradling the base of her wine goblet.

When the pizza had disappeared and Bibi looked drawn, Megan said, "Shall we head inside? Your room is ready, Eddie. I put your bags upstairs, and there are fresh towels and quilts in the dresser."

"Oh, we can't stay here. Edward told you that, yes?" Sylvia's eyes widened. She tilted her head toward Eddie, who seemed suddenly intent on studying the lines on Thana Moore's landscape painting. "We have reservations at Peaceful Summit Yoga Retreat Center and Spa."

"You're not staying with us?" Bibi stared at her son, openmouthed. "When I found out you had flown in, I made biscuits and gravy for tomorrow, your favorite, Eddie. And homemade biscotti for Sylvia."

It was Sylvia who answered. "I'm afraid this is a business trip, Bonnie. Edward should have told you that. I'm going to meet with local artists and artisans so I may bring some assets back to Milan." She looked at Eddie for confirmation, but his fingers were twisting around his napkin, an activity that seemed to require all of his attention.

Bibi said, "Eddie?"

Sylvia's smile was hard. "I made reservations at the Center. It's new. It's a business expense. We will see you for dinner later in the week, perhaps?"

"Oh," Bibi said, crestfallen. "I thought Eddie and I would spend this time together."

"I'm afraid that's not possible." If Sylvia was picking up on Bibi's disappointment, or if she cared, she didn't let it show. "Eddie is coming to the Center."

Megan watched the all too familiar way her father dealt with conflict — by escaping. He stood, kissed his wife on the forehead, and then gave Bibi a quick peck on the cheek. "I need to get our things," he mumbled. He nodded to Megan, avoiding her eyes.

"Yes, good." Sylvia sipped the last of her wine, scanning the faces around her with a fierce intensity. "The pizza was nice. Too cheesy, perhaps. And watch the sausage. It overwhelms the palate."

Clay gave her a half smile. "Thanks for the feedback."

Sylvia waved a hand languidly toward the paintings on the walls. Her gaze lingered on the portrait. "That artist. Thana Moore. I recognize her work. She's scheduled to show at the Center. I want her pieces to take back to Milan."

That was interesting. Megan hadn't seen her old friend Thana in ages — since that craft fair years ago. Before Mick died. Before Megan's life changed forever.

"I've heard Thana's work is tough to get these days. We bought these back when she was a nobody." Megan stared at that portrait, trying to keep her feelings out of her words. "You may need to order something well in advance if you really want a piece of her art."

Sylvia merely smiled. "I think she'll accommodate my requests. I look forward to meeting her."

"You're used to things going your way, aren't you?" Bibi asked, with no apparent attempt to hide the bitterness in her voice.

Sylvia glanced in the direction of the entry door, the very door through which Eddie had just exited. Her face darkened, although the shadow passed so quickly that Megan thought perhaps she'd imagined it. Finally, Sylvia said, "Yes, Bonnie. They generally do."

Megan found her father in the upstairs hall, outside the room he'd once shared with Megan's mother, Charlotte. Since Charlotte abandoned her family more than two decades ago, the room had been vacant. Back then Eddie, suddenly finding himself to be the too-young single father of a daughter under ten, had moved to a guest room. Their marital quarters remained empty for years, until Eddie relocated to Italy. After that, Bibi, not one for overt sentimentality but a great holder of grudges, made it into a sewing room. Any traces of young Charlotte Birch had been swept out with the dust bunnies.

"I met her, you know." Megan moved down the darkened hall toward her father. She watched him breathe deeply, square his shoulders. Always preparing for flight, it seemed. Even when there was no enemy in sight. "My mother, I mean."

Eddie's eyes widened slightly. "Oh?"

"Christmastime. Last year."

"Not since?"

"No. Not since."

"That's your mother, I guess." Eddie put his hand against the heavy wooden door and removed it quickly, as though the surface had burned him. "Unreliable."

"She wrote me a letter."

"She remarried, Megan. Has a new family." His words were almost a whisper. "I don't want you to get hurt."

"I know about her other children. And as for getting hurt, it's a little late for that."

Eddie picked up the suitcase that sat on the worn runner and nodded. "Well, then."

Just like Eddie, Megan thought. Leaving when the going gets tough. But, she reminded herself, he was the one who stayed all those years ago when Charlotte disappeared.

Megan said, "Do you really have to leave?"

"Sylvia made reservations. We just came for the evening, to freshen up and say hello."

"You can change those reservations."

Her father gave her a sad smile. "I don't think so, Megan."

"Bibi —"

Eddie's hand shot up. His eyes pleaded for understanding. "Sylvia's a good woman, Megan. I know she can seem high strung, but she's a visionary. She sees the positive where others see only failure, possibility where others see futility. She has a sharp eye for business."

"You love her?"

"Yes," Eddie replied. "Very much."

Failure and futility. As Megan watched her father disappear into the guest room to retrieve their bags, she wasn't so sure it was really Sylvia's business savvy he was referring to.

Two

Megan was still thinking about her father on Monday morning while she, Clay, and Porter attended to the farm chores. The tomato harvest had been strong despite the worst drought in years, and the trio undertook the painstaking process of pulling tiny cherry tomatoes off their vines. Although it wasn't even nine, the sun beat down with the brutality of a feudal overlord, and the air was thick with sticky moisture. Megan wiped her brow with the back of a gloved hand and glanced toward the house. Bibi was baking — her way of dealing with emotional turmoil — and the kitchen was scented with cloves, cinnamon, and vanilla. A glass of iced tea and a scone would taste good about now, but Megan had promised herself she'd work in the fields until noon. If only she could focus.

Clay knelt on the ground beside her and began plucking plump little yellow tomatoes with quick, deft motions. He popped one into his mouth.

"Still angry at your father?" he asked, chewing.

Megan smiled despite herself. Clay had always been good at reading people, but they'd spent a lot of time together over the past two years. He was getting damn good at reading her.

Megan gently placed a handful of tomatoes in the basket and stood, stretching. Gunther, her Polish Tatra Sheepdog rescue given to her by the town's veterinarian, Megan's boyfriend Dr. Daniel "Denver" Finn, lay to the side of the field, his attention trained on her. Beside him, Megan's mutt Sadie lay chewing a tennis ball: mouth on the ball, gaze on Gunther. Megan knew it would take only the slightest indication from Gunther that he wanted to play and Sadie would be off in a sprinting mass of joy. She lived to play, eat, and sleep . . . and in that order.

If only people were so simple.

"Angry with Eddie?" Megan said. "No. Yes. Oh, I don't know — maybe." Megan stomped a foot against the dirt. "He's only been back for a day and already I'm frustrated."

"With him or with her?"

"Her?"

Clay's look was one of amused exasperation. "Sylvia."

"How can I be angry with Sylvia? I don't even know her."

"And how can you get to know her if she won't spend time with the family?"

Megan shrugged. "It's her choice."

"You feel hurt. Your father left Bibi and this farm to be with Sylvia and she doesn't have the decency to spend a few days getting to know his family." Clay smiled to soften his next words. "She's kind of . . . mean."

Megan felt her shoulders slump. "You're right. Of course you're right. How could I not feel disappointed in Sylvia? It's the first time she's meeting our family, she could make some effort. And I guess I'm annoyed at my father for being spineless. He's always taken the path of least resistance, but I thought maybe he'd changed." Megan frowned. "You saw how upset Bibi was. She doesn't ask for much. And she's in there now baking enough scones to feed everyone in the tri-state area."

"I've eaten three this morning. She brought them out with a pot of coffee at the crack of dawn." He pulled a dozen or so tomatoes off the vine, letting the sounds of the farm fill the void. When he finally spoke again, he didn't look at Megan but continued to harvest tomatoes. "Is that what this is really about, Megan? Their trip to the Center? Bibi's reaction?"

Megan pulled her gloves off and studied her hands. "No."

Clay turned toward her. His eyes probed, persistent but kind. "Your mother?"

"My mother. My childhood. My desire to have one parent who's reliable. I have a runaway mother, a ne'er-do-well father, and now the quintessential mean stepmother." Megan laughed. "I sound about ten years old, don't I?"

"You sound human. And you have a right to your feelings." Clay stood. He bent backwards, and Megan heard his spine crack. "Go to the Center. Talk to him. Get to know Sylvia." His smile was warm. "If they're too busy to stay here, go there."

Megan considered this. They had a ton to do around the farm, but she could get away for a few hours tomorrow. That would give Sylvia and her father time to themselves first. She'd make reservations at the spa's new restaurant and take them to lunch. Megan pictured her father from the night before: defeated, sad, torn. Yes, she'd go meet them, alone. Without Bibi this time.

Without the pressure of the farm — and the reminders it surely wrought.

"You're pretty wise for someone so young," Megan said.

Clay laughed, and Megan liked the way his eyes crinkled. He'd make someone a good companion someday, she thought. She had to remind herself he was only in his mid-twenties, wise beyond his tender years. An old soul, for sure.

"Glad I could help."

Gunther let out a bark and took off toward the front of the property, tail waving wildly. Sadie ran after him, nipping at his ankles.

"Reaction like that from Gunther can only mean one thing," Clay said.

"Denver." Megan smiled.

The veterinarian wasn't due back from his trip for another day. Megan knew she should take her time cleaning up the garden tools, but she sprinted after the dogs instead.

"Megs!" Denver spun her around. He placed her gently back on the ground and kissed her. Stepping back, he said, "You're a sight to behold, with your dirty nose and your bonnie smile." Wiping the dirt off her nose with his thumb, he said, "Did ye miss me?" Denver's Scottish accent seemed even stronger — perhaps the result of his trip to his homeland.

Megan kissed him, longer this time. "As a matter of fact, I did." She took him by the hand and led him toward the house. Bibi would be happy to see him — almost as happy as Gunther had been. Denver had saved the pup from the hands of an abusive owner, and while Megan was the dog's true love, Denver would be his forever friend.

About ten feet from the porch entrance, Denver paused. "Megan, before we go in, I want to talk to you. Alone."

His tone made the hairs on Megan's neck stand up. Requests for private conversation from someone you loved were rarely a good thing.

"Sure, what's up?" She forced an airiness she didn't feel.

"It's my sister. She insisted I not come to Scotland. You know that, Megs. Said things were 'just fine.' " Denver sighed. It was then that Megan noticed the hollows under his eyes, the three days' growth of auburn beard on his strong chin. Denver's was a handsome face. Not pretty, but with enough furrows and lines and chiseled planes to be dangerously sexy. It had always been those blue eyes that captivated her, and they were holding her hostage now. He frowned.

"Things are very much not fine."

Megan waited. Denver's sister, his only real family other than his aunt who lived in Winsome, an aunt he nearly lost nine months prior, had been in a terrible car accident. He'd flown to Scotland against her wishes. Now, it seemed, the promises that her injuries had been minor had been said to reassure, not convey truth. Megan tightened her grip on Denver's hand. He squeezed back.

"Broken ribs. A sprained neck. Flesh wounds from the glass. No companion to help her, no kids around. It nearly killed me to leave her like that, but I had to get back and get the practice in order." Those blue eyes searched for understanding. "She needs me, Megs. For a bit, I think."

Megan felt the twinge tugs of pride and disappointment. No Denver? Just when she'd gotten used to having him in her life.

"You need to go," she said. "Of course you do."

"You understand, then. You won't be cross with me?"

Megan laughed at the serious glint in his eyes. "Of course not. I'll miss you, is all. When are you flying back to Scotland?"

"On Wednesday."

"That soon?"

"Aye. I have a nurse lined up to help her until then. I'm hoping to stay a fortnight, then if she's doing better, we'll arrange for another nurse's aide to help her out thereafter."

A fortnight. That wasn't so bad. Although he'd already been gone over two weeks.

"I'm sorry," Megan said. "About your sister. I know how much Eileen means to you."

"Ta." From the barn, Porter's voice called out, an admonition to Heidi, one of the Pygmy goats. Denver smiled — he had a soft spot for the goats — but his smile seemed wistful. "Come with me, Megs. Meet Eileen. See Scotland."

Megan felt herself tensing again. She wanted to go with him. Oh, how she wanted to drop everything and get on that plane, strapping in next to this man who'd been such a surprise in her life. He was leaving everything for someone he loved, why couldn't she? But how *could* she? How could she leave the farm during one of the busiest seasons of the year? How could she leave Bibi, or the café, or the animals? The new pizza farm? And what about Eddie and Sylvia? There she was complaining to Clay that they weren't spending time with her or Bibi and she was contemplating leaving them altogether during their one visit to the United States.

Denver was studying her, waiting. He rarely asked for much. His job, like hers, was demanding. A labor of love and commitment. Her heart screamed yes, but Megan, a lawyer by training and a farmer by choice, was a woman of the mind. And the gut. And both said she needed to stay.

"I wish I could, Denver. You understand."

His look said he understood all too well. He'd always be second in her life — second to Washington Acres. Second to her obligations.

Someday, Megan was afraid, second wouldn't be good enough.

The rest of Monday flew by, and by late afternoon, Megan, two crates of fresh vegetables, and a dozen scones arrived at the Washington Acres Larder & Café. After putting the scones out for her staff — their chef, Alvaro Hernandez, and Clover Hand — Megan began placing the tomatoes, Swiss chard, red peppers, lettuces, and cabbage heads in the café's walk-in refrigerator.

"Where is everyone?" she asked. Normally the café was a hub for the locals. Mealtimes were always crowded. Alvaro's simple but flavorful farm-to-table dishes brought people from Winsome and neighboring towns as well as tourists from New York and New Jersey, but despite the near dinner hours, the café was empty. Megan glanced at the chalkboard announcing tonight's fare. Roasted beet and goat cheese salad. Seared chicken breasts with chimichurri sauce, rice and beans, and fried plantains. Late summer vegetable stew served with Bibi's biscuits. A local cheese selection with baguettes and fig jam. Not too shabby for a hole-in-the-wall café behind an organic food store.

Clover mumbled something with a mouthful of orange scone.

Megan squinted in her direction. "Say again?"

Clover pointed across the room, to a stack of papers sitting on the café's long counter. Megan walked through the kitchen and into the dining area of the café. She picked up the top paper. Her eyes scanning the sheet, she sat down heavily at one of the café's copper-topped tables. It seemed her father and his wife were not the only people spending time at the Center.

Clover picked up another scone. "Today's the restaurant's grand opening."

Megan nodded. "I see that."

"And their dinner tasting is free."

"I see that too."

"That's where everyone is."

Megan's eyes widened. "I get that, Clover. Thank you."

Megan re-read the brochure. Indeed, it looked a lot like the free tasting Megan had hosted at the café when it first opened. Even the menu was similar. Suddenly Megan was thinking about the pizza farm Clay had built. They were counting on that to help keep the farm afloat during the long winter months, but if the Center became a local hotspot, both the café and pizza restaurant would suffer. Had she taken on more than the town's economy could shoulder? The Center could be real competition. It was twelve miles away — she'd checked — so hopefully the draw was the free food, emphasis on *free.*

Perhaps she had more reason to visit tomorrow than simply seeing her father and Sylvia.

Megan looked up at Clover. "Why are these brochures even here?"

A guilty shadow passed over Clover's face. "I put them there for Alvaro."

"Alvaro?"

Clover flashed an apologetic smile. "Maria got a job at the Center. She's an event coordinator. It's a big deal for her and

Alvaro. Maria's coordinating the art show the Center is holding in the Meditation Gallery. That's what they call it — the gallery. Pretentious, right? I really didn't see the Center as competition." She waved a hand toward the empty café. "I'm sorry, Megan. I really am."

Megan nodded, thinking. People liked new things, and the Center had been a buzz in the town for the last few months, since it announced its official opening date. More jobs in the area. A free meal. And attention for local artists and practitioners. Winsome townsfolk were understandably curious. And she could understand Clover's desire to help Alvaro and his wife, Maria. They were like surrogate parents to Clover and Clay.

"I have to believe that once the newness wears off, Winsome residents won't choose a twenty-minute drive to get their dinner."

Clover nodded. "I'm sure you're right." She paused. "Have you driven by the Center yet?"

"No, why?"

"It's really beautiful. Rolling pastures, fields of sunflowers and wildflowers, wooded hills, acres of walking trails. Horse barns. Classes on everything from yoga to Zen meditation to ethnobotany and Pilates. The

Meditation Gallery — that's the yoga and meditation building — is to die for." Clover looked wistful. "Really something."

Megan frowned. "Are you trying to make me feel better? Because if so, you're doing a helluva job."

Clover apologized quickly. Her head turned to track the progress of a customer, and Megan's gaze followed. The woman paused by the refrigerator section of the store, placed carrots and kale in her basket, and disappeared behind the canned goods shelves.

Megan said, "Well, hopefully the Center will ultimately be good for business. A fancy spa like that means tourists. And tourists bring in money."

Clover chewed on her bottom lip. Her hair was down today, and it cascaded around her face in soft muddy waves, making her look younger than her twenty-four years. "The owner is from Winsome, you know."

"Carly Stevenson? She's from Boston."

"Not Carly. Her business partner — Ray Cruise."

Ray Cruise. Megan's mind was suddenly flooded with a thousand unwanted images. A teenage Ray on horseback at her grandparents' farm. Ray in the river, laughing. Ray in the dark, his back pressed up against

34

a brick wall. Ray standing in the yellow glow of a mid-summer sunrise, his bare shoulders crisscrossed with red marks from the boards on which he'd slept. Ray Cruise's name on the bottom of a note. The kind of stupid note kids pass back and forth between them in school. The memories of youth.

"Megan?" Clover took a step closer. "You okay?"

The customer had made her way to the check-out counter and was waiting to be rung up. Megan forced herself to smile, first at Clover, then at the customer.

"I'm fine."

"You weirded out on me for a second," Clover said as she moved toward the register. She stopped. "You sure you're alright?"

Megan nodded.

Ray Cruise. Thana Moore. Back in Winsome — for good?

THREE

Tuesday morning was sunny and warm — too warm. Yet again, Megan found herself wishing it would rain. The crops needed a few days of steady drizzle to reap the benefits, but all the wishing in the world wasn't going to make it happen today. Megan would have to be content with a decent lunch and a pleasant visit with her father and his new wife. Megan left the farm at eleven wearing a newly-purchased plum-colored vintage sundress and strappy sandals — a departure from her normal work attire. She just wished she could shake the rock hanging out in the pit of her stomach.

Denver had agreed to join her for this impromptu lunch with her father and Sylvia. While the two sat quietly in Denver's 4Runner, watching the Bucks County pastoral landscape go by, Megan pondered her reasons for this visit. Yes, she was taking Clay's advice and seeking out time with her father. But as loathe as she was to admit it, there was a secondary reason for the trip. She wanted to see why all the fuss with the Center. And maybe, just maybe, she wanted a glimpse of Ray Cruise and Thana Moore.

"You seem quiet today, Megan. Everything okay?"

Megan turned toward Denver. She placed a hand on his forearm, appreciating the firm muscle beneath her fingers. "I'm fine. Just a little anxious about seeing my dad."

"Understandable. I've heard that his new wife can be a handful."

Megan laughed. "Is that so? Heard from whom?"

"During my rounds. You know, people chitchat about all sorts of things when they're bored or nervous. While I'm stitching up a horse or a puppy, they're carrying on about the Phillies season or the drought or the latest Winsome gossip."

"And Sylvia is the latest Winsome gossip?"

Denver glanced at Megan, his blue eyes crinkling in amusement. "Let's see. From a different country. Snagged a Winsome bachelor. And ready with her opinions on any topic ranging from the correct color to wear in winter to the political climate in Mozambique. Yes, I'd say she's the latest gossip."

"Wonderful." Megan sank a little lower in the seat. Even the air freshener hanging from the mirror couldn't mask the scent of dog in Denver's vehicle, and Megan tried unsuccessfully to stifle a set of sneezes.

"God bless you." Denver handed her a tissue from the glove compartment. "You never know when a situation will call for Kleenex," he said in response to her querying look. He pulled onto Orchard Hill Road, a curvy stretch of asphalt that eventually led to the Center, and let out a long, low whistle. "Someone was well-funded when they undertook this project."

Orchard Hill Road climbed steadily upward toward the sprawling inn at the top. On either side of the road were fenced-in horse pastures where horses lazed under shady oaks and maples. Megan could make out a new red barn in a meadow at the top of a steep hill. Fields of late-season lavender and other wildflowers blanketed the hilltops like a scene from Provence, and a wall of tall sunflowers surrounded the barn. As they continued to climb, Megan could make out a large swimming pool and glass-enclosed solarium.

Denver pointed. "That must be the restaurant."

Megan followed the gesture. The inn itself

was white and grand with clapboard siding, deep sills, dark green shutters, and imposing columns. It was built to look like a historic estate, possibly one more at home in Carly Stevenson's New England than the Philadelphia region. Along the side facing the woods was a grand covered porch twinkling with tiny lights and dotted with terracotta pots filled with geraniums and trailing ivy. Fans blew cooler air down, and gauzy sheets of fabric blotted the bright sunlight. Dozens of patrons sat at civilized tables adorned with milky-blue water pitchers and bouquets of lavender. It was a scene from a country club. Or a movie about a country club.

"Nice," Megan said. "Very tasteful."

"Very expensive."

"Well, I guess we get to see how the food is."

Denver nodded. "First things first. Since your father isn't expecting us, want to take a quick trip inside?"

"Of course," Megan said. They parked, and as they made their way hand-in-hand toward the porch, Megan found her gaze drawn to a group of people who were laughing and clinking glasses at a corner table. Not just any people — Winsome residents, including Merry Chance, Roger Becker, and

Anita Becker. Washington Café regulars. Megan swallowed the jealousy that she felt bubbling up to the surface.

Denver had spotted them as well. "The newness will wear off, Megs. Hard to compete with a farm-to-table café in your own backyard."

Not when the competition has fancy china, linen napkins, top-notch staff, and a breathtaking view, Megan thought. But she simply smiled and said, "Let's go inside. I want to see what the Center is really about."

They got as far as the lobby before Megan saw her father. He was standing by the concierge desk talking with a slender woman wearing a crisp aqua suit and a silver name tag. Eddie was sporting plaid Bermuda shorts, loafers, and a melon-colored Polo shirt. Megan had never seen her father in any shade of orange — or Bermuda shorts, for that matter. It took her a moment to adjust to the vision.

Eddie saw Megan, took a double take, and then smiled at his daughter with what looked like relief. He finished up his conversation with the aqua-clad woman before joining Megan and Denver by the entryway's massive cream couches.

"Megan, I'm glad to see you." Eddie

kissed her on each cheek, European-style. He looked at Denver questioningly, and Megan made introductions.

"Ah, my daughter has told me a lot about you. She didn't exaggerate, either."

The handshake lasted a little too long and was a little too hardy. Eddie seemed distracted and Megan said as much.

Eddie's attention turned toward the entryway. "It's just Sylvia. She had some errands to do at the art show this morning, and she was supposed to meet me here well over an hour ago. I'm afraid I lost track of time at the gym." He blushed. "I was late and I thought perhaps she'd come and gone."

"I'm sure she just got sidetracked. The Center is beautiful," Megan said. "It looks like it would be easy to get distracted."

Eddie's nod was noncommittal. "She does like to socialize."

Denver asked, "How are the rooms?"

"Simple, actually. Tasteful — but simple. Sylvia says that's in line with the Center's aesthetic." Eddie motioned toward the nearest couch. "Would you like to wait with me?"

Megan smiled. "We thought we'd take you to lunch."

"Sure." Her father glanced around. "If you don't mind waiting for Sylvia."

They all sat side-by-side on a long pale cream couch with no arms. An assortment of square, rectangular, and round pillows in soft shades of aqua, cocoa, yellow, and red served as back and arm cushions. The room itself had high ceilings and white trim with splashes of aqua here and there. Paintings had been hung on soft cream walls, and more paintings and sculptures were displayed on easels and stands around the large room.

The "welcome hall" — a lobby, really — was large and uncluttered enough to feel open, yet small enough to feel cozy. It seemed contemporary, while maintaining the character of the intended historic style. The colors were soothing but clean and fresh. Megan had to hand it to whoever designed this place. They'd had a vision, and kept to it.

"Have you taken any of the classes?" Megan asked her father.

He was glancing around the welcome hall. "Sylvia signed me up for yoga for beginners and a meditation class." He gave Denver a conspiratorial look. "I went to meditation. I told her I was going to yoga but had a smoke behind the horse barns instead." He shook his head. "No smoking here. Anywhere. Can you imagine? That would never fly in Italy. The Italians are still addicted to their cigarettes, and they don't try to hide it. One of the things I love about them."

Denver smiled. "Tough for a smoker here in the States."

"I'm not really a smoker. Just the occasional cigar. But yoga? I'd rather have a root canal."

"Then why in the world are you here?" Megan asked. She pictured her father doing Downward Dog and laughed. "Seems like this isn't quite your thing."

"Because it's good for me to broaden my horizons," Eddie said, tongue-in-cheek. He placed one leg over the other and sat forward, his hand tapping rhythmically against a hairy knee. "Tonight we have the sweat lodge. And Thursday? A regimen of liquid meals followed by high colonics."

Megan laughed. High colonics — a fancy name for enemas.

"Makes me glad I'll be on a plane for Scotland," Denver murmured.

Eddie took out his phone. "I'll text Sylvia again, and then would you like a tour, Megan? No use sitting around here feeling nervous. I'm sure she's off making deals and sweet-talking artists."

Denver raised his eyebrows behind Eddie's back. Megan stifled a laugh — she wasn't quite seeing Sylvia sweet-talking anyone either. "Sure," Megan said. "As long as we have time for lunch."

"We'll have to put our names on the waiting list anyway," Eddie said. "It seems like everyone from the surrounding towns has come to the Center today." He stood and straightened his shorts. "Apparently the Center is the new 'it' place in Bucks County."

They'd toured the main building and were dining outside on the restaurant's porch when Sylvia finally joined them. She sat down with a flourish. She wore a slim-fitting black pants suit, and her bright red hair was pulled into a neat chignon. Several loose strands flew around her face. Megan couldn't help but notice the large diamonds in her ears or the diamond embedded in the jade pendant around her neck. More diamond than Megan was used to seeing, even on the wealthy tourists who flocked to Winsome in the autumn. The diamonds clashed with the bits of mud and pine needles caked on the edges of Sylvia's strappy flats. A hazard of the countryside, Megan figured.

"Ah," Sylvia gave a tight smile. "Have you ordered? The salmon mousse is spectacular.

But I had that yesterday." She slipped on smart black-rimmed readers and stared at the menu for all of thirty seconds. Like Eddie, she seemed distracted, even a bit frazzled. She checked her phone twice then seemed to push it away reluctantly. "The fruit plate for me. With a glass of Pinot Grigio. And some sparkling water." She glanced over at Megan and Denver, as though for the first time. Her smile brightened. "Who is this, Megan?"

Megan introduced Denver. He stood, towering over Sylvia's petite form.

Sylvia met him around the table and kissed him on each cheek before staring into his eyes for a moment. "You're Megan's beau, no?"

Sitting back down, Denver smiled. "I am."

"You can get her to reconsider her vocation, perhaps?" Sylvia squeezed his hand. "Farming is no life for a young woman. She's a solicitor by training? A lawyer? She spent a lot of money to put herself through law school. Or someone spent a lot of money." Eddie reached out a hand to stop her, but Sylvia waved him away. "Youth of today don't understand the value of security. Why throw away a good career to pursue something that will lead to the poor house? You like to grow things? Have a garden. But this life?" She shook her head and made a *tsk, tsk* sound. *"No."* She squeezed Denver's shoulder this time. "You're a doctor. You understand what I'm saying."

The waitress arrived. With one last insistent look at Denver, Sylvia sat back down. Denver seemed about to respond, but Megan caught his eye. She wanted this to be a pleasant lunch and fighting with Sylvia about farming wasn't something she was about to do.

The waitress — dressed in a pale aqua shirtdress and matching one-inch heels — took their orders with the seriousness of a surgeon preparing for her first procedure. No pad — she simply listened to their selections and nodded.

When she'd left, Sylvia made another *tsk, tsk* noise with her tongue. "When wait staff do that, they never get it right. Just write the orders down." She placed those perfectly manicured hands on the table. Megan saw a slight tremble, and Sylvia quickly placed her hands under the table, on her lap. After a few seconds, she grabbed her phone, glanced at it, and frowned. "This restaurant is so crowded. How is one supposed to relax?"

Eddie placed a hand on his wife's arm. "Are you okay? You seem agitated about something."

"I'm just hungry. You know how I get when I haven't eaten, and that Cream of Wheat we had this morning was more like gruel. Megan, Denver — tell me, do you like the Center?"

"It seems nice so far — what we've seen of it," Megan said.

"It's . . . over the top," Denver said. "But is there substance beneath the pretty façade?"

To Megan's surprise, Sylvia agreed. "Yes. It is supposed to be a center for health and spiritual and physical rejuvenation. One would expect soothing quiet, an emphasis on the individual. This grand opening, with all its pomp and circumstance, makes a mockery of that notion."

"And the art," Eddie said. "There must be hundreds of thousands of dollars-worth of art in the Meditation Gallery alone."

"Yes, the art." Sylvia glanced at her phone, clearly longing to pick it up. Instead she said, "It's in the Gallery, but also around the Center. On the walls. In the rooms."

"Someone coughed up a lot of money to fund this place," Denver said. "Even without the art."

"Speaking of art," Megan said, "did you meet with Thana?"

The waitress arrived with their drinks, and Sylvia took a long sip of her wine before responding. "No, not yet. I'm afraid she's been busy."

Megan couldn't help but feel a tiny frisson of satisfaction. She figured getting an audience with the now-famous Thana Moore would be hard — even for someone used to getting her way.

A short time and a few awkward silences later, the meals were served. Megan's sea bass was delicious, although she noticed the vegetables were rather lifeless in taste and color. Denver's beef Wellington looked good, and Eddie's salad — ordered for him by Sylvia ("the heart knows when you're cheating, Darling"), was passable.

"Decent food," Denver whispered, "but no match for Alvaro's cooking."

Megan looked out over the porch rails, at the stretch of rolling pasture and forest beyond. No, the food was no match for Alvaro's slow-cooked wonders. But that view, Megan thought. The café could never compete with the sheer size and grandeur of this place.

As Sylvia was taking care of the bill — she'd insisted on paying — Megan thought about how to broach the subject she'd come to discuss. She wanted to spend more time with them, and she wanted Eddie to reach out to Bibi to spend time with her as well. Business trip or not, Eddie hadn't been back in the States in two years, and now that he was here, he was making no effort to see them. Clay had been right. How could Megan expect Eddie and Sylvia to know how much that hurt if she didn't share her feelings?

Before Megan could bring it up, Alvaro's wife Maria stopped by the table. Maria was an elegant older woman with impossibly broad, sculpted cheekbones and a toothy smile, but today she seemed drained of energy, a shell of the person Megan was used to seeing. For a rejuvenation center, no one seemed very rejuvenated. Maria hugged Megan and Denver and shook hands with Sylvia and Eddie.

"I saw you come in," Maria said to Megan in her accented English. Like Alvaro, she'd moved to the United States from Mexico many years ago, but her words still held the beguiling lilt of her birth land. "But I was tied up with the art show. How do you like the Center? It's quite grand."

"It's beautiful."

"Yes. We are so busy I barely see it any-more." Maria looked back, toward the entryway into the kitchen, and frowned. Her eyes looked red and swollen. "Well, I have to go. We have a charity auction tonight. Paintings donated by a few of our artists. Several sculptures too. I have to take care of some things before I leave for the day. Will you be staying for the auction?"

"I'm afraid not." Megan explained that she had to go back to work at the farm. "But Sylvia and Eddie will be there, I imagine."

Sylvia's face tightened. "No, unfortunately. We have reservations at the sweat lodge for tonight. It's the couples retreat. Eddie insisted."

Megan looked from Sylvia to her father and back again. Eddie insisted? The Eddie she knew liked football games and softball picnics. His only retreat was to the back room to catch a Phillies game or a nap. And if this was a business trip scheduled to buy artwork for the boutique, why was Sylvia skipping the auction for a sweat lodge?

Megan chose to let it go. She said goodbye to Maria and watched the older woman make her way across the restaurant, her aqua dress floating around her like a shroud.

The pull of the phone was too great and Sylvia was back on it. "I have to go make some calls," she said. She stood to leave. Remembering her manners, she spun back around and gave Megan and Denver each a perfunctory hug. "Darling, I'm exhausted," she said to Eddie. "Would you mind going to Pilates alone this afternoon? I have business to attend to and then I think I may take a nap."

Eddie's eyes brightened and Megan knew he was envisioning cigars behind the horse barns. "Sure. Get all the rest you need."

When Sylvia was gone, Megan tried to bring up the topics she'd come to discuss, but Eddie was already on to other things.

"Dad," Megan said, hoping the name of endearment would garner his attention, "Maybe dinner at the farm tomorrow? Or you and Sylvia could spend some time with Bibi at the Café if you want a more neutral spot. It would mean the world to me and to Bibi."

"Sure, whatever you want," Eddie said. "I'll talk to Sylvia."

And Sylvia will say no. Megan sighed. She watched her father fidget in his seat like a toddler who'd been strapped in a high chair too long. Some things really never changed.

After Eddie had returned to the bowels of the Center, Megan and Denver needed to leave. Denver had rounds to make before his flight left for Scotland, and Megan didn't want to hold him up. Still, while they walked to his 4Runner, she looked around

51

for Thana Moore or Ray Cruise. Just a glimpse of them was all she wanted. To assuage her curiosity, she told herself. Nothing more.

FOUR

"Turn on NBC! Isn't that the girl you went to school with?" Bibi's voice carried from the kitchen, through the hall, and into the sitting room where Megan and Denver were cuddled on the couch watching *Secondhand Lions.* Denver pushed a strand of Megan's brown hair back from her eyes and kissed her forehead. Megan enjoyed the warmth of his body, the weight of his arm around her shoulders. She didn't want to move.

"NBC!" Bibi's voice came from down the hall again, more insistent this time. "The artist!"

Reluctantly, Megan stretched across the small space, grabbed the remote, and flipped channels. Sure enough, the face on the screen was one she recognized. Heart-shaped jawline. White-blond hair fashioned into a pixie haircut. Impish smile — all teeth, thin lips. A neck so slender it seemed to be a stalk barely holding up her head.

Megan moved to a sitting position on the couch, her attention now glued to the screen. The banner below the image on the screen said "Suspected homicide in Bucks County." Flashing lights, dark woods, a lone reporter standing by a police car.

"You know her?"

Megan said, "I did, a long time ago."

Denver also slid into a sitting position. He took the remote from Megan and turned up the sound.

Mesmerized, Megan watched as the reporter talked about the death of Thana Moore, one-time Winsome resident and burgeoning artist.

The facts were sparse.

Her minivan had been found a mile from the Peaceful Summit Yoga Retreat Center and Spa, tucked between the trees on a lonely stretch of unnamed drive off Orchard Hill Road. Thana Moore's lifeless body was inside. Her last known whereabouts had been the Center. Police were investigating.

They'd already declared it a homicide.

Thana Moore, dead? Megan thought of those paintings in the renovated barn, of the young girl she'd shared her dreams with. Megan hadn't seen Thana in years, but she'd heard about her and her exploits, she'd followed her career from afar.

Another murder in the area. Not Winsome. Nevertheless, this one felt close to home.

Bibi joined them in the sitting room. Denver flipped from channel to channel, searching for more about the death of Thana Moore. But that was it: five minutes on the local news. Megan scanned the internet on her phone, reading piece after piece, but each was noncommittal in its conclusions and stingy with the facts. Thana had died sometime between late morning and early afternoon, on an unnamed back road near the Center. Not even the means of death had been disclosed.

After a while, Denver stood up. Gunther joined him and they paced up and down the front hall.

"Want to go for a walk, Megan? Gunther here would like some fresh air, and after that, I would too."

Megan agreed. What Denver hadn't mentioned was that he was leaving tomorrow, heading back to Scotland to be with his sister for the foreseeable future. This was their last chance to be alone.

"Do you want your dogs to stay with me?" Megan asked once they were outside. She tried to shake the newscaster's face, the harbinger of more death and misery. Thana Moore's murder seemed abstract — a fact Megan was still trying to process. Megan would do what she always did in the face of emotional upheaval: she'd focus on tangible things she could *do*. Bibi had her baking, and Megan had her action items.

Denver had five rescue dogs, all of whom would need care while Denver was away, and Megan had grown close to the pups over the past year. What were five more dogs when you were already caring for two dogs, two goats, a barn cat, and a whole flock of chickens?

Only Denver didn't need her help. "Ta, Megan, but my assistant at the hospital will be staying at my house. No need."

"Which assistant would that be?"

"Are you jealous, Megs? Well, put your worries to rest. It's Mrs. Hathaway. I think Mr. Hathaway would kill me if I made any advances toward his wife."

Megan smiled. Denver had three assistants: a man and a woman, both in their twenties, and an older woman whose husband worked at the prison two towns over.

"Mrs. Hathaway is staying at your house?"

"Said she needed a vacation from Hank. Can't say I blame her. She'll have quiet, at least. And that teepee if she wants to feel like she's in the back woods."

Denver had kept the large teepee given to him by a grateful client the winter before. He pretended that he didn't want it anymore, but it had become their own little secret spot. A space that neither of their lives or jobs infringed upon.

The air outside had cooled to an almost comfortable eighty-four. A few stars shone overhead, and other than the hoot of a barn owl, the night was dark and still, the blackness absolute. The pair followed Gunther on his rounds, quietly watching the dog as he went from barn to goat enclosure to chicken coop, his natural inclination to guard propelling him forward.

"Tell me, how did you know that woman who died?"

"We were childhood friends."

"As in young lassie childhood, or older?"

"The awkward years."

Megan headed toward the barn. More specifically, she walked toward the new pizza farm Clay had installed in the newer side of the building. She pulled the key from the pocket of her jeans, shined her phone on the lock, and opened the door. Inside, she flipped on the lights.

Denver moved behind her and placed his arms around her waist. "Wow, Megan. It's quite beautiful. Clay did an amazing job. You must be thrilled." He disengaged and walked around the hostess station, pausing to look around. "I love it. Winsome will love it."

"I want you to see something."

Megan walked over to the wall, where Clover had hung paintings on a white-washed paneling. She stopped before the paintings Thana had done so long ago. Denver joined her. Holding her hand, he contemplated the artwork.

"These were painted by the woman who was killed?"

"Thana. Yes. I was visiting Bibi after Mick and I got married. We went to a fall craft fair and there was Thana selling her paintings. Mick bought these for me. He said having them would be cathartic."

"Cathartic? Why would paintings be cathartic?"

"Thana and I had a falling out. Mick had been part of it." Megan shrugged. "Silly kid stuff."

Denver traced a slender, calloused finger down the length of the wooden frame. "Well, they're . . . unusual."

"That's one way to describe them."

Megan looked at the two paintings with fresh eyes. The landscape was painted in vibrant primary colors, the fields and hills and buildings of Winsome captured in a landslide of oil paint. It wasn't a large canvas, but it was beautifully framed and, Megan had to admit, made a lovely addition to the restaurant. She found the portrait more unsettling. It showed an older woman sitting on a hill overlooking a town. The woman had her legs up and her dress bunched around her knees. She held three dandelions in one hand. Her expression was wistful. There was a familiarity to the set of the wide jaw, the round eyes, and ivory skin.

"It's you, you know," Denver said. "The portrait is of you."

Megan's head swung toward him. "It is not."

"Aye, it is. Same eyes, same chin. Same complexion. Aged, of course, with different hair. But that's you, Megs."

Megan stared at the portrait. Perhaps she'd realized all along that Thana had used her as the model for this piece.

"You must have been close once," Denver said. "For her to do this."

"We were close. Once upon a time."

"You said you had a falling out?"

Megan's smile was tinged with sadness. "You could say that."

Denver drew her close. Kissed her. "You're

being awfully closed up about this."

Megan sighed. "It's not a big deal, Denver. She was a close friend when I was younger. Kids grow apart." She shrugged. "I moved on, she moved on."

Denver's head turned back toward the portrait. "Only I'm not so sure she moved on. And now she's dead."

Back inside, Bibi had made warm milk with honey and laid out a plate laden with her signature scones. Six different kinds. Denver thanked her and took two — a cinnamon and a blueberry. Bibi insisted he take a third "for the road." Megan declined the scones but accepted a mug of the milk. Sadie, perhaps sensing Megan's quiet angst, pressed herself against Megan's leg. Gunther sat by Bibi, aware, Megan was certain, that Bibi was the weakest link when it came to food — despite her own strict rule against feeding "people food" to the dogs. Apparently if you thought no one saw you do it, it didn't count.

"Thana Moore. Haven't heard that name in a while." Bibi "dropped" part of a scone on the floor and the very helpful Gunther cleaned it up. "I used to see her around Winsome, Megan, but not in quite a while. Come to think of it, not for several years.

Her father's still here; I see him at the post office every once in a while. Losing his wife aged him."

Tiny Bibi was still in her bridge-playing clothes: brown pants, an ivory blouse, and the string of real pearls her late husband had given her. She'd tied a "Winsome Rules" apron on over her blouse — a left-over from Eddie's failed Winsome souvenir shop, which Megan had turned into the Washington Acres Larder & Café — and pulled a tissue from the apron pocket. Crackers fell out with the tissue, and Gunther helped himself to those as well.

Looking at Denver, Bibi said, "Thana was always a quiet girl. Rather awkward, if you ask me. She hung around Megan, star struck half the time."

"That's not true, Bibi."

"It is. Megan and that boy. What was his name, Megan?"

"Ray Cruise. He opened the Center, Bibi. He's one of the owners."

"He always liked you too. They followed you around like two lost puppies."

"That's not how I remember it."

Bibi's smile was soft. "You were clueless in your own way. Thana would dress like you, if you liked a band, she liked a band. She and that boy were here all the time.

Aside from becoming an artist, whatever became of her? I asked her father how she was doing once, but he only shook his head and walked away."

Megan felt a tinge of defensiveness, pushed it down. "We were teenagers, Bibi. We lost touch. How should I know?"

"You have that portrait she painted of you. Clover hung it up in the new barn."

Megan threw down her napkin and stood up. How had everyone seen the resemblance except her? "Anyone want more milk?"

"What did I say?" Bibi asked, looking genuinely confused. "Are you okay?"

"I just don't want to talk about Thana, Bibi. I haven't seen her in years, and now she's been killed." Another loss in her life, another tragedy for Winsome. Megan closed her eyes, then opened them. "I'm tired."

Bibi gave Denver a furtive glance, one that Megan caught. "Denver has a flight to catch tomorrow. He needs to get packed and ready to go."

"Why don't you go with him?" Bibi suggested. "Give him a hand."

"Yes, why don't you do that, Megs?" Denver asked.

Megan was quite sure Denver had things other than packing on his mind, and despite the queasiness that rose in her gut at the thought of Thana Moore, she wanted to join him. "It's late."

"It's nine o'clock. Do you turn into a pumpkin, Megan?" Bibi asked, smiling gently. "I'm fine here. I'll clean up and watch some shows. Go."

Megan conceded. She'd go to Denver's. After all, it would be a while before she saw him again.

"Come with me, Megan. To Scotland."

"Denver —"

"I'm not asking for me, mind you. It's about you — in case you've realized how much you want to try some haggis." Denver turned over in the bed, pulling the blankets up over Megan's bare shoulders. They'd started the evening in the teepee and after swatting a few too many mosquitos, moved to Denver's bungalow-style house. "And perhaps rumbledethumps."

"Rumbledethumps?"

"Delightful things, they are." He grinned, and a dimple popped up on the left side of his face. She felt his strong legs wrapped around her own, his hand on her arm. "You'd love Scotland."

"I'd like nothing more than to join you, haggis and rumbledethumps and all." Megan snuggled closer, wishing he didn't have to leave. She felt herself drifting in and out of sleep but knew she didn't have the luxury of dozing. Not here, not tonight. "I wish I could, but it's not in the cards."

Denver kissed her. "All work and no play."

"Someday I'll be able to get away," Megan whispered. She pulled him closer. "Someday."

FIVE

Wednesday came and went like a camera's flash. Denver's plane took off on time, and Megan, sad to see him go, busied herself preparing for the upcoming opening of the pizza farm. All permits and licenses were in place, but the farm still needed more parking and an area for patrons to wait. While Clay and Porter sectioned off a portion of the yard near the driveway for cars, Megan planted flowers along the walkway that led to the barn. The goats, Heidi and Dimples, were gracious enough to help.

After the third time one of them stole a glove, Megan picked up Heidi and carted her off to the goat enclosure. Her sister followed obediently behind. When they were tucked inside their pen, Megan returned to the flower bed. She was just transplanting some impatiens when she heard her name being called.

"Megan!" It was Bibi calling from the

kitchen. "Megan, your father needs to talk to you."

Megan pulled off her gloves and hustled down the hill toward the house. She was wondering what could be so important when Bibi rushed outside and handed her the house phone. "I'm sorry to interrupt you. He said it was an emergency."

Giving her grandmother a questioning look, Megan took the phone. "Dad?"

"We have a situation, Megan."

A situation? What could have happened at that luxury resort masquerading as a health spa? Was he stuck in Downward Dog? Had Sylvia fainted mid-colonic?

"What is it, Dad? My hands are full of —"

"It's Sylvia." His voice was tight. "The police are here. They won't tell me anything, but they're talking to Sylvia. In a private room." Each word gained in pitch until "room" was said at a crescendo. "A *private room.*"

"You need to calm down." Megan paused, giving him a chance to settle. "They'll be talking to a lot of people. Someone died nearby and Thana was last seen at the Center. The police will want a sense of timing, who may have seen Thana, that sort of thing." Megan kept her voice controlled to

66

counter her father's hysteria. "It doesn't mean anything."

"You don't understand. This is the third time they've questioned Sylvia. I think it's more than just procedure."

"Don't be ridiculous. Why would they suspect Sylvia of all people?"

When her father didn't answer, Megan sat down on the stoop. "Dad?"

"I don't know, Megan. I don't know! Can you come here? Please?"

Megan took a deep breath in and let it out slowly. She was sure her father, who'd always had a flair for the dramatic, was blowing this all out of proportion. Nevertheless, she agreed to go. She'd had some experience with murder investigations. If nothing else, she might be able to help him calm down.

"What do you mean they're questioning Sylvia?" Bibi asked.

Megan had quickly changed from her grungy work clothes into a black pencil skirt, slides, and a crimson wrap-around sweater — an attempt to look professional. Now she was putting on some lip gloss in her bathroom while Bibi stood outside, questioning her.

"You're putting in a lot of effort just to

talk to your father. What aren't you telling me, Megan?"

Megan put down the lip gloss. Softly, she said, "Dad seemed upset and I don't know what's going on. Thana's dead and somehow the Center is implicated. Am I going over as a daughter or a lawyer? I don't know, so I'd prefer to look presentable." Seeing the worry on her grandmother's beautiful face, Megan forced a cheery smile. "And I didn't think muddy knees and a grass-stained butt was a good look."

But Bibi's lips remained pressed into a frown. "Do you think that woman has gotten Eddie into some sort of trouble?"

Megan sat down on the bed to pet Sadie, who had curled herself up on the old quilt. "Sylvia is a grown and responsible woman. My father is overreacting. He'll be fine."

"What if he's not?"

"Then I guess he's not and we'll — he'll — deal with it."

Bibi looked neither comforted nor convinced. Megan knew her father was Bonnie Birch's kryptonite. Bibi had a tough life. Married young, she worked in one form of physical labor or another most of her years. Her husband hadn't been an easy man, and their one son wasn't easy either. And when Megan's mother left, Bibi took up the yoke of parenting all over again. But Megan didn't think Bibi had ever quite allowed Eddie to grow up, and as a consequence, even in his late fifties he was immature — and Bibi was protective. So at the first cry of "foul," Bibi wanted to turn into Mama Bear.

Not on Megan's watch. It was time for her father to . . . be a father.

Megan stood. "I'm heading there now. I'll call you."

"I'm coming too."

"Do you think that's a good idea?"

Bibi pursed her lips, giving her the recalcitrant expression of a teenager Megan knew all too well. Megan hung her head. "Fine. I'll meet you downstairs in five minutes."

Megan's head started to throb. Dramatic father, obstinate grandmother, and Sylvia. What could ever go wrong?

"Where's my son, Eddie Birch?" Bibi asked one of the two women running the front desk. "Please tell me where I can find my son."

The younger of the two women looked at her colleague over ivory-rimmed glasses. The pair wore matching aqua suits — the hue of which coordinated with the pillows and window treatments in the welcome area and had the effect of making them blend with their surroundings. A wave of aqua.

In a flat voice, the younger one asked, "Is he a guest here?"

Bibi crossed her arms over her chest. "He is."

"My father is here with his wife, Sylvia Altamura. They've been staying since Sunday." Megan spelled their last names. "I think Sylvia has been involved with the art show you have going on."

"Ah, I see them here." The representative punched a few keys on her computer before looking up. "I can't give you their room number, but I can call them for you. Privacy."

"Yes, call their room please. My father isn't answering his cell. Tell Mr. Birch his daughter is here."

"And his mother," Bibi chimed in. She rocked back and forth on her toes, pulling herself straighter with each motion.

Megan glanced at Bibi, frowning "And his mother."

A few seconds later, the young woman hung up the phone. "I'm sorry. They're not answering their room phone. He's probably in a treatment or at the fitness center."

Megan tried him on his cell again. No answer. She debated whether to mention the police. She'd seen the black and whites

70

parked around the side of the main building and figured the Center had tried to keep their activities quiet. She didn't want her father and stepmother branded by the staff, assuming they were unaware of what was going on — which seemed unlikely.

As Megan was deciding what to do, Bibi said to the aqua minions, "Sylvia is being questioned by the police." She lowered her voice. "About that young woman who was killed. Thana Moore."

Megan saw the representatives exchange another look, this one loaded. "Give me a minute," the younger one said. She disappeared somewhere behind reception.

The older one contemplated Megan and Bibi with a frosty gaze. She had long, gray-streaked hair pinned back with a black barrette. She tugged at a strand of hair with a multi-ringed finger and looked like she was about to say something when a young couple approached the counter. Megan took advantage of the distraction and stepped away from the desk.

"What do you think of this place?" Bibi whispered. She glanced around and then jutted her chin toward one of the ivory couches. A woman sat cross-legged on the cushions. She wore fuchsia and royal blue yoga pants and was studying a Kindle. Her face was pulled so tight that her eyes began nearly at her hairline. "These people have too much money and not enough to do."

"I imagine the rooms are expensive."

Bibi harrumphed. "I don't know why Eddie and Sylvia needed to stay here. We have a perfectly good guest room at the farm. And breakfast better than what they serve here, I bet."

"I bet you're right about the breakfast, Bibi. As for why they stayed here, you heard Sylvia — business."

"Nonsense. That was just her excuse. That woman has Eddie wrapped around her finger. Eddie can't do anything for himself, and now he has her to make decisions for him."

Megan bit her lip so hard she could taste the metallic drops of blood. Who was to blame for Eddie's lack of independence? The younger spa receptionist finally arrived — not a moment too soon.

"If you want to come with me, Ms. Sawyer, I'll bring you to Mr. Birch." With a sidelong glance at her colleague, she sashayed away for Megan and Bibi to follow.

They went through the door behind reception and into an inner chamber of sorts. Down a long hallway, they passed four glass-enclosed offices, all currently empty of people but filled with boxes. At the end of a hallway was a conference room devoid of furniture. The receptionist waited for them by the conference room. When they joined her, she opened the door to the office across the way — a larger room whose glass was obscured by blinds.

She remained in the hallway. "Mr. Cruise will see you now."

Mr. Cruise. Mr. Ray Cruise.

"We want to see Eddie, not Mr. Cruise," Bibi said.

"Mr. Cruise will help you."

Megan and Bibi entered a spacious office. The room sported a wall of windows, which looked out upon the tennis courts and the hills beyond. Unlike the other rooms, this one was fully furnished. State of the art standing desk. Large, flat computer monitors. Streamlined keyboard. Three chrome and white chairs with a chrome table between. A sound system currently playing Blues. No aqua here — just shades of white and all that metal.

"Megan." The man standing behind the desk walked around to the other side and leaned against it. He held out his hand. "It's been a long time."

Megan shook Ray's hand. Firm grip, smooth fingers. He held her hand for a beat

73

too long before moving on to Bibi. If Bibi recognized Megan's old friend, she didn't let on.

"Excuse our appearance," Ray said. "Our investors demanded a certain opening date and we had to prioritize. I'm afraid some of the backroom stuff isn't finished yet."

"It's quite something. The Center, I mean."

Ray nodded. "Been in the works for years. This area needed something like the Center. Something to bring in upscale clientele. Tourists benefit all the businesses. The locals don't always like it, but with tourists come money. And jobs."

Megan studied her old friend. He'd been a lanky teenager. Now he was medium height and very toned. The biceps under the pressed French-blue button down strained against the expensive material, the breadth of his chest said he was no stranger to bench presses. His hair, still brown but flecked with gray, had thinned, but he kept it short. His once-angular face had gotten a little fleshier, his eyes a little lined, but overall, time had been kind to Ray Cruise. Megan was surprised to realize she was glad.

Cruise said, "Megan, Mrs. Birch, please sit."

Bibi protested. "We're looking for Megan's

father, Eddie —"

"I know, Mrs. Birch. And I'll take you to him in just a few minutes. I just want to ask you and Megan a few questions first."

Bibi sat, but Megan chose to stand. "We'd really like to see my father now, Ray, if you don't mind."

Ray held a hand up. "Water? Coffee?"

When neither woman responded, Ray smiled. "Mr. Birch is talking to Detective Lewis. I know this is awkward, but it seems that your stepmother, Ms. Altamura, was the last person to have seen Thana yesterday."

Megan tensed at the mention of Thana, especially from this man's mouth. Memories flashed again, unbidden and confused — a collage of childhood images and feelings.

"Once she tells this Detective Lewis what she knows, she should be finished, right?" Bibi sat on the edge of her seat, her tone challenging. "Being the last to see Thana is not a crime."

"No, it isn't." Ray looked faintly amused, a fact that irritated Megan. "But Thana and Ms. Altamura had words."

"Words?" Megan asked. "What does that mean?"

"Other patrons heard them arguing. They saw Ms. Altamura storm out."

"That still doesn't mean anything," Bibi said. "People argue. So what?"

"You're right, of course. There's more, but I'll let Mr. Birch tell you the rest."

Ray — this composed, self-assured Ray, so different than the boy she'd known — made a phone call. He said nothing, but rather he listened and hung up quickly. "Your father will be down in a moment."

"Thank you."

They waited, the room blanketed by a stiff silence. Finally Ray said, "Thana told me you'd moved back to Winsome. To start an organic farm." That look of amusement again.

"Thana told you that?"

"Yes. She followed your career."

Megan pulled her gaze away. "It's been two growing seasons now."

"I never saw you as a farmer."

"I never saw you as the owner of a health resort."

"A 'health resort.' I like it." Ray walked toward a framed painting that sat propped on a box toward the back of the office. It was one of Thana's landscapes — Megan recognized the style. The subject was a small house, a hovel really. The building sat on a hill. Around it were the vertical lines of a broken-down fence and, in the near distance, the looming presence of a water tower. The sky had been painted in purple and gray pigment, with only the faintest suggestion of the sun hovering behind the clouds. Gloomy — yet not altogether devoid of beauty. Or hope.

Megan recognized the house. She could tell by the expression on Ray's face that he knew she knew Thana had captured his childhood home. One painting said a lot about Ray's upbringing. Lay-offs. Divorce. Alcoholism. If one looked closely enough, Megan thought, it was all there, laid bare on canvas.

Before either could say anything, the door swung open. Another young, aqua-clad staff member walked in with Eddie behind her. Bibi rushed over to her son and gave him a hug before sitting back down.

"Thank you, Delilah." Ray dismissed his employee and offered Eddie a seat.

Eddie sat heavily in the chair. He wore expensive, tailored gray pants and a white button-down linen shirt, but his shirt was rumpled and his pants creased. Worry lines marred the skin around his eyes, which looked deep-set and shadowed. His mouth was pressed into a resolute line.

Ray moved toward the door. "I'll give you some time to talk to your father in private."

Surprised by the courtesy, Megan thanked him. Once he'd left, Eddie placed his face in his hands and sat that way, bent over.

"Eddie —" Bibi started to rise again and Megan motioned for her to stay put. She was afraid her grandmother's attempt to assuage whatever Eddie was going through would derail his train of thought.

"Dad, what happened?"

Eddie sat straight in his chair and took a deep breath. "Sylvia's been with the police most of the morning. They're not telling me much."

Megan frowned. "Surely they've told you *something.*"

Eddie shook his head.

"Ray mentioned that Sylvia had an argument with Thana. Is that true?"

"I don't know. If she did, she never mentioned it to me."

Megan said, "Did Sylvia say anything about Thana? About her paintings? I know she wanted to purchase some for her boutique."

"Not a word. She seemed subdued last night, not really herself. I was worried she had a migraine — she gets those occasionally — but she denied it. I suggested we skip the sweat lodge couples night and to my surprise, she agreed. We watched television

78

and ate in our room." He looked at Bibi. "We didn't find out about Thana until this morning when Ray and a detective knocked on our door." Eddie started to rock back and forth in his chair, and with each movement Bibi looked more distressed. "They told us then, while we sat in our suite wearing nothing but robes and slippers."

"How did Sylvia react?"

Eddie threw up his hands. "How would you react if someone interrupted you at seven a.m. and that someone was a cop?"

He had a point. Megan tried a different tact. "Ray said there was more to the story than the argument, Dad. What else happened?"

Eddie stayed silent for a long moment. Megan could hear voices outside, in the hallway. Through the window, she watched as an older couple in matching whites volleyed a ball back and forth on the tennis courts. They looked red and sweaty. Inside, the air was so chilled she shivered.

Eddie said, "I don't know where Sylvia was yesterday morning."

Megan said, "Before our lunch?"

Eddie nodded. "Sylvia told me she met with Thana at eight thirty at the Meditation Gallery. They argued — or so people say. Then Sylvia just sort of . . . disappeared. I tried her cell, I called the room. I even asked the concierge to help me find her." He closed his eyes. "No one could locate her. And then out of the blue, she showed up at lunch." He reopened his eyes and stared at Megan. "You can see how that looks given the timing."

"She told us she'd never met Thana." Megan frowned. Why had Sylvia lied? "I'm sure she can explain."

"Can she?" Bibi asked.

Eddie's face paled. "She claims she went for a walk in the woods. To clear her mind."

Megan remembered the mud and pine needles she'd seen on Sylvia's expensive shoes. She mentioned it to Eddie.

Eddie shrugged. "Makes sense her shoes would get dirty. She says she was on the path in the woods."

"Remember," Bibi said, "the news said Thana died on an unnamed road not far from the Center."

"A wooded road," Megan added. "That may be why they're talking with her. It doesn't mean anything, Dad. Sylvia was outside around the time this happened. She could have seen something important. They have to be thorough."

"Aren't there security cameras on the property?" Bibi asked. "They should show that Sylvia's telling the truth."

Megan snapped her fingers. "Good thinking." She'd seen a camera in the reception area. Surely there were others.

Eddie sighed. "Afraid not. The Center struggled to open on time. Some things were put off."

"Like security?" Bibi looked aghast.

"It's scheduled for next week." Eddie's smile was weak. "Ironic, isn't it?"

Indeed. Megan leaned against the window, watching the couple who were now playing a serious game of tennis. The woman had a powerful serve. "Sylvia is an intelligent woman," Megan said. "I guess we'll just have to see what she says about yesterday."

When Megan turned around, her grandmother was holding Eddie's hand. He seemed not to notice.

"Have the police questioned you?" Megan asked.

"Briefly — shortly after they came to our room. Mostly they asked questions about my recollection of the day Thana died."

Hoping he'd contradict Sylvia's accounts, Megan thought. She watched her father sitting there in his white shirt and his wrinkled linen pants and hoped that he and his wife hadn't done something unforgivable.

Six

It was Ray Cruise rather than one of his aqua minions who led Megan, Bibi, and Eddie across the main building and out to the Meditation Gallery.

"This is where the police have set up temporary headquarters," Ray said. He looked pained. "We have private rooms for individual instruction. They're borrowing them." He used finger quotes around "borrowing."

"I bet that's not great for business," Bibi said.

"No, it's not ideal."

Megan had to hand it to Ray — he seemed to be maintaining his composure. She knew what it was like to be a new business and dealing with police activity. It wasn't that long ago that a dead body appeared in her own barn, where the new pizza farm would be. And it wasn't until now, until Clay reclaimed the structure with fresh purpose and fresh paint, that she could feel some of the emotional ghosts dissipating.

Thana hadn't died on Center property, but people wouldn't remember that. They'd remember her association with the Center just as the deceased Simon Duvall would always be tied to Washington Acres.

Megan looked at Ray with renewed empathy.

They walked across an open courtyard planted with tall sunflowers and dotted with birdfeeders and ornate stone bird baths. It was a lovely spot and would have been a nice retreat were it not for the police tape strung across the entrance to the adjacent building. A wooden monolithic building tucked toward the back of the property behind the courtyard, the Meditation Gallery was more Asian revival than New England Colonial. Ray went through a set of large wooden doors and the group followed.

Inside, they made their way through a vaulted entryway. The building had slate floors and richly stained wooden walls. A velvet rope cordoned off the vestibule from the main portion of the gallery. A single slate-topped table stood against one wall of the entry and on it were brochures — for horseback riding, yoga, and any number of special spa treatments. Mats had been laid out on the slate and several pairs of shoes sat on the mats. Eddie was already slipping off his loafers.

Ray flashed him a smile of appreciation. "I'm sorry, but no shoes inside."

"We figured that," Bibi quipped. She bent to untie her sneakers and Megan felt for her grandmother. At her age, nothing was as easy as it once had been.

Shoes removed, Ray continued into the main hall. Megan held her breath and let it out in a slow whistle. The meditation hall was a soaring wooden room. The floors, the ceilings, the walls — all were made of the same tropical wood. One wall consisted entirely of windows, and the windows had been strategically positioned to take advantage of the majestic view. With the monochrome walls and floor, it was as though the meadows, sloping woods, and pastures beyond were part of this great room. The effect was breathtaking. Or would be once the room was empty.

Today the room held art. Paintings had been secured to easels and displays all along the perimeter. Watercolors, oils, collages. Everything from portraits and still life artworks to jarring modern pieces. And along the floor near the walls, sculptures sat on felt mats. Megan glanced at Ray and he nodded.

Ray said, "We need to wait here. We'll be called when Detective Lewis is finished."

Megan's pulse kicked up a few notches. She wandered around the room, looking at the art, to quell the jitters.

Every piece of artwork had a small card containing information about the artist. Megan presumed everything also had a price — although none of the prices were on the cards.

Megan was staring at another piece by Thana, a watercolor of a particularly abstract barn in the throes of what appeared to be a snowstorm, when she felt a presence right beside her. She smelled Ray's musky aftershave, saw his expensive Italian loafers. A familiar pull threatened, and Megan didn't turn to look at him.

"She had a style, I'll give her that." Ray's voice was husky with emotion. He moved away from Megan, closer to the painting, before continuing to the next Thana Moore painting beside it — a portrait of a young girl dressed solely in winter white. He stood quietly for a moment. "Do you see the magic of her work?"

"I'm not much of an art connoisseur."

"I'm not sure Thana was either. Maybe

that was her gift — she captures a certain naiveté in her paintings. The world as it should be rather than how it is."

"The critics liked it."

"Actually the critics didn't like it. The people liked it. She had more popular support than critical acclaim."

Megan turned her head in surprise. "Yet you asked her to be a feature artist during the Center's opening week."

Ray's smile was twisted. "Did I?"

"Didn't you?"

"I suppose. In a manner of speaking it was my idea for her to come." He looked back at the painting. "She was talented, but not educated, if that makes sense. We thought we could capitalize on her local popularity."

Megan watched Ray's face for an understanding of subtext. Why was he being coy? She glanced at Ray's hand. No ring. Had he and Thana been an item? Had they ever stopped being an item?

All at once it dawned on her that he could be grieving Thana's death. Not just as a professional whose business was impacted, but as a friend. Or even lover. She was surprised to find that after all these years, it mattered to her whether they were together. And she despised herself for it.

"My father's wife," she said, her voice

sounding twisted, even to her. "Sylvia. Can we see her now?"

Ray's gaze lingered on the portrait for another moment. "I'll check." He disappeared behind what appeared to be a panel in the wall.

Megan walked to the vestibule where Eddie and Bibi were sitting on a wooden bench. Bibi was clutching her brown leather purse as though someone was actively trying to poach it.

"What's taking so long?" Eddie asked.

Bibi glanced at her watch. "That poor woman has been in there much of the day."

Megan thought it amusing that Sylvia had gone from the Witch Who Stole My Son to that "poor woman" in the course of twenty-four hours.

Megan said, "Ray's checking with the police."

"All this art." Eddie glanced around the room. "Sylvia's passion. I'm afraid I just don't understand."

A few moments later, Ray materialized from behind the secret panel. With him were three people: a stocky, bearded man in his fifties with a long, crooked nose and a sizable mole below his left eye; a younger woman wearing gray dress pants and a white blouse that contrasted elegantly against her dark skin; and a very irritated-looking Sylvia.

Eddie ran to his wife. She brushed him off with a firm head shake that left Bibi frowning.

Ray said, "Megan Sawyer, Arnold Lewis and Jasmine Jones from the Templeton PD. Megan is an attorney."

Megan exchanged head nods with the officers.

"Are you Ms. Altamura's lawyer?" Detective Jones asked.

"Yes," Eddie said.

"No," Megan corrected, "but I'll be finding one for Ms. Altamura — assuming she needs one. In fact, I'd like a word with you in private, if you don't mind."

The detectives exchanged a look. Finally Detective Lewis nodded curtly. "Five minutes." Without another word, he walked back through the panel. Megan started to follow, but when Eddie and Bibi moved forward too, Detective Jones held up a hand.

"Afraid not," she said.

Megan didn't wait around for an invitation. She ducked through the panel and into a hallway. Like a spa, the lights were dimmed and the hallway had multiple unmarked, closed doors along one side. Also like a spa, the hall smelled of lavender.

An odd place for a police interrogation.

Detective Lewis led Megan into the room at the end of the corridor. The eight-by-eight space had been set up as a temporary conference room. A square brown table had been placed in the middle of the wooden floor; four folding chairs sat around it. Pads of paper, granola bar wrappers, and dirty water glasses littered the top. Unlike the hall, the air inside the room smelled of body odor and onions.

Detective Lewis sat down heavily on a chair. "What do you want?" he asked with a tired sigh.

"What's going on? Ray said you've been talking to Sylvia half the day."

"We had a lot to talk about."

"Is she a person of interest?"

"Are you a criminal defense attorney?" Lewis's look was challenging.

"No." Megan sat back. She decided to placate Detective Arnold Lewis. "An environmental attorney."

"Barred in Pennsylvania?"

"Illinois. I practiced in Chicago."

Another sigh. "Look, I don't generally talk offline with the relatives of people we're questioning and I'm not about to start, lawyer or not. But I will say this: we'd like Ms. Altamura to remain in the United

States. If you can't see to that, then she needs to stay somewhere that folks can babysit her."

"In other words, you'll lock her up."

"Can you make sure she stays in the area?"

"My father's wife didn't kill anyone, Detective, and without evidence you can't detain her. Why would she hurt Thana? She has no motive to kill Thana Moore, a woman she didn't even know until yesterday."

Detective Lewis inspected his fingernails, which had been chewed to the quick. "You're smarter than that. You and I both know people do inconceivable things for rational reasons, and conceivable things for irrational reasons. Crime rarely makes sense."

"Nevertheless, unless you're dealing with a sociopath, there would likely be some reason behind Thana Moore's death. You're barking up the wrong alley with Sylvia, and in the meantime you could be letting the true killer get away."

Detective Lewis stood. "Our five minutes is over."

Megan found herself missing Winsome's young Chief of Police, Bobby King. "So you're telling me Sylvia needs a lawyer."

Detective Lewis said, "She *needs* to stay local."

"You'd *like* her to stay local." Megan stood up. With heels she was nearly the same height as the detective. Her eyes drifted to one of the pieces of crumpled paper laying on the table. She could make out one word in messy print: Maria.

Maria? Another guest? Or Maria Hernandez, Alvaro's wife?

Megan started to ask Detective Lewis another question, but before she could utter a syllable, he had left the room, sucking any air along with him.

SEVEN

Sylvia refused to remain at the Center, so she and Eddie drove back to the farm in their rented Ford. Once there, Sylvia stormed upstairs without another word to any of them. Eddie was left standing in the large farmhouse kitchen with three oversized suitcases and Sylvia's baby blue satin wrap.

Megan almost felt sorry for her father. *Almost.* Hadn't he been making poor choices for years? Wasn't it about time he faced up to those decisions? And his new wife was one of those decisions. Megan couldn't see how Sylvia could be involved with Thana's murder, but clearly Sylvia's personality wasn't making any of this easier.

Megan's frustration with her father dissipated a few moments later when he sat down at the kitchen table, head in his hands, and said, "Once in a lifetime, God forgives you for all of your mistakes and sends you someone who helps you see clearly for the first time."

"And Sylvia is that person?" Megan said softly, knowing that's whom he meant.

"You don't see what I see in her."

"You're right," Bibi said. "We don't."

Megan filled a tea kettle with water and placed it on the stove. From her vantage point near the window, she could see Porter in the far side of the yard. He was hauling hay bales around the outside edge of what was to be parking. Gunther stood watch near him, his gaze on the chickens pecking around their yard.

"We just don't know Sylvia well," Megan said. She pulled three mugs from the cupboard and placed a Breakfast teabag in each. "It hasn't helped that you chose to stay at the Center rather than here."

"Sylvia didn't want to impose."

"I thought it was all about business," Bibi said.

"Business. Respect. Privacy." Eddie looked at his mother, clearly exasperated. "Had we stayed here you would have complained that she was too demanding, too picky. We didn't stay here and we were punished for that. We couldn't win, Mother. Sylvia knew that. Even I saw that."

Megan had to admit, he had a point. When Bibi didn't care for someone, she had trouble hiding it. Eddie and Sylvia were damned whatever direction they'd chosen.

The tea kettle whistled. Megan poured the boiling water into the mugs and placed one in front of her father. It was well past lunchtime, and Bibi was bustling around the kitchen, fixing what looked to be egg salad on toast, so Megan placed her mug on the counter. She took a seat across from her father.

Megan said, "The question is what to do next."

He glanced at her with surprise. "Next? What next?"

"Detective Lewis didn't give me the sense that his inquiries were over."

"Why?" Eddie's eyes widened. "What did he say?"

"Nothing. That was the problem." Megan knew she had to tread easy here. If her father got excited, calming him down would take energy she just didn't have. "He wants her to remain in the area, though."

"Meaning?"

"The United States. Winsome — or nearby."

Eddie pushed a hand through his hair. "Come to think of it, he mentioned as much to me too."

"Did Sylvia say anything, Dad? Maybe in

the car while you were driving back here? Anything that would indicate why she and Thana fought? Why she was tromping around in the woods?"

Eddie shook his head. His eyes looked heavy, his skin gray. "Just that Thana had been insufferable, but that didn't mean she killed her."

"But why was Thana insufferable? What had she done?"

He shrugged, his mind clearly elsewhere. "She wouldn't say, Megan."

Megan drained the last of her tea, thinking. "You should get some rest. We can talk more later."

"Uh-uh. First you eat," Bibi said. She placed a hand on his shoulder to keep him seated, and she put a plate in front of him. He looked at the sandwich, chips, and carrot sticks as though she was trying to dispense cow manure.

"I'm not hungry."

"You'll eat." Bibi walked away to grab her own lunch and the one she'd prepared for Megan.

"And this is why we stayed at the Center," Eddie whispered to Megan. He took a few half-hearted bites of a carrot stick.

Megan, on the other hand, felt ravenous. She wolfed her sandwich down while contemplating the rest of her day. There wasn't much she could do for her father's morale, but Alvaro needed kale, potatoes, and onions at the café, so she could run those over. She knew Clay would take them, but he and Porter needed to finish up the yard for Saturday's grand opening — and maybe Alvaro would know something about what was happening at the Center. At this point, she planned to move forward with the pizza farm. Reservations were booked, and she didn't want to disappoint.

"Megan," her father said, "what if they're seriously considering my wife for this murder? Who do we talk to?"

"She needs a lawyer. We should find one now."

"Can you do that?"

Megan nodded. She watched as her father took a bite of his sandwich under the mindful eye of Bibi. She'd call Lara Bjorn, a woman she knew from law school. Better to have someone lined up . . . just in case.

"In the meantime, it would be nice to have more information," Bibi said. "About the investigation and whether those detectives are really looking at Sylvia as a suspect."

"Are you thinking what I'm thinking?" Megan asked her grandmother. They'd been through this a few times, so Megan suspected they're thoughts were aligned — in this, at least.

Bibi said, "Call Bobby King?"

"Yep. I'll do that now." Megan glanced at her watch. Late afternoon. Perhaps Winsome's Chief of Police would be willing to talk to her for a plate of Alvaro's never-on-the-menu secret specialty of farm fresh *huevos rancheros.*

And if not, maybe he'd make time at the station. The way Megan saw things, King owed her a favor or two.

The café was crowded. Megan looked at the full tables and the wall of backs sitting along the food counter with a degree of relief. She knew that nothing brought Winsome residents together like a tragedy, but she was glad to see so many familiar faces in her store.

She made her way to the kitchen amidst nods and greetings. King had agreed to meet her there at six, once he was off work. He also agreed to make a few calls beforehand to see what he could learn about Thana's death and the Dartville investigation.

For now, she'd help Clover and Alvaro with the dinner crowd.

After putting the vegetables in the walk-in

cooler, Megan donned a dark green Washington Acres Farm Café apron and washed her hands in the commercial sink. Alvaro was busy at the stove, hovering over a large pot of something fragrant while flipping grilled sandwiches on the griddle.

"Roasted corn chowder," Alvaro grumbled. "Did you bring me the kale?"

"In the cooler." Megan peaked over the rim of the giant pot. "Smells amazing."

"I need the potatoes. I have six orders of the Cubano, which comes with potato salad and sautéed kale." He lifted a lid off a steaming pan and looked inside. "This is the last of the kale. If you want to be helpful, chop some up."

Amused, Megan obeyed. Her chef was as known for his curmudgeon-like personality as for his talent in the kitchen. He'd been the chef at the commune where Clay and Clover Hand grew up. When Megan's first chef quit, she'd hired Alvaro, unsure what to expect. He'd never failed her. And in time, she'd gotten used to his salty personality.

She was chopping her first bunch of rinsed kale when she noticed the chef staring into space while the Cubano sandwiches sat untouched on the griddle.

"Hey, Alvaro," Megan said, "I think those

sandwiches may be burning."

Alvaro jumped. Deftly he pulled the Cubanos off the stove and slid them onto plates. She watched as he sliced the sandwiches, eyeing the layers of ham, slow roasted pork, and melted cheese. To the plate he added a scoop of red-skinned potato salad and a large pile of fragrant sautéed kale with garlic and cumin seeds. Despite the sandwich she'd eaten recently, her stomach rumbled.

Alvaro rang a bell that sat on a slim counter by the stove. Within seconds, Clover joined them in the kitchen. She balanced three of the dishes and left the room with a smile. She was back a few seconds later for the remainder.

"Keep it up, Alvaro," Clover said. "They love the Cubanos. And Mrs. Henry wants a bowl of roasted corn chowder."

Alvaro filled a deep ceramic bowl — made by a local artisan — with the creamy soup. To that he added a dollop of sour cream, some freshly ground pepper, and chopped fresh chives. He rang the bell again, but it was barely a *ding* — not the exuberant ring she was used to hearing.

Once Clover had come back in and left again with the soup, Megan put down the chef's knife and turned to her cook. "Spill it. What's eating you?"

Alvaro continued sautéing garlic and spices, his back to her.

"Alvaro?"

"Nothing, Megan. I'm fine."

"Something's bothering you." She walked around the side of the huge gas stove so she could see his face. Bags under his eyes, a day's growth of white beard. Very unlike Alvaro. He was always impeccably groomed and on his game. "Alvaro?" Megan said softly. "Are you okay?"

Clover called out, "Two more Cubanos, one with no pickles."

"Then it's not a Cubano," Alvaro barked.

"Hey, don't shoot the messenger." To Megan, Clover said, "Bobby's here for you. He wants those *huevos rancheros* you promised."

In addition to being Winsome's youngest-ever police chief, Bobby King was also Clover's boyfriend. She was a free spirit, he tended toward uptight. She grew up on a commune, the daughter of a house cleaner and a father she never knew; King's father was a Lutheran minister, his mother the pianist at the local church. Clover had never been to a party she didn't like; King preferred football games and quiet nights at home. The two were as opposite as they came, but somehow it worked.

As Winsome's police chief, King was earnest and fair. Megan hoped she could pick his brain about what was happening at the Center. One glance at Alvaro told Megan that her chef was in no mood to make the wonderful egg dish he was known for. Megan asked Clover to see if a Cubano would work for Bobby, with some soup — all on the house.

Clover returned quickly. "That'll be fine, especially if you top off the meal with a serving or two of Alvaro's Dulce de Leche."

Megan said, "Another Cubano, then, Alvaro."

Alvaro nodded, and Megan knew she wasn't getting anything but food out of her chef tonight. Whatever was bugging him would have to wait.

Megan placed a bowl of soup and a slice of Bibi's bread in front of the Chief of Police, thanking him for coming. He smiled broadly and picked up the spoon, digging in immediately.

After a few spoonfuls, he looked up at Megan and said, "That detective Lewis is a hard ass."

"Tell me about it."

"The other one, Jones, isn't much better,

but she at least called me back."

"And?"

"And there's not too much to say at this point." King put down his spoon and took a long swig of the sweet tea Clover had brought him. "Thana was strangled in her van. Pretty cut-and-dry from a detective's point of view. What I mean is that it was clearly homicide."

"That's awful."

King nodded. "They think whoever did it was either someone she knew and she was giving them a ride, or they snuck in the back of the van when the back hatch was closing. She had one of those newer vans, the kind with a button that slowly closes the back hatch. Based on what Detective Jones said, I'm betting on the latter, and I told her that."

"Why?"

Clover arrived with King's Cubano and he stared at the plate for a moment. "What's the green stuff?" he asked, making a face.

"Kale. It's good for you." Clover leaned down and kissed his forehead. "Eat it."

When she walked away, King said, "Want this?" to Megan. He pointed to the kale.

She laughed. "No, but it's actually pretty tasty. And you'd better eat it or Clover will have you sleeping outside with our goats."

Bobby raised his eyebrows in mock agreement. "Yeah, she's decided I have an unhealthy lifestyle. I'm surprised she's letting me eat the pork at all."

Megan noticed that the sandwich did look slimmer than what Alvaro typically put together, and wondered whether Clover had made some adjustments once beyond the purview of Alvaro's watchful eye.

"So back to the van, Bobby. Why do you think someone snuck in the back?"

"Because according to Jones, Thana was a pack rat. Her minivan was a portable art studio. She had canvases and containers of paint and boxes of finished and half-finished work in there."

"A mess, or organized?"

"Organized. It's a newer minivan. She had the third row folded into the floor and the back fairly packed. There were things on the seats but the aisles were clear."

"Things on the front passenger seat too?"

Bobby nodded. "If she'd intentionally given someone a ride, it seems more likely that one of the seats would have been cleared off."

Megan considered this. "So whoever killed her got into the van when she was loading it at the Center, waited until she pulled over along the road on that unnamed stretch, and strangled her?"

King was eating the last of his potato salad. The kale remained untouched. He said, "Sounds that way."

But something about that scenario bugged Megan. "Why would Thana pull over along that stretch? And if someone was in the van for the express purpose of hurting, or even threatening Thana, wouldn't they be taking a risk that she'd drive to somewhere public and they'd be discovered before they could act?"

"Good point."

Clover, who had been cleaning off one of the copper-topped tables, glanced over at Megan and Bobby King. When she saw the kale, her expression went from pleasant to annoyed. She threw down the rag and joined them.

"Seriously? Eat the kale."

"I don't do kale."

"Yeah, well, I'll be skinnying down the things I 'do.' "

"Damn it, Clover." Like a child faced with an unpleasant chore, King took a tentative bite of the greens. Finding it not as awful as perhaps he'd thought, he followed it with several more. "Happy?"

Clover said, "No kale, no dessert."

"And what might that be?"

"Alvaro's Dulce de Leche."

"Oh, you know that's my favorite. A whole serving, or are you going to skimp out on me like you did with the pork?"

Clover smiled. "I'll let Megan serve it."

"I don't know. You women tend to stick together." But King finished the kale. He gave Clover a self-satisfied smile. "I did it."

As she walked away with his plate, Clover leaned down toward Megan. "*Who* did it?"

Megan smiled. Echoes of her father and Sylvia. Thinking of Sylvia brought her back to the business at hand.

"So here's what I'm thinking," Megan said.

Bobby held up a hand. "First, dessert."

"Help me and I'll get it for you." She paused, waiting for him to agree. He nodded and she said, "I'm thinking, what if the killer snuck in while at the Center. Thana opened the hatch, did what she needed to do in the back, and then hit the button to close the rear door. Not suspecting that someone was watching her, she slides into the front seat and starts the engine. Meanwhile her killer slides in the back and hides behind the seat or the canvasses."

King said, "Thana wouldn't be expecting anyone to do something like that, so it would make sense that she wouldn't notice."

"Exactly." Megan fingered the edge of a white napkin, visualizing the scene. "Then the killer steadily moves closer and wraps something around her neck."

"At that point she'd drive off the road. You've been on Orchard Hill Road. It's a mess of curves."

Megan waved her hands. "Ah, but what if the killer only places the object around her neck — doesn't tighten it. He or she threatens Thana with a knife or a gun. Whatever. Makes her drive to the secluded spot."

"Then kills her. Yes, I could see that."

"Did they find the murder weapon, Bobby?"

The corners of King's mouth turned down. "It was in the van. A woman's scarf."

"Did they identify whose scarf?"

"Jones didn't say. She just said the scarf was still around Thana's neck when they found her. And that it had been pulled from behind."

"Can you get more information about that scarf, Bobby?"

"Are you worried it belongs to Sylvia?"

"It would make it more understandable that the police spent so much time questioning my father's wife."

Bobby appeared thoughtful. "It would. And come to think of it, they were pretty

106

circumspect about the scarf. But honestly, Megan, I'm crossing more than a few lines even having this conversation with you. If they told me it was Sylvia's scarf, I couldn't tell you."

Clover approached the table carrying a tray. From it, she placed a mug of coffee and two miniature Mason jars filled with a creamy caramel-like pudding topped with whipped cream and chocolate shavings in front of King.

"Thought I'd save you a trip, Megan. Did you want one too?" Clover asked.

"You mean one's not for me?" Megan grinned. These were Alvaro's mini "tasting" desserts. Two barely added up to one full dessert — but neither she nor Clover would tell King that.

"Sorry. Bobby earned the second dessert. I had Alvaro give him extra kale."

Bobby rolled his eyes while Clover walked away. "See what I put up with?"

"Could be worse." But Megan's mind was back on that scarf. "Did you learn anything else from Detective Jones? Anything you *can* share?"

King took a mouthful of his dessert and closed his eyes, savoring it. Finally, he said, "Just that several people had been in arguments with Thana the day before and the day of her death."

"Yes. Including Sylvia." Megan felt anxiety creeping over her. "They told us that."

"Not just Sylvia." King stared down at his Dulce de Leche. His lips pressed into a frown. "The former boyfriend. And several of the staff." He looked up, and his expression was sad. "Including Maria Hernandez."

Stunned, Megan stood up. The words were a knife to the gut. Alvaro's wife. No wonder her chef seemed upset. No wonder Maria's name had been on that paper.

"And every one of them is a person of interest?"

King nodded. "They're looking at everyone who spent time at that Center the day Thana was killed and had a potential beef with the artist. The security cameras weren't working yet, so it's a painful process of interviewing people, checking and cross-checking facts. I don't envy them the job. May explain why they're being so difficult."

"It sounds like the investigation could take a while."

"Yes," King said, now onto his second dessert. "The question is, will the killer break in the meantime?"

EIGHT

The call Megan had been expecting came the next morning.

"Ms. Sawyer? This is Detective Jones from the Dartville Police Department. My partner and I, Detective Lewis, would like to meet with you."

Megan was tending to the chickens, but she'd stuck her cell phone in her pocket in case King called with more information. She stopped feeding the birds long enough to get the particulars of where and when she was to meet the police. They wanted to see her at their headquarters, not at the Center.

Although not even ten a.m., the day was already hot and humid. Megan was dripping with sweat, so she ran inside to take a quick shower. She changed into dress pants and a linen blouse before heading out to her truck. She felt grateful that Bibi hadn't been at lunch with Denver and her the day of the murder. Otherwise, she'd be taking her grandmother in for questioning as well. Been there, done that, and it wasn't a stress she needed to experience again.

The Dartville police headquarters wasn't much bigger than Winsome's. A brick one-story rectangle, its entryway was off the town's main street. Geraniums in plastic green pots lined the walkway in a lame attempt to spruce up the place, but other than that, the building felt starkly institutional.

Within minutes of arriving, Detective Lewis met her in the waiting area. He led her through a Linoleum-floored hallway and into a small windowless conference room. Megan sat at a scarred wooden table, across from the officer. He ignored her, writing notes in a spiral bound book rather than engaging in any type of interaction. A few seconds later, Detective Jones arrived.

"Ms. Sawyer," Detective Jones said. "Thank you for coming in today. When we asked for the roster of known guests at the Center the day of Ms. Moore's death, imagine our surprise when we saw your name on it. Last we spoke, you didn't bother to mention you'd been there that day."

"You didn't ask, and it didn't seem relevant. Plus, I didn't arrive until lunchtime."

Detective Jones said, "To the knowledge of the staff. That doesn't mean you weren't there earlier."

"I announced myself as soon as I arrived. I was looking for my father."

Detective Lewis's eyebrows shot up. "Well, let's try for full disclosure today, shall we? Then we aren't left to guess." He slid on a pair of black-framed readers and opened his notebook. "Please tell us when you arrived, who you were with, and what you did while there. Include times." He looked at Megan over the readers. "Be specific. You're a lawyer; you know the drill."

Megan went through the day in excruciating detail, including such banalities as when she used the restroom and what she ordered for lunch. The detectives did not appear amused.

"Yes, yes, we get it," Detective Lewis waved a thick, hairy hand, his mouth pressed into a frown. He flipped through back through a few pages of notebook. "And Dr. Daniel Finn? According to the receptionist at his practice, he seems to have left the country."

"He's in Scotland attending to his injured sister."

"Seems rather convenient," Detective Jones said. "The two of you arrive the day of Thana Moore's death and he leaves immediately after."

"He couldn't very well coordinate when his sister's accident would impact his life, Detective."

"He could plan when he wanted to leave the country."

Irritated, Megan said, "Neither Dr. Finn nor I had anything to do with Thana's death."

"Nevertheless," Detective Lewis said. "Can you give us a number where we can reach him? We've tried his cell to no avail."

Megan pulled Denver's sister's number from her mobile phone. Detective Lewis jotted it down on a separate pad of paper and handed the pad to Detective Jones. Jones left the room.

"Let's see if the doctor's rendition of what happened corresponds with yours." Lewis's tone was flat, but his eyes bore into Megan's.

Megan smiled. "By all means."

They sat in silence for about ten minutes, Megan staring at her hands and Lewis scribbling in that damn notebook. Finally Detective Jones came back. She gave Detective Lewis a curt nod before leaning against the back of a chair.

"Anything else you can think of from that

day? Perhaps a conversation you may have had with your stepmother?" Jones was all smiles and kindness now. "Or maybe a discussion with your father?"

"I talked to Sylvia at lunch. I told you that. We discussed mundane things. My job, the Center's decor. Otherwise I didn't see her or talk to her all day."

The officers looked at each other. "And your father?"

Knowing this may not help Sylvia, but needing to be truthful, Megan said, "He seemed genuinely not to know where his wife was. As I told you, I found him in the lobby talking with staff. Sylvia was late and he was worried. I'm sure the staff can corroborate."

Officer Lewis nodded. He jotted something down in his notebook, closed the book, and pushed his chair away, as though they were finished.

Megan started to rise.

"One last question," Detective Jones said. Her tone was studiously nonchalant, which gave Megan — familiar with courtroom techniques — pause.

Megan tilted her head. "Yes?"

"You have a history with the deceased?"

Bingo. The question Megan had been expecting. The fact they'd waited this long made her think they thought it far more important than it was.

"I would hardly call it 'a history,' Detective."

Detective Lewis opened his notebook. Without looking up, he said, "You grew up together. Had some sort of falling out about sixteen years ago. Have not been close since."

"Sounds like you have the whole story."

Lewis removed the readers. He sighed. "Don't be coy. You and I both know that revenge can be a prime motive for murder. And often an old grievance grows more malignant over time, not less so. At least in the mind of the aggrieved."

"I wasn't the aggrieved."

"That's not what Thana's father told us." Detective Jones crossed her arms over her chest. "He felt like maybe you've held a grudge since high school."

"Then he told you wrong." It was Megan's turn to sigh. "Look, it was pretty simple. I was dating Ray Cruise."

Detective Jones sat forward. "The owner of the Center?"

Megan nodded. "And Thana and I were close friends. Thana had a crush on a boy named Mick Sawyer. Mick and I were also friends, Thana didn't like that, and she went after my boyfriend, Ray, to retaliate. Kids' stuff, Detectives, and so long ago that none of it matters."

"You never forgave her for going after your boyfriend, who is conveniently back in the area?" Detective Lewis yawned, as though the motive was so common as to be a boring cliché. "Perhaps the two of you cooked something up?"

Megan's smile was genuine. "Mick Sawyer became the love of my life and later my husband, Detective. It was a stupid teenage love triangle that ended in hurt feelings. But in the end, it was a blessing. I married my best friend. I don't think I had any reason to seek revenge."

Detective Jones said, "And Ray and Thana? Did things fare well for the two of them?"

"I have no idea." Megan collected her bag. She knew her rights, and this conversation was over. "If you want to know more, I'm afraid you'll have to ask Ray yourself."

By the time Megan reached the truck, her hands were shaking and tears had sprung to her eyes. Not because of the detectives' tactics. They were predictable. But because of all the baggage their questions brought to the surface. The pain of losing a best friend. The crush of having a trusted boy-friend betray her. Her own shame at encouraging Mick when she knew full well there was chemistry there — and that Thana had liked him. The guilt of not really regretting any of it because without that betrayal there would have been no marriage, tragically short though it was.

But most of all, the soul-wrenching ache of losing someone you love. Just when she thought she'd made progress, when she was learning to let go of the hurt enough to move forward with life, back it came. Mick's death. A tsunami of feelings.

As she'd done so many times when she first moved to Winsome, Megan drove now to Mick's grave on the outskirts of Winsome. She shifted the truck into fifth gear and wound her way around the street until she was at the cemetery by the Presbyterian church. Once she'd parked, once she'd run across the paved lot to the grave marked with an American flag and the flowers she and Bibi had planted on July Fourth, only then would she give into the need to cry.

Only the tears wouldn't come.

Instead, Megan felt anger overwhelming her. Anger toward her father for once again bringing turmoil to their home. Anger toward Sylvia for getting them into this

116

mess. Anger toward Thana for seeking revenge all those years ago. Anger at Mick for dying.

But most of all, anger at herself for what she knew where unproductive, unfair, and not wholly rational thoughts.

She wished she could talk to Bibi, but her grandmother's inability to be objective when it came to Eddie prevented that.

She wished she could talk to Denver. But he was part way around the world — how could she burden him with this when he was dealing with his own family's issues?

She wished she could call her mother.

As she walked back to the truck, Megan remembered the card that sat unopened in her dresser drawer. Her mother had given her that letter at Christmastime, and like a small child unwilling to face up to reality, Megan had hidden it away. She was afraid of what it said. Or didn't say.

I can do one thing right today, Megan thought. I can open that damn card.

She drove away from the church and Mick's grave knowing what he'd want her to do.

NINE

Back at the farm, Megan's attempt to beeline to her bedroom was thwarted by her father in the kitchen. He was still in pajamas and a blue bathrobe. His graying hair was in disarray, and he had what looked like a coffee stain on the lapel of his top.

"Have you heard anything, Megan? Anything at all?"

Megan, still smarting from her mental tirade, said, "I just got back from the police department."

Panic flashed across his face. "They want to see Sylvia again?"

"They questioned *me* about *me*, Dad. Remember — Thana and I were best friends once upon a time. I know you're wrapped up in what's happening with Sylvia, but this affects other people too." Her father's crestfallen look made her regret her harsh tone. "I'm sorry. I know this is hard for you."

"No, you're right. I'm sorry you're part of this. I screw everything up, don't I." It was a statement, not a question, and Megan didn't respond.

Morning had given way to afternoon, and Megan had a laundry list of things that had to get done before Saturday and the pizza farm opening. She didn't have time for self-pity, and she didn't have time to assuage her father's angst. But she knew something that would. Work.

"Come on," she said. "Get dressed and come outside."

"Why?"

"You can help me pick corn."

"Corn?"

"Yes. Corn." Megan tugged on her father's arm. "Come on. Some sunlight and fresh air will do you good."

Eddie shook his head. "I can't leave Sylvia."

"Then bring her out too."

That made Eddie smile. "Sylvia picking corn? I don't think so." Like that, his demeanor changed again. "You go, Megan. I'd just mess it up somehow. And Sylvia needs me. She's just up there, fretting on her computer. I'm worried that this is too much for her."

"It's kind of ridiculous. She's innocent.

119

She should be up and out, doing her best to enjoy her time here. There's not a thing she can do about what happened. The truth will vindicate her." Even as she said it, Megan heard how trite that sounded. After years of practicing law, after witnessing several murders in her beloved Winsome, she knew the truth did not always act as a shield.

Eddie had walked out of the kitchen and into the hall, the ties of his bathrobe trailing behind him. "You're right, of course. She's innocent. But Sylvia can be bull-headed. She had big plans for this trip. It was going to be the start of a new chapter for her boutique. Now it's ruined." He shrugged. "Or at least she thinks it is."

Megan watched as her father drifted down the hall, his shoulders slumped in defeat. She wondered why he seemed so despondent. Even more, she wondered why Sylvia had simply given up.

Megan took the steps two at a time with Sadie behind her. She saw her father's back as he retreated into the bedroom he shared with Sylvia, then turned toward her own room. Bibi was helping Alvaro at the café, but she would be back soon. Megan only had so much time.

She lifted the card from the drawer. It was

thin, light. Charlotte had left it for her at Christmas, by the hospital bed occupied by Megan's Aunt Sarah. Unable to face its contents then, now she sat on the bed and tore open the dark green envelope, careful not to harm what was underneath. Her hands betraying her, she pulled out the card. Made of heavy cardstock, it was a tasteful print of a dove carrying a sprig of holly. Inside was the preprinted message "Wishing you a season of peace and joy."

On the left side of the card was a hand-written message. Megan scanned it, then read it more slowly.

Dear Megan,

I've written this card in my head a million times, but no words ever seemed adequate. I want to ask for your forgiveness, for no child should feel abandoned by a parent. I want to tell you I've been watching you from afar and am awed by your accomplishments. I want to tell you I regret leaving, and not being there for you for the joyous occasions — and the heartbreaking ones. I want to tell you that I never left you; it was me I was escaping. I want to tell you that not a day went by that I didn't love you and wonder what was happening in your life.

You may be asking yourself why I never reached out, never called or wrote. Another of my failings, I'm afraid. As time went by, I convinced myself that you'd forgotten about me. That reaching out would reopen old wounds. But now I know better. Wounds like that never really heal, and they need the sun's light and the whisper of hope in order to start to mend.

It's Christmas, Megan, and like every Christmas since I left, I am thinking about you. Would you meet me? For coffee, for brunch, for Easter dinner, for a walk along the Winsome Canal. For whatever time — and in whatever capacity — you think you can manage. Or not at all. It's up to you, Megan. Whatever you decide, I will love you always.

Charlotte

Megan placed the card back in the envelope and tucked it all into her dresser drawer. She sat on the bed for a long time, Sadie beside her, and watched through the window as the afternoon turned to dusk and, eventually, to evening.

It was nearly dark before she realized that Bibi had never come home.

TEN

While Megan was nursing her hurt and her hope, her phone, left in another room, was collecting voicemails. One was from Clover. Alvaro had to leave the café suddenly — very unlike him — and Bibi and Clover were staying to fill in. "Just grilled cheese, fruit salad, and soup," Bibi said in her third voicemail. "It'll have to do. These old bones can't multitask like they used to."

Megan wasn't so sure about that, but she was less worried about the café menu than her cook. Why had he left so suddenly? And without word?

After quickly feeding the dogs, Megan slipped on a pair of flip flops and hustled outside into her truck. She felt lightheaded and woozy, leftovers from a day spent wallowing. And in the meantime, the café needed her, and there she was hiding out in her bedroom.

By the time Megan arrived at the café, the

last of the customers were finishing their meals and Bibi and Clover were cleaning up the kitchen. Emily, a family friend, was working the register, her daughter Lily, now over a year old, sleeping in a Pak-n-Play next to her.

Megan donned an apron and pitched in with the dishes. "I'm sorry," she said to Bibi. "I got caught up in some things at the farm."

Her grandmother gave her a probing look before peering into a pot of tomato bisque. "Everything okay?"

"Sure."

Bibi ladled tomato bisque into a bowl and slid it across the counter, toward Megan. "You don't look fine. Here, have some soup."

Megan took it. She grabbed a spoon from the silverware bin and tasted the creamy concoction. Smooth and delicious, with overtones of fresh basil and black pepper. She just wished she was hungry.

"I'm worried about Alvaro," Megan said. She covered the bowl and placed it in the refrigerator for later. "Did he say why he left?"

Clover bounced into the kitchen with an armful of dirty dishes. Depositing them in the sink, she said, "Maria."

Megan's stomach clenched. "What about Maria?"

Clover shrugged. "You know Alvaro. A closed book."

More like a locked vault, Megan thought. She returned to her chores, her mind on Detectives Jones and Lewis.

"Is Bobby around tonight?" Megan asked Clover.

"Softball tournament. He'll be at Otto's Brewery afterwards if you need him." She pulled a broom out of the closet. "Why?"

"Just thinking about Thana Moore's death. Wondering if he's heard anything more."

Clover stood the broom straight and leaned against it. "I'm sure he'll tell you what he knows, if anything. He's relieved Thana wasn't killed in Winsome. We've seen tragedy."

"Dartville's not far," Megan said. "But at least it's not his jurisdiction."

Bibi stared angrily at the soup. "I wish they would find the monster who did it already."

Clover pushed the broom across the floor. "We all do, Bonnie. It's hard to feel safe."

"I did hear they're looking at Thana's boyfriend," Clover said. "They were recently estranged and he'd been seen arguing with

125

her at the Center."

"I didn't know she had a boyfriend." Emily popped her head over the counter, a now awake Lily on her hip. The baby's sweet face looked on the verge of a howl. "Someone's awake and hungry."

"I'll mash her some sweet potato," Bibi said. "Would she like some noodles too? Or maybe some soup?"

"Just the sweet potatoes. Thanks, Bonnie." Emily turned her attention to Megan. "And what's this about a boyfriend?"

"His name is Elliot Craddock." Clover started sweeping. "He's also an artist. Lives in the city but had been staying on and off at an apartment on Chelsea Avenue."

"That's near your place," Megan said to Clover.

"That's why I know. He and his buddies have a reputation for playing loud music, getting into brawls, that sort of thing. Bobby's officers have been called out many times." Clover slammed the broom down harder than necessary. "Sometimes by me."

"Isn't he a little old for that type of behavior?" Bibi asked. "Thana was Megan's age."

"Thanks, Bibi," Megan said dryly. "Calling me old?"

"Elliot is a younger man." Clover bent

126

down to reach under the counters with the broom. "Can't be much older than me. But yes, still old for that kind of behavior."

Bibi handed Emily a bowl of warm, richly scented mashed sweet potato and a small spoon. She leaned over the counter toward Lily and brushed her finger against the child's cheek. Lily grinned. After Emily's father's death almost a year before, Emily had become like a Birch family member. She stayed at Washington Acres while getting her life back on track. Now she had her own place to live, but she and Lily were frequent visitors at the Farm, and Bibi was Emily's first choice for babysitter.

Emily had been through a lot in the past year, little of it good. Megan was worried that talk of murder wasn't doing Emily's psyche any favors.

Not surprisingly, Emily said, "I'm going to feed Lily by the register. You guys go on with your conversation, but the fact that there's another killer in the area is giving me the creeps."

When Emily and Lily were gone, Megan asked Clover, "Have you met Elliot?"

"Several times. Usually at his friends' apartment — when he's drunk and I'm angry."

"Would it surprise you if he had hurt

Thana?"

Clover didn't respond right away. She took her time sweeping up by the stove. When she'd picked up the last of the crumbs, she said, "He's rough around the edges. And young. And if his peers are any indication, impulsive. But I don't know, Megan. I think maybe I've lost the ability to judge people. And I've only met him a few times and under less than ideal circumstances."

Megan knew exactly what she meant. If the last year taught her anything it was that people were not always as they seemed. Some could surprise you in the worst ways possible. Others could awe you with their selflessness.

Bibi seemed to still be stewing by the stove. She had cleaned up the sweet potato and was now putting away her grilled cheese ingredients, but the scowl on her face told Megan she wasn't thinking about food.

While Megan washed the last of the pots, Bibi left the kitchen. She sat in the café, at one of the tables positioned closer to the register, and seemed to be watching Lily as the baby played with some blocks on the floor.

"I can finish up here," Clover said. "Go talk to your grandmother."

Megan thanked her. She left the final dry-ing to Clover, took two organic sweet teas out of the refrigerator, and, joining Bibi at the table, slid one across to Bibi. Then she settled opposite her grandmother.

"What's on your mind? Now it's you who looks glum."

Bibi cocked her head, her gaze on Lily. "That child is growing so fast. Before you know it, she'll be driving."

"She's sixteen months old, Bibi."

"You blink and they're grown."

Megan put a hand over her grandmother's. "Is this about my father?"

"When Eddie was a boy, he was always in trouble. Always. Once he got picked up by the police for lighting an old shack on fire. It was empty, thank the Lord, but the police didn't find that any consolation. Nor did your grandfather." She watched as Lily stacked the blocks, one on top of the other, before knocking them all over the floor. "As a teenager, he was restless. Never stayed with anything more than a few months. Weeks, even. Would fall for any half-baked scheme that came along. Would've bought land on Mars had someone offered it."

Bibi turned her attention to Megan. "When Charlotte left, a small part of me was relieved that it wasn't Eddie that quit the marriage. Isn't that horrible, Megan?"

129

She wrapped her arms around her chest. "All you were going through, and I was relieved because it wasn't my son who quit."

"That's understandable, Bibi."

"Is it? Well now he's found himself in another pickle. I'm watching that little one play with blocks, so cute and focused. That was my son not that long ago. A few years later it all changed. I couldn't seem to do right by him then, and I'm no better off today."

"Dad's not in trouble. There's nothing for you to do."

Her gaze was caustic. "But he's fallen for a con artist. And it's going to be his undoing."

"My father is an adult. Maybe it's time to treat him like one. Let him succeed or fail on the basis of his own choices." Megan said the words softly, as kindly as she could. Still they tasted bitter in her mouth. "He loves Sylvia."

Bibi stood up, her hands flat on the table. She looked at Megan with sorrow and something like pity in her eyes. "Things aren't always so simple, Megan. You think I don't know your father is a grown man? That I've coddled him in ways that proved ultimately to be a disservice? I know that. Maybe I was trying to make up for the things he didn't have — warmth from his father, a loyal wife. Maybe in trying to help him, I hurt him." Her voice cracked. "The right choice isn't always so clear, and someday I'm afraid you'll learn that the hard way."

Thinking of her mother, of the letter sitting in her dresser, Megan wondered if that wasn't a lesson she'd already been taught. Before she could respond, her grandmother had walked off. As she made her way down the aisle between rows of canned corn and organic nuts, she looked old to Megan. In fact, for the first time in ages, Bibi seemed older than her eighty-five years.

Megan pulled a stool up next to Bobby in the brewery that once belonged to Winsome native, Otto Vance. Since Otto's untimely death last fall, the pub had been run by his daughter, Hedy Vance, and she smiled when Megan sat down. Springsteen's "Born to Run" blared from the loudspeakers. A crowd had gathered by a large screen television on the far side of the room and cheers broke out when the Phillies scored a hit.

"Things never change around here," Hedy said with a smile. The petite blonde looked good — better than she had ten months ago when she'd first taken over the business.

"Good to see you, Megan. What can I get you?"

Megan ordered a house brew.

"Make that two," Bobby King said. He turned around on his stool and nodded at Megan. He was wearing shorts and a t-shirt, and his six-foot-five frame towered over her, even while sitting. It was nice to see him out of uniform and in something more humanizing.

"Let me guess," King said to Megan, "You ran out of work at the farm and decided to celebrate by drinking yourself silly at Otto's Brew Pub."

Megan smiled. "Nope."

"You decided farming is too hard a career and you'd rather apply for a waitressing gig."

Megan shook her head.

"Hmm." King grinned. "Our good Dr. Finn is out of town, so you're here trying to pick up another man. While the cat's away and all that."

"Good guess, but another no."

King took off his baseball cap and pushed his thick, blonde hair back off his forehead. "Well, you got me, Megan. What brings you to Otto's — and alone at that?"

"You."

"Did Clover send you to fetch me? That woman —"

Megan laughed. "She told me where to find you, but that was it." Hedy returned with two beers and a bowl of salty pretzel bites, and Megan thanked her. When she was out of earshot, Megan said, "Just checking in on Thana's murder investigation."

Some of King's good humor appeared to fade. "Yeah, that. I hear Detectives Lewis and Jones are making friends all over the place."

"What does that mean?"

The Phillies batter struck out, giving them three outs. Booing ensued, and King waited out the noise.

When the crowd was only mildly rowdy, King said, "They've been through Winsome, questioning anyone and everyone with a connection to the Center the day Thana died. You know Thana's parents are from Winsome, right?"

Megan nodded. Bobby was too young to remember when she and Thana had been pals.

"Her dad's still alive, and word is he's devastated — as any parent would be."

"Wesley Moore. I remember him from when Thana and I were kids."

"Yeah, well, Wesley called me to complain about the detectives' tactics. I guess in the process of questioning folks they've been digging up dirt on the deceased. They insinuated to Wesley that his daughter wasn't always well-liked."

"And he was upset?"

"Sure he was. Problem is, there were lots of folks in Winsome with a connection to Thana, either because they knew her well — like her daddy — or because they were at the Center the day Thana died." King grabbed a handful of nuts and popped them into his mouth, one at a time. He followed the nuts with a swig of his beer, wiping his mouth with the back of his hand. "You, too, from what I hear."

"They dragged me in this morning."

King was silent for a moment, his eyes on the game. Not looking at her, he said, "How'd that go?"

"Fine. Once we got past their attitudes."

"They've got a right to be suspicious, I guess. Dead body says so."

"Perhaps. Do they have a lead suspect?"

"Nothing new, I'm afraid. Your stepmother is on the list."

"She's my father's wife."

"Ah, I forgot how sensitive you can be. Yes, Sylvia is on the list. Some others." He made a disapproving face. "Including Maria Hernandez."

Megan pulled her stool closer to King.

Keeping her voice low, she said, "That's why I wanted to come find you. Alvaro left the café early today, Bobby. He never leaves early."

"That's probably why. The Dartville police called her in for questioning again."

"Do you know why they're so focused on Maria?"

Bobby's jaw clenched ever so slightly. "I really can't say more, Megan. I'm walking a thin professional line as it is."

"Maria? Come on, Bobby. We both know Maria Hernandez is as likely to kill someone as Bibi is."

"Under the right circumstances, your grandmother could pack a wallop." His gaze became serious. "Really, Megan. If you or your father were threatened, Bibi wouldn't hesitate to protect you, I'd bet a year's pay on it."

"But we're not talking self-defense. Thana Moore was murdered. In cold blood." Megan shook her head. "Maria would never do that. For god's sake, she was like a second mother to Clover and Clay growing up."

Bobby swallowed more beer before signaling Hedy for another. "Think about that, Megan. What if someone — Maria, anyone — thought they were acting in self-defense, even if the harm was in the past, or anticipated again in the future? When does self-defense slide into revenge?"

Hedy handed King another beer. "Anything else for you?" she asked Megan.

Megan thanked her but declined. "Bobby, unless you're not telling me something, revenge hardly seems to apply here. What in the world would Maria be seeking revenge for?"

King chewed on his lower lip. "What if I told you that Thana got Maria fired."

Stunned, Megan sat straighter. "Fired? Why would she do that?"

He shrugged. "She lodged a complaint that morning. Accused Maria of trying to steal one of her paintings. Maria was called in to account for her actions."

Megan thought back to the Meditation Gallery and all of the work displayed there. Ray never mentioned this. "You said trying to steal."

"The painting was found." King leaned in toward Megan. "Look, I'm trusting you with this. You can't repeat any of it. To anyone."

"Of course."

King took a deep breath. "The night before her death, one of her portraits went missing. Initially Thana believed it was a

136

theft, but the painting was found."

"I'm confused. Why does she think Maria was to blame?"

"They'd had a disagreement the day it went missing. An ongoing disagreement, really. Maria was an event planner. She'd set up the show, and Thana felt like she deserved more space, more recognition, a gold-plated toilet, whatever. She complained to Maria, and Maria put her in her place. Then Thana complained to Carly Stevenson, one of the owners."

"A painting went missing after that and they tied it to Maria? Wouldn't that be rather obvious? Maria's an intelligent person. She would never do something so transparent."

"It went missing and later showed up . . . ruined."

Megan sat back. "Ah, the revenge you mentioned. So the police think Maria argued with Thana, was ratted on, management took Thana's side, so Maria took the painting as revenge, ruined it, and when Thana again reported her, she killed her?" Megan let out a whistle. A man next to her glanced over and she smiled an apology. "Wow. That feels like a hell of a stretch."

King shrugged. "The fact remains that Thana Moore was murdered. You and I both know that they'll look at means, opportunity, and motive. Maria definitely had opportunity. She was at the Center and her job allowed her to come and go as needed. In the eyes of the police, she had motive, and from what I understand she had no confirmed alibi for the period in question. Back to the security cameras. Without proof of where she was on the Center's grounds, she has only her word to go by."

"And the murder weapon was a scarf."

King drained his beer, grimacing. "Right. As for means, Maria is not a weak woman. She's a runner and she helps Alvaro out in the gardens. Thana was slight. It's conceivable Maria could have overtaken Thana, especially with the element of surprise on her side. And, as you said, the murder weapon was a scarf." King rubbed the back of his neck with a beefy hand. He looked suddenly tired. "Opportunity. Motive. Means. Arguably Maria had all three."

"And Sylvia?"

King took an audible breath. "Get her to be more specific about where she was and why she was arguing with Thana, Megan. Otherwise it's possible she has all three as well."

"She says she was on the walking path."

"No one can confirm her whereabouts."

"Why would she want to kill Thana? I just don't see a motive."

King frowned. "They argued that morning and Sylvia won't say why."

"That doesn't amount to motive. And as for means, Thana may have been slight, but Sylvia is tiny. I doubt she weighs a hundred pounds." Megan's eyes widened. "So there must be something else. Something that ties her to the murder." She snapped her fingers. "That scarf. The scarf did belong to Sylvia." King didn't respond but he didn't need to — his face was the color of his Phillies hat. Megan felt her temples begin to pound. "She could have left that scarf somewhere. Or someone could have stolen it."

"Sure. Anything is possible."

Megan rubbed her own temple. Anything *was* possible. Little consolation. Two women. Each close to someone she cared deeply about. Each with baggage making them viable suspects.

Megan watched the Phillies game for a few minutes while her mind cleared. One of King's teammates had wandered over to chat with him, and Megan took the time to consider what she'd learned. She was pretty sure Bobby was tired of this conversation, and she didn't blame him. The whole thing was giving her a headache.

When Bobby's buddy was gone, Megan leaned toward Hedy. "I'd like to buy one more for Bobby," she said.

Bobby thanked her. "But I'm sure there's a price attached."

Megan smiled. "Just one more question."

King popped a pretzel in his mouth. "Shoot."

"How about Elliot Craddock?"

King's eyebrows arched in surprise. "The boyfriend?"

"Yep. I heard he's bad news."

"Elliot's okay. Kind of a drifter. Hangs around with an obnoxious crowd." King smiled. "You must have been talking to Clover. She can't stand any of them. Their choice of music disturbs her delicate sensibilities."

Megan smiled. Sounded like Clover. "Is Elliot under suspicion?"

"I suppose everyone's under suspicion. He wasn't at the Center that day, as far as I know." Bobby shrugged. "But they had separated recently. And someone saw them fighting at the Center, so I guess it wouldn't surprise me if he was on the detectives' short list. Then again, I heard Thana was a spitfire. The rumor is that she cycled through boyfriends like some people go through paper products. Which is why Wesley Moore was upset." The Phillies scored and cheers and catcalls swallowed the quiet. King stood up and whistled.

Megan mouthed "thank you," left a twenty on the counter, and headed for the door. The Thana she remembered from their school years had been quiet and shy, more passive aggressive than spitfire. One thing was for sure, a lot had changed in the intervening years. Perhaps that was where Megan needed to begin.

ELEVEN

"Everything's set." Clay rubbed his hands together in a gesture of accomplishment. "Oven's ready, kitchen's ready, plates and trays are clean." He ran through the list of things that needed to be finished for the farm pizza kitchen to open Saturday night. "And Clover has the reservations ready. Alvaro and I will cook, Clover will play hostess and waitress along with Emily. You and Bonnie can wander, greet people, and fill in as needed."

"Do we have enough staff?"

"We're only allowed to have forty guests at a time under the terms of our permit, so I think we'll be fine." He glanced at a clipboard. "We have two seatings, one with seventeen guests, and the other with eighteen. If they overlap a little, we're fine."

They were outside, under the ancient, giant oak that separated her house from the greenhouses and the abandoned Marshall

142

house next door. Bibi had made them a pitcher of iced tea and they were lounging under the maple's shade — their version of a meeting. The Marshall house stood still and dark beyond the tree, it's solid form a testimony to an era when houses were built to last. But the vestiges of time and neglect had taken their toll, and the Marshall house — once part of the Washington Acres parcel but empty and abandoned for years — seemed an empty shell of what could have been.

Megan had been eyeing up that property for a long time. She just wished she could afford to buy it before someone else did.

"Do we have room for two more people?" Megan asked, glancing at the reservation list.

"Sure. Who?"

"Just note two more. I'm not even sure they'll come."

"Five o'clock or seven o'clock?"

"I don't know. Can you pencil two in for both?"

Clay gave her a funny look but jotted something down on his list. "Done. That's it, though. We're at capacity."

"Are you excited?" Megan asked. "This is a big deal, and you were the impetus behind it."

Clay grinned. "Yes, as a matter of fact, I'm very excited. I've been wanting to do this for quite a while."

"You have." Megan glanced out, over the stone fence that lined a portion of the property and toward the road beyond. She missed Denver, and found that she wished he was here with her — more so than she might have liked. "I'm impressed."

"Clover did a lot of the work. She held me to a schedule. She can be a stickler for planning."

"The incredible Hand duo." Megan smiled. She was wearing jeans and a fitted Green Mountain College t-shirt. She pulled a caterpillar off the sleeve of her shirt and tossed it into the grass, on the hump around the tree's roots. "Funny that someone who grew up so unconventionally can have such conventional attitudes."

Megan was teasing and Clay smirked back at her, happy to play along. "What, you don't think commune life is a conventional upbringing? We had Alvaro. He was pretty conventional."

At the mention of Alvaro, Megan thought about Maria. Alvaro had returned to work, but he was surlier than usual. Surly and quiet. Every attempt to draw him out was met with stony silence.

"Tell me about Maria," Megan said.

Clay seemed surprised. "What do you want to know?"

"I know her now as Alvaro's chattier better half, and as the put-together, professional events coordinator, but Clover's hinted that Maria wasn't always that way."

Clay lay back on the grass, using the hilly area around the tree to prop up his upper body. He studied Megan for a few seconds before turning his attention to the flawless sky.

"Jeez, Megan, I'm not sure where to even begin. Maria's story and our own intertwine."

"Then start there."

"Yeah, okay." Clay placed one hand behind his head, and he picked at the grass with the other. "My mother had a good heart. She was young when she had me, and Clover followed right behind. We never really knew our father, and Mom joined the commune when she was only twenty. I was two, Clover was one. The community was all we knew."

He paused and Megan waited. Gunther sat at attention a few feet away, his focus on Megan, and Sadie snored softly in a dappled patch of sun nearby.

"That's the beginning of the happy children's book version of our lives," Clay said. "In that version, the commune was like one large, supportive family and my nuclear family never wanted for anything. I could stop there. I think that's the version my sister tells herself." Clay readjusted so both arms were behind his head. "The truth is a little more sordid."

"Sordid in what way?" Megan had been sitting cross-legged on the grass. She shifted so her legs were outstretched in front of her and tilted her head toward the sun.

"I wouldn't call the commune a cult, but it did have a fairly rigid social structure. It recognized marriages and long-term relationships, and single parents, especially mothers, were looked upon as charity cases. My mother had no interest in another relationship, and she earned her keep by baking bread and cleaning up the kitchen after meals. In return, we had a small apartment — just one bedroom for my mom and Clover and a living area where I slept on a couch — and Clover and I attended school. My mom was . . . quirky. Eccentric. She meant well, but her judgment wasn't always the best." Clay sighed. "Anyway, life in the commune was strictly regimented, which I think is why my mom liked it. She didn't have to make decisions. But as part of the regimen, men and their families ate first, so by the time we ate, much of the healthy stuff was gone." His smile was tinged with melancholy. "Much of the food was gone."

"That must have been hard," Megan said. She pictured young Clay and Clover waiting for the dregs in the cafeteria. The image tugged at her core.

Clay agreed. "Don't get me wrong. People were nice enough. It wasn't like we were abused or anything. Or starving. But the commune was poor, and we knew the pecking order and the elders, as they were called, made it clear that we were on the bottom of the list. Unless my mother wanted to marry one of the single men, that is. It was like relationship blackmail." Clay tilted his head so he was looking at Megan. "I guess it's why I consider myself a feminist. I know what my mother went through to maintain her freedom of choice. She had no power because she lacked a certain piece of anatomy — and she refused to marry a man she didn't love."

Megan pondered that. Clay's mother had chosen to live in that environment, had made the decision to stay, and yet Megan didn't hear bitterness in his voice. "And Maria?"

"Yes, Maria." Clay put his head back on

his hands, and Megan felt like he was on the therapy couch. A first — normally he was the one listening to her. "Maria and Alvaro worked at the commune, but they weren't really part of it. Alvaro was the chef and Maria ran the kitchen. Mostly we saw Maria storming around looking purposeful and stern. One day she found Clover crying outside the meal room. She asked what was wrong and I told her my sister was hungry."

Clay smiled at the memory. "Maria's face turned bright red and I thought for certain she was angry at us. The next thing you know, she disappeared inside and came out with a bag. She took us to a quiet spot and fed us meat-filled sandwiches and milk and fresh fruit, which we never got — especially the meat and fruit. After that, she saw to it that we were well fed." He sat up, shook his head. "She never acknowledged us publicly. No special treatment that could give our friendship away. But always, always, she found us and made sure we got protein and fresh fruit and vegetables."

Which explained Clover's unrelenting loyalty toward Alvaro and Maria. Watching out for children — and risking her own job to do so. Hardly the character of a killer. "Clay, I'm worried about Maria. She was at the Center the day Thana Moore was murdered." Megan went no further. She had promised Bobby King.

"So?" Clay looked confused. "You're afraid she's a suspect?" He watched Megan's face, and when she didn't deny it, he said, "Ridiculous."

"Maybe not so ridiculous. You'll have to trust me on that."

Clay shook his head vehemently back and forth. "It can't be true, Megan."

"If it is true, if the Dartville police are looking at Maria for this heinous crime, how would Alvaro react?"

Clay seemed to consider the question. "I doubt it's true, Megan. Maria is quiet, but she's an angel. Literally. But if she was somehow implicated? Beware the wrath of Alvaro. Maria is his life."

Clay's words stayed with Megan for the remainder of the morning. Maria as an angel — an image so at odds with the suspicions cast her way. Megan decided to drive by the Hernandez's home. Perhaps if Alvaro wouldn't talk with her, Maria would. Megan was worried about her chef, and if Clay was right, and Maria was ultimately implicated, she wanted to know how to help him.

She decided to call first. Maria had

enough on her plate without a drive-by, however well-intentioned. Megan tried their home number and when no one answered, she got Maria's cell phone number from Clover. Only Maria didn't answer that, either. Megan left a message. She hoped Maria would call her back.

It didn't help that Thana Moore's death was all over the news. The media portrayed Thana as a local artist who had been on the verge of a blossoming career. They noted her packed shows, the interest of larger art houses and wealthy patrons, the commissions she had been receiving for many of her paintings, especially her unusual portraits. But every article Megan read said very little about Thana Moore as a person.

Budding artist? Local hero? Relationship addict? Vocal complainer? All of the above?

The problem was none of these sides of Thana Moore matched the girl Megan had known. Megan knew people could change, but they had already been young adults when they parted ways. By that age, certain aspects of a personality were formed. Megan could remember Thana doodling on the notes she'd pass to her in class. Or drawing the ski club mascot. But significant paintings? Works that would be considered true contributions to the art world? Even the paintings hanging up in the pizza farm were less sophisticated than what Megan had seen at the Center. Clearly Thana's work had been evolving. But where did the passion come from?

Thana must have found her calling later in life, and it saddened Megan that she knew so little about someone who had once been her best friend.

A little before noon, Megan left the barn and headed back to the house. She found Bibi gone — presumably helping out at the café — and her father and Sylvia in the kitchen drinking coffee. Sylvia wore a long turquoise, red, and yellow skirt and a silk turquoise tank top. Her hair hung loose around her face, which was minimally made up. She looked tired, but some of the feistiness had returned to her expression.

Eddie, on the other hand, seemed distracted. He barely glanced at Megan but was staring down at the local paper, which had Thana's elfin face plastered on the front page.

"Well, good morning," Megan said. She poured herself a large mug of coffee, added cream, and sat down at the table with them. "Nice to see you two up and around."

"We're going to the Dartville Police Station," Sylvia said drily. She took a long sip of coffee while watching Megan over the rim of her mug, as though daring Megan to challenge her.

Eddie brought a mug to his lips before lowering it without drinking. "They want to talk to Sylvia again."

Megan reiterated the name of the attorney she'd sent her father. "She's the best I know in the area."

"Sylvia doesn't need an attorney." There was a slight whine to Eddie's voice. He placed a hand over his wife's. "Right, sweetheart?"

"Don't be ridiculous. Of course I don't need an attorney. I didn't do anything." Sylvia disentangled her hand from her husband's. "We should get going, Edward. We don't want to be late."

Eddie stood up obediently.

"Do you need a ride?" Megan asked.

"No. We have the rental." Eddie patted his pocket, then looked to his wife. "We're hoping they'll tell us she's been cleared. After everything, I think we both just want to go home."

Go home. The words stabbed at Megan. This was no longer home for her father.

"I understand," she said. "It's been difficult, I'm sure. Not the vacation you were planning."

"Business trip," Sylvia said. "While it is lovely to see you, Megan, and meet your friends, this was always meant to be a business trip. And I'm afraid we haven't done much business."

Sylvia drew close to Megan. Even with the three-inch strappy heels Sylvia was wearing she didn't clear Megan's shoulder. And Megan wasn't particularly tall.

"Perhaps next time you'll visit us in Italy." Sylvia's words were more command then request. "And you can see how well your father is doing."

Doing what? She didn't realize her father was doing anything. But Megan nodded. "Sure." She figured she was as likely to get away to Italy as she was to Scotland.

"Good." Sylvia grabbed her expensive handbag and slipped on a pair of oversized sunglasses. She looked more like a movie star posing for the paparazzi than a woman on her way to a police station. "We'll be back for our bags."

Eddie turned around and gave her a long hug. "I'm sorry, Megan. I'm making a mess of things again, aren't I?"

"You're fine, Dad. Go deal with your wife."

Eddie's look was wistful. "You have your mother's patience."

It seemed an odd thing to say about a woman who had run away from home, but Megan simply replied, "Do I?"

Eddie nodded. "I'll let you know what happens. Sylvia thinks we'll be done with this. I'm not so sure."

Megan watched them climb into their rented Ford. She wasn't so sure either.

TWELVE

Friday afternoon at the café was slow, in part because Alvaro was once again missing, having departed unexpectedly at one that afternoon. He'd left Megan a message, but her return calls went unanswered. Bibi had graciously taken over as the cook and had limited the menu to grilled chicken and cheddar Paninis with red-skinned potato salad, a black bean soup that Alvaro had stored in the freezer, and her ubiquitous grilled cheese. Bibi was an excellent cook in Megan's opinion, but the local customers had come to expect Alvaro's creative flair, and a simple grilled cheese with potato chips was not quite up to par.

Bibi didn't take it personally. "I cook food that nourishes," she said as she placed carrot sticks on a plate next to a grilled cheese and tomato on whole wheat. "They want fancy, let them go to that yoga center."

Megan forced her eyes not to roll. The

whole point was that she didn't want them to go to the Center. Megan washed a dirty pot, then hung it above the work station. The café's kitchen wasn't huge, but it was a comfortable size and had ample storage. She pulled a smaller pot from a cupboard.

"Do you want me to make more potato salad?" she asked her grandmother.

"No, I think we have plenty in the refrigerator."

Megan checked and sure enough, Alvaro had left them well-stocked. "Alvaro's Mexican coleslaw is in here too. That would go well with the Panini." Megan loved Alvaro's take on coleslaw. Red and green cabbage. Red peppers. Black beans. Fresh corn. Cilantro. Just a few dices of jalapeño. A little mayonnaise, sour cream, lime juice, and his secret seasonings. Every vegetable sang.

"I don't know what's wrong with plain old coleslaw," Bibi said. "I've been making it the same way for sixty years and not once has anyone complained."

Megan hung her head. "Your coleslaw is delicious too." And it was. But Megan needed her chef back.

Megan said, "Do you need me here, Bibi?"

They both glanced out past the lunch counter, toward the café's small dining room. Merry Chance, the town nursery's owner, sat chatting with Roger Becker and his wife Anita. All three were eating black bean soup. None of them seemed in any hurry.

Bibi shook her head. "Clover's here. I think we can hold down the fort. Emily is coming to run the register in an hour."

Megan thanked her grandmother for stepping in. She had somewhere to go, so she excused herself. She'd decided not to wait for Maria to call her back. While her head screamed "invasion of privacy," her heart had a different take on the matter. Picturing Alvaro's deadened stare, Megan climbed into the truck and set out for another town.

Alvaro lived about seven miles outside of Winsome, in a small hamlet called Brightonburg. Brightonburg was closer to Dartville than Winsome, and the entire town consisted of a handful of large working farms, a convenience store, an old mill, and a spattering of fifties-style brick ranch homes. The Hernandez family lived in one of the brick ranch homes, on a two-acre lot off the main road. The house was a tidy replica of its neighbors' homes, except that a huge garden took up much of the side yard. Megan could make out potato plants, corn, and Swiss chard alongside rows of

157

bean vines growing up ornate trellises. Flowers lined a path to the front door, and the side beds overflowed with late summer color. It was a quiet home on a quiet street — except for the cars parked in the lot.

Megan had never been to her chef's home. Alvaro was a private man, and she respected that. But given what she knew from Bobby King, she was concerned — about him, about Maria, and about the effect on Clover and Clay should something happen. Megan parked the truck several houses down from Alvaro's place, parallel to the curb. She recognized Alvaro's older Saab and his wife's Honda. Behind their cars was a plain black sedan with official plates. An unmarked. Megan's worries were confirmed.

She killed the engine and was debating what to do when the front door of the Hernandez home opened. Detectives Lewis and Jones came outside with Maria between them. She wore no handcuffs, and her attractive face was a mask of indifference. Behind her stood Alvaro, short frame rigid, hands clasped in fists.

Lewis walked ahead. Detective Jones hovered next to Maria, as though afraid her charge would run. Only Maria walked slowly, shoulders back, not hurrying, even when Detective Jones prodded her along.

An arrest or more questioning? It wasn't clear. The older woman climbed into the back seat, retaining her regal posture despite the situation. Megan saw her turn to Alvaro and smile lovingly before Lewis closed the door.

The police car pulled away.

Alvaro stood in the doorway a long time, watching an empty road. If he saw Megan's truck, he didn't react. But Megan suspected he only had eyes for his wife, who was by now long gone.

After a drawn-out internal debate, Megan decided to leave Alvaro alone. She watched as he re-entered their home and closed the door, and then she called her father's cell phone. If Detectives Lewis and Jones were here, they were no longer with Sylvia. And if they were still questioning Maria, they had not arrested her father's wife. So what was going on?

Eddie didn't answer on the first try. Megan hung up and called again. And again.

When Eddie finally picked up, he sounded weary. "This is never-ending, Megan. She certainly hasn't been cleared. Is it alright if we remain at the farm?"

"Of course."

"And that attorney . . . we may need her."

"I think that's a good idea." Megan gave him her name and number again and paused while he recorded the information. "Did the police give you any indication of what was happening?"

"Not really. But they questioned Sylvia for more than two hours. And they had a warrant for her phone and computer."

"I'm sure she has nothing to hide."

Eddie didn't respond. Megan heard a dog bark, and she figured they were back at Washington Acres. "Do you need me to come home?" Megan asked.

"No," Eddie said quickly. "We're fine. I think we may go for a walk. I'd like to get Sylvia out for some fresh air."

Another call rang in. Megan recognized her Aunt Sarah's number. Stomach tightening, she let it go to voicemail.

"Call the lawyer, Dad. It will make you both feel better. Especially if they've taken Sylvia's phone."

"I will. I will." He sounded noncommittal and Megan thought she'd have to call the lawyer herself. "Okay, I'll see you later? I should be with Sylvia now."

"Yes, of course. The pizza restaurant opens tomorrow, so it's a big day. Come, be part of it. Maybe it will help take your mind off things."

"Yeah, sure." Megan heard a door close, the hiss of water. Then her father said softly, voice barely a whisper, "I'm afraid she's not telling me everything, Megan. Sylvia's not acting right. I think something happened between her and Thana, something she's hiding." The water stopped and Eddie's voice lowered even further. "Thana was your friend. What could it have been? Can you think of a reason someone would want her dead?"

Megan wondered the same thing. "I just don't know."

A door opened and Eddie's voice became unnaturally cheerful. "Okay, then, Snicker-doodle. We'll see you tonight." He clicked off.

Eddie Birch hadn't called Megan Snicker-doodle in twenty years. Something was definitely going on.

THIRTEEN

Megan still knew the route by heart. Through Winsome by way of Canal Street, past the post office, left at Winnie's Hair Loft, down Long Mill Road, past Vinnie's Coffee Shack and Car Wash, and through the gated entrance to Deer Meadow Estates. The gate had long since gone the way of Vinnie's Coffee Shack and Car Wash, and it sat in rotted pieces by the side of the pitted drive. The Moore home was the last house on Winter Road, near Deer Meadow Pond. And if history was any predictor, Wesley Moore would be sitting outside on the porch of his modular. Or he'd be down at the pond.

It didn't take long to see him. Same hulking shoulders. Same full beard.

The day was hot and soupy, with no rain in sight. The pond, like much of Winsome, was suffering under the drought, and rings now marked the previous water lines. A dock extended into the water like a hand on a clock, only it now sat two feet above the surface. A man sat on the dock in a hunter green folding chair, a thermos by his side, a fishing rod in his hand, the line dangling into the murky water below.

Megan approached slowly.

"I was wondering when you'd come around," Wesley said. He reeled in the line, then cast it right back out. It was then that Megan noticed the absence of bait on the hook. "I see you made good here in Winsome."

"I'm sorry about Thana."

"I'm sure you are."

There was no hint of rebuke or sarcasm in Wesley Moore's tone. He wound in the line again, but this time he attached the empty hook to the reel and placed the rod on the wooden dock. He turned his chair around so it was facing Megan.

Thana's father had to be in his early sixties now, but he looked like a man two decades older. His once shaggy gray curls were white and thinning. His beard was spotty in places, and red, irritated skin shone through in patches. His eyes looked rheumy, and his nose bore the bulbous, reddened veins of an alcoholic. Megan felt her resolve wane. How could she add to this man's troubles?

"I'm glad you came by, Megan. I haven't seen anyone from Thana's old days. Not one person."

"I'm sorry to hear that."

Wesley looked out, over the woodland that surrounded the pond and toward his own home. Deer Meadow Estates had been built in the eighties to look like a mountain vacation resort. Unlike the gate that once protected it, the woods and pond had remained, but now only about half of the faux log cabins seemed to be occupied. Like his neighbors' homes, Wesley's was a modular with cheap vinyl log cabin siding and red window trim. His lawn was brown and uncut, and a mess of weedy perennials lay in various states of decay around his front porch.

"The missus has been gone three years now," Wesley said, following her gaze. "Those were her flower beds. I haven't had the heart or the back to maintain them." He turned to look at Megan. "My daughter was murdered."

"I know."

"I told the police it was that boyfriend of hers, Elliot." Wesley picked up the fishing rod and began polishing the wooden handle with a handkerchief, as though it was a gun.

"I'd been telling Thana to leave him for months. She finally did it. And this is what happened." His voice stayed steady, but the rheumy eyes moistened. "For once she listened to me and it got her killed."

"It wasn't your fault."

"Easy to say."

True, Megan thought. "So you told the police about Elliot?"

"Lewis and Clark?" He smiled at his own joke. "Yeah, they were here. Asking all kinds of questions about Thana. Her lifestyle. Did she take drugs? Had she pissed someone off lately? Did she sleep with strange men? As though she was the one on trial."

"That's often how these things go, Mr. Moore. Sometimes the victim's life holds the key to what happened."

He regarded Megan as though he were just seeing her for the first time. "I forgot that you went off to law school." His eyes narrowed. "Did you and Thana ever patch things up? I was sad to see your friendship end, you know. You were good for her. After you ended your friendship, she wasn't the same. I hope you were able to let go of your grudge."

"I never held a grudge."

"Then why didn't you call her? Try to see her? She never forgot you, Megan."

"Things changed. I was sorry for what happened back then." Megan didn't want to go there. She didn't want to get into a discussion about who had hurt whom. She figured they'd both done their fair share of damage. "I'm sorry we lost touch."

"She never did tell us what happened. We figured it was some silly teenage thing." His eyes searched Megan's for an indication that this was the case. "Me and Konstantina, we hoped you'd patch things up."

"I always liked Thana's mother. She was like a parent to me."

Wesley's eyes looked far away. His attention turned to the lake. "She's gone three years now."

"I'm sorry for your loss."

"And now my daughter."

"Mr. Moore, why do you think Elliot hurt your daughter?"

The mention of Elliot's name seemed to return him to the present. "They were always fighting. Elliot liked to pretend he was Mr. Casual, never a care in the world, but he is as controlling as they come. Got to the point that he didn't even want Thana to come here."

"She told you that?"

"She told me, and I witnessed it."

"Was he ever aggressive with Thana in

front of you?"

Wesley's hand flew to his face. He dabbed his sweaty skin with the handkerchief he'd used on the fishing rod. "Not exactly." He hesitated. "It was more like possessiveness. She'd stand where you are, and he'd be standing over her. She'd get a phone call and he'd want to know who it was right away. I even caught him reading her text messages." Wesley tucked the handkerchief in his pants pocket and examined the rod handle. "It was like he didn't trust her."

"Did Thana ever complain to you? Express fear of Elliot?"

"The police asked me the same thing. No, not exactly."

"Not exactly?"

"Once I saw a hint of it. More than a hint, I guess." Wesley looked uncomfortable. "They'd stayed at the house for a night. It was after my surgery — I had to have a hip replaced and needed some help for a week or so. Thana came and he joined her one evening. I didn't like that, not that she asked me." Wesley's skin flushed. "They were in the room next to mine. I . . . I heard them."

Wesley's obvious discomfort was making Megan squirm. "It's okay, Mr. Moore. You don't need to say anything else." Megan could imagine what he'd heard.

"No, it wasn't like that. And it needs to be said." He scrunched his face into a visage of resolve. "She was crying out. I heard a thump, arguing. Something smashed against the wall and shattered. Finally I had to bang on the wall and threaten to call the police. You know what that's like? I couldn't walk. I had to bang on the wall to help my daughter." He sat straighter, gripping the fishing rod so that his knuckles were white. "He left the next morning before I was up. It was the last time I saw them together. She left him a few days later."

Slowly, wearily, Wesley rose from the chair, his awkward movements underscoring the long healing process. "I asked her the next day if she was alright. She said Elliot was just angry about one of her paintings. That he wanted her to sell it to someone she didn't want to sell it to."

"I heard Elliot was an artist as well."

Wesley's laugh lacked any discernable humor. "So he said. Never saw anything he made except some tin can garbage he called modern art." Wesley scowled. "He saw himself as her manager — part of that controlling thing. That's ultimately why Thana left him. The truth was my daughter paid him to frame her work. That's how he made money."

"Did he frame others' work as well?"

"Don't know. Maybe. Had to pay the bills somehow."

Megan thought about this. An up and coming artist dates someone who's been described as rough around the edges — at best. Maybe abusive. And an aspiring artist whose career was going nowhere. Was her success enough to set him off?

"What about Ray Cruise, Mr. Moore? Was Thana still friends with him?"

"Ray who?" Wesley looked genuinely confused.

"The man who owned the Center in Dartville. We were all friends in high school. Thana, me, Mick Sawyer, and Ray Cruise."

"Thana never mentioned him." Wesley started to fold his chair. "I'm going inside for a bite to eat. Would you like to join me? I made meatloaf, and it's not half bad."

Megan smiled. "Thank you, Mr. Moore. Maybe another time."

He nodded, already shuffling toward the walkway that led to his house. "Don't be a stranger, Megan," he called over his shoulder.

"I won't." She watched her old friend's father disappear inside, his chair and fishing rod left behind on the porch.

Megan got into her truck and glanced at the clock on her dashboard. Almost dinner time. Bibi, Clover, and Emily could hold down the fort at the café, and the farm was in the capable hands of Clay and Porter. She wanted to call Denver but realized he was likely asleep. She sent him a quick email telling him how much she missed him and then decided to make one more stop for the evening.

Elliot Craddock. Although an internet search only turned up an address in Philadelphia, she had a general idea of where she might find him. A text to Clover gave her an exact address for his beer-loving buddies. Megan pulled out of Deer Meadow Estates battling a feeling of sadness. For her childhood. For Wesley Moore and his lost family.

Evening was pressing down and the blue sky was beginning to darken. The air, thankfully, had cooled a few degrees and the humidity had lessened. Megan rolled down her window, grateful for the rush of air against her skin, and thought about Wesley Moore. Such a lonely figure. He'd said Elliot was abusive, but could his impressions be trusted? He'd also had no recollection of Ray Cruise, but yet he remembered Megan immediately. Ray, Megan, and Thana had once been the three Winsome musketeers. Had Ray made less of an impression, or was Wesley an unreliable witness? He certainly loathed Elliot — and his story held the ring of truth. Clover didn't seem to care for Elliot either, but Bobby King said he was an okay guy.

She needed to see for herself.

Clover and Bobby King shared a Colonial-style duplex in a neighborhood off Canal Street, in the busier section of town. Their house was painted gray and white, and both sides were uniformly neat. Trimmed lawns, mended fence, newly painted trim. Bobby's parents lived in the other half of the duplex, and they rented half to King so he could save for his own home. In return, Bobby and Clover kept up the shared yard and exterior maintenance. It was an arrangement that seemed to work. Except, according to Clover, for their neighbors.

The Kings' home abutted an apartment complex, one of the few in Winsome. More specifically, it abutted a sprawling Victorian that had been added on to in haphazard ways over the years, before Winsome's Gestapo-like zoning board took over. The result was a peach-colored monstrosity with multiple balconies and a yard consumed by parking spaces. As Megan pulled in front of Clover's house, she saw a group of men sitting on one of those balconies, drinking Budweiser and tossing pennies into a can on the ground. Megan took a deep breath. She never liked dealing with drunk people — especially groups of drunk men barely out of adolescence.

Nevertheless, she marched forward.

One of them cat-called. "Coming to party?"

"Hey, bring our pennies up here?" another yelled. "And we'll give you a beer."

"No thanks," Megan yelled up. She tried to see their faces, but the low-lying sun shone in her eyes. She cupped a hand over her brow and shouted, "But if you can tell me where to find Elliot Craddock, I'll buy you a case of Bud."

The group went silent. Megan could make out six guys, all in their twenties. Two wore baseball caps. One wore a Drexel t-shirt and a pair of khaki shorts. Another had on a ripped black Rush t-shirt that framed heavily tattooed arms. The other two were leaning up against the exterior wall of the house, faces in the shadows.

"Who wants to know?" Drexel yelled.

"A friend of Thana Moore's."

More silence.

"What friend?" Drexel yelled. He leaned over the balcony railing. "I didn't think Thana had female friends."

"I was a school mate of Thana's. I'd really like to talk to Elliot."

Drexel said, "Sorry. No Elliot here."

"Yeah, well, I just want to give him my condolences," Megan said. "If he shows up, can you tell him Megan Sawyer stopped by? Thana knew me as Megan Birch."

No response. Drexel moved back, under the awning.

Realizing she wasn't going to get anymore from these guys, Megan walked back to her truck. It wasn't until she'd pulled away from the curb that she realized the pennies had stopped flying and the men had disappeared inside. Suddenly the party was over.

FOURTEEN

Megan stopped at her Aunt Sarah's cottage on the way back to the farm. Sarah Birch, who wrote award-winning mystery novels under the pen name Sarah Estelle, lived on the outskirts of Winsome in a cottage nestled in the woods. The house and yard had storybook charm, with their masses of perennial gardens, tiny fairy villages, and brightly painted bird houses. As Megan walked up the steps toward her aunt's house, she felt some of the day's anxiety wash away.

No one answered her knock, but eventually her aunt called from somewhere inside the house and told her to come in. Megan twisted the knob and found it unlocked. She wandered through the small house until she spotted her aunt sitting at her dining room table, laptop open, typing madly away. An orange tabby sat placidly next to the computer, bathing himself in a slice of sunlight.

The cat opened its eyes when Megan entered, then closed them languidly once more.

"Sit," Aunt Sarah said. "Let me finish this scene."

Megan accepted a chair. She pulled out her phone.

"No phone," Sarah said without taking her eyes off the screen or her fingers off the keyboard. "Distracting. And don't pet Harley. He'll start purring again and that will distract me."

And so Megan sat at the table listening to the *click, click* of Sarah's short nails hitting the keys. After a few minutes, her aunt removed her yellow-and-black-striped readers and rubbed her eyes.

"I apologize for that," she said. "Deadline."

"Sorry to have disturbed you."

Sarah smiled. "Nonsense. I'm always happy to see you." And she did look happy. Sarah Birch was her great aunt — her grandfather's younger sister. A tall, sturdy woman, Sarah had long gray hair she often wore in a braid or pinned up on her head. She was fond of shapeless, comfortable clothes and kaftans, and this evening she wore a yellow linen kaftan embroidered with tiny red, blue, and black flowers, and a pair of flowing black pants. Her size ten feet were bare, nails painted red. Her hands were large and strong, and unlike her toenails, her fingernails were clear of polish and had been trimmed almost to her fingertips. She wore no rings.

"Do you ever think of dating again?" Megan asked, the question surprising her as much as it did her aunt.

Sarah laughed. "No. Men my age are looking for women twenty years younger, and men older than me need more care than I'm willing to give." She leaned in, giving Megan that piercing stare that Megan had become accustomed to. "Why are you asking me this?"

"No particular reason."

Sarah stood, stretched, and walked out of the dining room. Harley followed her. From the kitchen, she said, "There's always a reason, Megan. You just might not know it yet — or want to admit it."

Sarah returned with two glasses of iced tea. "So what brings you by on a Friday night?" She sat back down in a different seat, away from her computer. "And where's that handsome doctor of yours? Have you had a falling out?"

Megan smiled. "No, he's traveling." She told her Aunt Sarah about Denver's sister in Scotland. "He wanted me to go, but —"

"But you're far too needed and important to leave for a week."

Megan smiled at the implied rebuke. "Something like that."

"Life is short." Sarah took a sip of iced tea. "Which is why I'm having a steak for dinner. Would you care to join me? We can throw two on the grill. I have some nice broccoli from your farm, as it happens. And a good Pinot Noir."

"I can't stay."

"You can. You choose not to."

"Were you always like this?"

Sarah laughed. "You're thinking it may be why I'm no longer married? Well, I tell it like it is. I guess I've done it my whole life, but as one gets older, they grow more like themselves. At least that's my belief." She pushed her tea away and steepled her fingers. "Okay, so I'll be eating alone and you'll be missing your beau. What else?"

"Did you get my message?"

Sarah looked momentarily confused, and Megan thought perhaps she'd forgotten to leave a message. Then Sarah brightened. "Ah, the pizza restaurant opening night! I did, but I was on page 346, a pivotal scene, and couldn't respond right then."

"Did you have a chance to call my —"

Megan couldn't quite bring herself to say the word.

"Mother? Unfortunately she's about to be a grandmother. Not a good time."

The words were wounding. A grandmother. From a sibling Megan had never met. And Aunt Sarah said this all so matter-of-factly, as though Charlotte needed to buy pantyhose or wash her car.

"I see."

Sarah frowned. "Megan, you and your mother haven't had a relationship in almost twenty-five years. You can't get upset now. This — the baby — has nothing to do with you." Sarah's expression softened. "You're feeling left out. I'm sure this continues to be a shock. Little Sean should be born tomorrow. C-section. After that, I'll call her."

"You never called her?"

"Of course I never called her. She would drop everything to see you, and she has other obligations right now. Surely you see that."

Surely. Megan looked out the window. She watched a fat Robin perched on a branch outside Sarah's house. The bird cocked its head and flew away.

Megan stood. "Thanks, Aunt Sarah."

"I always upset you."

"That's not true." *Yes, you do.*

"Your mother wants a relationship with you. She's made that clear. She's waiting on you, Megan, but it's not fair to expect her world to stop when you're ready to get onboard."

"I just wanted to invite her to the farm. I had no idea about the baby."

"I know you didn't." Sarah took a deep breath. "How about if we try to schedule something later. Maybe a brunch or a tea? We could do it here."

Megan couldn't think of a worse idea. "No, no, it's fine. I'll wait a week or so and reach out to her myself."

Sarah nodded, but the worried look remained in her eyes. "I'll be there tomorrow. I'm looking forward to it."

"Thank you."

Sarah walked Megan out to her truck. "I heard about that young woman, Thana Moore. Bonnie said she'd been your childhood friend. That must be hard."

"I hadn't seen her in years."

"It doesn't make it not hard."

"No, it doesn't." Megan opened the truck door. "Did Bibi also tell you about my father's wife? The police suspect Sylvia could have had something to do with Thana's death."

"Bonnie left that part out. But you know your grandmother when it comes to her son."

Megan didn't need to say anything. Bonnie Birch's soft spot for her only child was notorious. "And Alvaro's wife, Maria, is on the hot seat as well."

At this, Sarah's eyes widened. "Maria Hernandez? Whatever for?"

"She worked there. Had a disagreement with Thana over some art work — at least that's the word on the street." Megan dared say no more.

"Hmm. Maria's no killer. The papers aren't saying much, but it sounds like whoever did this did it in cold blood."

"Yes. Strangulation. With a woman's scarf." Sylvia's scarf to be exact.

"That doesn't mean anything."

"I know that and you know that," Megan said. "But try telling it to Starsky and Hutch over at the Dartville PD."

Sarah smiled. "I write mysteries, remember."

"Well, maybe you'd like to help solve a real one."

Sarah seemed to consider this. She pushed an invisible hair away from her face and looked around the yard. "I don't have time to get involved, the deadline and all, but I will tell you that Thana was doing some work for the New Beginnings Ministry in Brightonburg. You might want to talk to the pastor there. Her name is Elizabeth Yee. Maybe she can tell you something about Thana that will help."

"Thana did work for a ministry?"

Sarah nodded. "She was donating her time to paint a mural on the outside of the church. They do a lot of youth outreach. They wanted something edgy but regional." Aunt Sarah's hands flew up. "Something to attract the millennials."

"And you know this because?"

Sarah smiled. "Who else?"

"Merry."

They both laughed. Merry Chance's nosiness was as famous in Winsome as her holiday dinner parties.

The sun had mostly set and the mosquitos were out in droves. Megan slapped one on her arm. "I'll talk to Merry. Maybe she knows more."

"She'll be there tomorrow. You might be able to catch her then."

Megan said good-bye and climbed into the truck. She realized she felt tired and hungry, and while she was disappointed that her mother wouldn't be there tomorrow, she also experienced a frisson of relief. Her mother meant pressure and emotional angst she didn't need. Not for such a big day.

She rolled up the window and put on the air conditioning. The radio was tuned to a local news station, and she caught the tail end of an update on Thana Moore. "No arrests yet," was what she heard. "And anyone with information is urged to come forward."

No arrests yet. Megan figured that was a good thing.

By the time Megan got back to the farm, the sun had set completely and a sliver of moon shone in the sky. Megan pulled on a light long-sleeved jacket from the back of her truck to protect against mosquitoes and walked back toward the barn. She'd check on Heidi and Dimples, the goats, and make sure the chickens were tucked in for the evening. She could hear Gunther clawing at the porch door, so she let him out and he accompanied her on her rounds.

Heidi and Dimples were curled up in their pen. They ran to her as she entered and began pushing up against Gunther — their way of teasing the dog. He stood there placidly and took it, a farm dog to the end.

"Hey girls," Megan mewed. "What are you doing?"

A white form leapt over the goat gate and

the barn cat, Mutton Chops, joined them. Cat and dog had an understanding. Dog pretended that cat wasn't something he'd like to chase, and cat pretended she didn't hate dog. This meant they mostly ignored each other, although if Gunther got too close, Mutton Chops would hiss.

Today she jumped on the hay bales the goats liked to stand on and began a personal grooming regimen, keeping a wary eye on the dog.

Megan scratched Dimples behind the ears. Sometimes she swore that goat thought it was a dog. "Now if only people could set aside their differences the way dogs do."

"Will never happen."

Megan looked up to see Sylvia standing in the weak glow of the outdoor light. Sylvia smiled. "I was taking a walk. Your father's watching a game."

Megan opened the gate, and the petite woman walked through. She glanced around the pen looking only slightly put out before taking a seat next to the cat on the hay.

"My grandfather was a farmer," she said. "A small fig farm in Verona. Perhaps that's why I'm such a romantic."

Megan wasn't sure she'd compare her father's marriage to Romeo and Juliet, but who was she to judge? "It must be beautiful there."

"You'll see when you visit. It's breathtaking."

They sat in silence for a moment, Megan on the ground with the goats and Sylvia on the makeshift bench. Mutton Chops rubbed her head against Sylvia, but she ignored the cat and eventually it settled down next to her denim-clad leg.

"I need you to do something for me," Sylvia said. She slid something across the floor toward Megan. "There is a number on there. Please call it. The woman who will answer is named Chiara. She's my aunt. Just tell her to send the money." Sylvia's curt tone belied the pleading in her eyes. "Don't tell her about me and this legal nonsense. Don't tell Eddie I'm asking this of you. Don't say anything to Chiara except that I could not contact her myself and she should send the money. She will know what to do from there."

Megan stared at her. She sat there quietly, absorbing Sylvia's request, until her eyes were throbbing and she felt Heidi gnawing on her knuckle with her bony gums.

"Sylvia, why can't you contact your aunt yourself?" she asked quietly.

"Because I am under suspicion by the

United States government —"

"The police, but okay."

"And my lawyer whose name you gave us, she said not to contact anyone if it would seem suspicious." Sylvia shrugged. "Plus, the police took my phone."

"Then maybe you shouldn't be contacting your aunt at all if it seems suspicious." And asking for money certainly sounded suspicious, even to Megan. "Why do you need the money? To pay the attorney fees?"

"It doesn't matter. I just need to get in touch with Chiara. You will call, no?"

"No." Megan slid the number back across the floor. A curious Heidi sniffed it and started to pick up the paper.

Sylvia's eyes widened in surprise. She snatched the number. "I thought I could count on you."

"Then tell me why you need the money."

Sylvia closed her eyes. When she spoke again, there seemed to be genuine regret in her voice. "I'm afraid I can't. You will need to trust me, Megan. I have done nothing wrong. The need for the money is legitimate."

Sylvia stood. She walked to where Megan was sitting and placed the paper down in front of her. "*Ciao,* Megan. Whatever you decide, please don't tell your father about this conversation. Trust me on that at least. It's for his own good."

Megan tucked the paper into the pocket of her jacket. She wasn't sure what she'd do with it, but she was too tired to decide that now. For now, she'd sit outside with the animals and wait until it was late enough — or early enough, if you were in Scotland — to call Denver.

It seemed the animals were the only sane ones in her life.

FIFTEEN

Saturday brought with it sunshine and a break from the humidity — but still no rain. Today, though, Megan wasn't complaining. It was a perfect late summer day for an event, and hopefully the breeze would keep the bugs at bay. Megan spent the morning tidying up the house and yard and checking and rechecking to make sure everything was in order.

Denver called her at two to wish her good luck. "I wish I could be there, Megs," he said. "I know this is important to you."

"And to Clay. This was his baby, and I think his ego is tied into the outcome."

Megan was in the small commercial kitchen they'd set up in the old barn, chopping red onions from the farm for use in the house salad. Tonight's menu would be simple. Every adult would receive a field green salad tossed with Bibi's maple cider vinaigrette and a personal wood-fired pizza with their choice of local products as toppings. Caramelized onions. Morgan Farms sausage, barbeque chicken, and pepperoni. Red and green peppers. Even goat cheese. Anything, really. And Alvaro's amazing tomato sauce. Children under ten could opt for crudités with ranch dressing and a smaller personal cheese pizza for free. The kids' wood-fired pizzas were adorable; Clay had practiced making them until he could master the crust on such a small oblong shape.

The onions caused Megan's eyes to tear. She dabbed at them with a napkin. "How's your sister?" she asked Denver.

"Not too well, I'm afraid. Still having difficulty with basic tasks." He sighed. "I know she'll get through this, but I wish I could make it better for her. She has a long road of physical therapy ahead of her before she'll be running more marathons. Before she can walk to the front stoop, for that matter."

Megan had never met Denver's older sister, but she'd heard about her eccentric personality and her love of running. "She's lucky to have you," Megan said. "I hope you're finding some time to enjoy Edinburgh."

"If by enjoy you mean checking in on every one of Eileen's friend's pets, I am. It's funny how many Scottish dogs, cats, and horses, and even a rather cantankerous iguana, need a vet's attention this time of year."

Megan laughed. She bet that these requests for house calls from his sister's friends had more to do with his status as a handsome, single practitioner than the maladies of their furry and non-furry companions. "At least you're staying busy."

"And at least I don't have to cook. While my sister may be wishing for some lovely haggis accompanied by tatties and neeps, she'll have to make due with a spot of whiskey and some of her friend Bridgette's homemade tuna noodle casserole. You heard right, Megs. Or maybe her other friend Dolores's very traditional Scottish sauerkraut and pork, which she brought yesterday in a Crock-Pot large enough to feed the entire bloody country." Denver laughed. "Apparently Dolores did some research on the region of Pennsylvania in which we live and saw German heritage was common. I should be touched, right?"

Megan smiled. "As long as there is no actual touching, yes, you should be touched."

"You don't have to worry about that. My heart is loyal. Now if you had come with

189

me this problem would be a non-issue, you know. These ladies would see the beautiful farmer Megan Sawyer and stop visiting with their sluggish reptiles and their Betty Crocker recipes."

Megan pulled another onion out of the bin, wiped it with a damp cloth, and peeled off the outer layers. "But then you'd have to cook, although there is always takeaway. Pizza, I understand, is available everywhere."

"True." Denver paused. When he spoke again, his tone was serious. "Did you hear from your mother? Will she be attending tonight?"

Denver was the only person aside from Aunt Sarah who knew she'd invited Charlotte to the wood fired pizza opening. "No, she's busy."

When Megan didn't say more, Denver let it go. "And your father? He and Sylvia will be there?"

"As long as Sylvia isn't arrested first." Megan described recent conversations with her father and his wife — leaving out the bit about the request for money. "I have to admit, I'm worried about her and about Alvaro's wife, Maria. Have you heard from the police since they called you to confirm the details of your visit to the Center?"

"No, thankfully they've not called again. The first discussion with that Detective Jones was unpleasant enough. A lot of me cracking witty jokes and her not laughing even a little bit. But she must have realized there was no time to strangle an artist between the time I lounged in the reception area, or whatever they call it, and that first delightful bite of my Beef Wellington."

"You did go to the bathroom."

"True. Although the three minutes that took was barely enough time to *find* a scarf, much less use it." Denver's voice had lost its bantering tone. "It is awful, the poor woman. Do you have a sense that the police have any clues beyond Sylvia and Maria?"

"Just Thana's ex-boyfriend, but that's my hunch." Megan told Denver about her conversation with Thana's father and her visit to Elliot's hang-out. "He seems like a possible candidate."

"So you have a local artist on the brink of fame, and possibly fortune. Suspects? An envious and controlling ex. An Italian visitor with no apparent ax to grind. And an upstanding local citizen who got into a tiff with the deceased."

"That about sums it up."

Megan cleaned her chopping block and the knife and pulled a scrubbed and peeled carrot out of the cooler, her mind on Thana. She started to slice the carrots for the kids' meals. "Don't forget all of the as-yet-unidentified people with something to gain from killing Thana. Whether or not she was rich off her paintings doesn't matter. It's the perception that counts."

"Were any paintings missing from her van?"

"I don't know if they had an inventory of what was in there. Based on what Bobby told me, the van was like a traveling studio — half-finished work, supplies, and the like." Megan placed a row of uniform carrots sticks into a large container lined with paper towels. "I'll have to ask Bobby if there was any sign of theft."

"And no theft from the Center?"

"None that I'm aware of." Except the painting Maria supposedly took, but Megan kept that mum. "It makes me wonder, though — who else was angry at Thana? If she was difficult enough to anger Maria, who by all counts is Bucks County's answer to sainthood, then she must have ticked off others."

"Only one way to find out. Ask around."

Megan put her head back and closed her eyes. "How I wish you were here."

Denver laughed, and the sound was like

music to Megan. "You could use a massage. And maybe some heavy beef stew. Make an appointment at the Center. Use the facilities."

"And sneak around. I like it." Megan grabbed several more carrots and poised the knife over their bright orange bodies. "The tuna did you good. Brain power."

"I didn't take a bite of Bridgette's casserole," Denver said. "Pork and sauerkraut is more my thing."

"Four cancellations, two additions, and otherwise ready to go." Clay stood by the big wood fired oven. His long hair was up and tied in a ponytail. He wore khaki shorts, a blue Washington Acres Farm t-shirt, and a blue and white "Winsome Rocks" apron, courtesy of Bibi's stock of leftover Winsome souvenirs. He held a wooden pizza panel in one hand. "And now I just need my co-chef."

"Alvaro's not here yet?" Clover looked up from filling the glass Parmesan cheese shakers and the vegan "cheese" shakers. "I assumed he was in the kitchen, putting the finishing touches on the sauce."

Clay shook his head. "And he didn't answer the phone when I called. I tried him twice."

Megan frowned. Alvaro was always punctual, always reliable. She pictured him as he'd been the day before, standing in his door as the detectives took away his wife. She wished she had talked to him then, had gone inside and provided some comfort. He and Maria had no children. This would be devastating, and he was likely too proud to ask for help. She had little doubt today's absence was tied to Maria.

"Try him again." Megan finished arranging the flowers in the Mason jars. She plucked out a sunflower with a broken stem and replaced it with a fresh bloom before wiping her hands on her own apron. "Leave him a message asking him to call me as soon as he can."

"And tonight?" Clover asked. She looked around the renovated space, and Megan's gaze followed.

The picnic tables were pristine, the hostess station was gleaming, and even the wooden floor shone from the cleaning the team had done the day before. Megan glanced at Thana's paintings. She wondered if she should take them down, but opted not to. For better or worse, they would remain a testament to her former friend's talent.

"Tonight we go on," Megan said. "Clay

can make the pizzas. Porter will help in the kitchen and as needed by the oven. You and Emily can waitress. Bibi can seat our guests and I'll fill in as needed."

"Your dad doesn't want to help?" Clay asked.

"Help?" Megan smiled. Even if Eddie were to get involved — and he certainly hadn't offered — getting him up to speed would take half the evening. "He may show up to eat."

The barn door opened and Megan saw Bibi's head pop in and out. When she finally came in and closed the door behind her, she let out a long sigh. "Those dogs! They follow me everywhere."

"Which means you're carrying candy in your pockets again." Megan held out her hand. "Give it up, Bibi." She thought of Bibi's last medical appointment — and the results of her grandmother's bloodwork.

Bibi waved away the request. "Nonsense." But the skin on her face had colored to the shade of roasted beets. Bibi liked her sweets, and unbeknownst to her, Megan was aware of the not-so-secret stash of Hershey bars she kept hidden in a kitchen drawer. "It's almost showtime. Are we ready?"

Megan, exasperated, nodded. "Are you ready?"

Bibi walked around in a circle, hands out. She'd donned lavender sweat pants and a tie-dyed lavender sweatshirt for the occasion. "Tie-dye one on in Winsome" had been embroidered in a deeper shade of purple across the chest. "Ready and energized."

"Because of the sugar?" Megan frowned at Bibi, but it was a playful reproach. Chocolate hoarding was as much a part of who Bonnie Birch was as baking and Bridge. "Alright, Bibi, you'll manage the cash register. No freebies."

"No freebies here. We need the income, I know that." She glanced around. "Where's the old man?"

"Alvaro's not here yet." Megan didn't want to explain now and worry her grandmother. "Hopefully he'll arrive before the guests."

Bibi nodded, but her eyes clouded with concern. "That's not like him."

"No, it's not," Megan said.

Clover handed Bibi the clipboard with the reservations. "It's not at all like Alvaro. And I'm really worried."

Before she could say more, they heard tires on gravel. The first guests had arrived.

Sixteen

"Megan, this is the best pizza I've had in a long time." Merry Chance wiped her mouth daintily with a cloth napkin. She had half of a wild mushroom pie in front of her, and she pushed it forward, toward the center of the table. "Clay is a genius."

Megan picked up the tray. "I'm glad you liked it."

Merry was sitting with Roger and Anita Becker, and Bruce Holiday, Winsome's only architect. They all nodded.

"Delicious," Bruce said. He was a medium-sized, middle-aged man with thin lips and delicate hands. Bruce's most distinguishing feature was the ring of flaming red hair around his head, which contrasted with his perpetually pale skin. He'd finished his Winsome Pot Luck pizza, a combination of all the available toppings. "Nothing left to take home."

"Will this be a regular thing?" Anita

Becker asked.

"We hope so." Megan picked up the remainder of Anita's plain pie. "Just on Saturday nights during the summer. Maybe more often as the weather gets colder. At least that's the thought now."

"Well, Clay did a great job," Roger said. He glanced around. They were on the second seating, and the barn was full of people, chatter, and laughter. "Where's Alvaro? Not interested in moonlighting at the farm?"

"He couldn't make it tonight." Megan's stomach churned. She'd checked her phone a dozen times — no call from her chef. "Hopefully he'll be here next week."

"Doesn't look like his absence hurt sales." Bruce pointed toward the line at the reception counter.

Five people were standing at the counter, talking to Bibi. Others were milling about, looking at the décor or the art on the wall or talking to neighbors at nearby tables. The atmosphere was festive, the smells from the wood stove intoxicatingly delicious. Megan just wished she could enjoy it. The spots she'd saved for her mother, father, and Sylvia sat empty. Sylvia had a headache and Eddie was tending to her. Sarah had stopped by, stayed for a quick bite, and left. And then there was Alvaro.

Bibi's wave caught Megan's eye.

Megan gave her a one-second signal, handed Anita and Merry's pizzas to Emily to wrap, and made her way through the crowded barn to Bibi. The barn door opened and another group of people walked in.

"What's up?"

Bibi nodded toward the couple standing in front of her. "They heard about the event tonight and were wondering if we had any seats left."

"Or maybe we can get a pizza to go," the woman said.

Megan glanced at her watch. 8:16. The last of the pizzas had been served and patrons were beginning to leave, but Clay was still back at the ovens. "Let me check with my chef."

As she made her way through the picnic tables, she let herself enjoy this moment. Everyone seemed to love Clay's cheesy wood-fired creations, and the restaurant was a great way to showcase the farm's vegetables and other ingredients from small, local farms. She'd resisted this idea for so long, and now it seemed to be part of the financial answer they were looking for.

This farm was a treasure, but it was also a

money pit. Megan smiled at the use of the word treasure. Hadn't Simon Duvall died because of a supposedly buried treasure on this property? Megan had thought perhaps the real treasure lay under the new section of the barn, but the renovations hadn't turned up anything. Ah, well. Old-fashioned hard work — and this pizza farm — and maybe the Marshall property would be theirs someday.

Megan's thoughts returned to the here and now when she saw Clay at the oven. His face was red, his forehead covered with a fine sheen of perspiration, but he looked happy. Megan explained what the customers requested.

"No problem," Clay said. "I can throw a few more in. Just let me know what they want."

As Megan made her way back toward Bibi and the small crowd of new customers, she heard the front door slam and a deep voice say, "What the hell are you doing here?"

Another voice said, "I could ask the same about you."

"I belong here."

Megan couldn't see the speakers, but she recognized the source of one of the voices. Alvaro. She pushed between the people standing between the picnic tables until she was at the front of the room. Alvaro stood by the door. White hair was in disarray. Plaid shirt stained and untucked. Days' worth of beard shadowing his chin.

"Get out." Alvaro wasn't yelling, but the tone of his voice — practically dripping with threat — left little about his state of mind to the imagination. "Now."

Megan caught a glimpse of the man Alvaro was reacting to. Broad and muscular, he had dark, wavy hair that had been combed up, away from his face. Chiseled chin, dark eyes under heavy brows. He wore cargo shorts and a slim-fitting gray t-shirt, and tattoos snaked up his arms, around his biceps, and disappeared underneath tight sleeves.

Undaunted, Alvaro marched up to the taller man until his face was just inches from his chest. He let out a string of what Megan assumed were expletives in Spanish.

That's when Megan intervened. Long used to dealing with hostile witnesses, Megan kept her voice calm and her shoulders strong — projecting tranquility, strength, and confidence. Aware of all the eyes on her, and the sudden hush in the room, Megan inserted herself between Alvaro and the younger man. She placed a hand on Alvaro and quietly but firmly told him to come with her.

Alvaro's gaze locked on the man.

The guy started to speak. Megan silenced him with her stare. He backed away, hands up.

"Come on, Alvaro. Let's let Clay deal with this guy. I need to talk to you. Come with me."

After another moment, Alvaro's gaze wavered. He seemed to see Megan for the first time, and a flush crept over his face and neck. "Yes, yes, okay."

Megan and Clay exchanged a look. He immediately walked over to the younger man.

"Who else wanted pizza?" Clover asked, speaking to the huddle of new guests by the door. She clapped her hands. "We'll make some to go. On the house."

The younger man called out to Megan. "You wanted to see me," he said to Megan as though he needed to get in the last word. "I'm Elliot."

Megan, who by now was near the back of the dining area, nodded but didn't stop leading Alvaro toward the small kitchen. She could feel Alvaro tense under her touch, and she knew pausing to answer Elliot meant risking another outburst. She had no idea whether Elliot saw her nod over bodies standing between them. She just hoped he was still there when she came back out.

Porter was in the small kitchen washing dishes at the deep stainless steel sink, but he left without a word when Megan and Alvaro entered. Megan closed the door and turned to her friend and chef.

"What just happened in there . . . that's not you, Alvaro. What's going on?"

Megan stood with her back against the door. She looked down, realized her arms were across her chest, and placed them down by her sides. She waded through Alvaro's stony silence, aware that pressuring him wouldn't help.

She could hear nervous laughter through the door. The sound of Clover's voice above the fray. The clanking of silverware against the trays as Clover and Emily cleared the tables.

Finally, Alvaro said, "Maria was arrested at 5:17 today."

Megan's breath stuck in her lungs. So many things crossed her mind. Anger for Alvaro and Maria. Confusion at the detectives' decision. And, she hated to admit it, relief that they weren't arresting Sylvia. "I'm sorry, Alvaro. This must be a shock."

"They're wrong about Maria." He

punched a fist into his other hand and closed his eyes. "With the very last breath I take, I will insist that they're making a grave error. Whatever they think Maria did, they're wrong."

There was no seat in the stuffy kitchen, and Alvaro looked like a man who needed to sit down. Megan led him out the back door of the kitchen, into the older part of the barn. From there they found the rear barn entrance and escaped outside. The night air felt good against Megan's skin, and after hours in the barn, she felt grateful for the fresh air.

She walked to the hill in front of the old oak and sat on the ground. From this vantage point, she could see the side of the renovated portion of the barn, the greenhouses, and the old Marshall property, but not the entrance or the comings and goings of the evening's guests. She and Alvaro had some privacy, at least. After a moment, Alvaro joined her on the ground. He sat with his legs crossed, his body pin-straight, facing the old Marshall house.

"That pair of knit-wits showed up today and arrested Maria. She didn't react, but that's Maria. I, on the other hand, did not control myself so well." Alvaro turned to Megan. Even in the murky evening light she could see the pain portrayed in his features. "I told the cops exactly what I thought of their actions. Idiots."

"Do you know why they arrested her?"

"Because they think she killed that artist."

"Why do they think that, Alvaro?"

"They didn't tell me anything. Maria says it's because of the painting."

"What painting?" Megan thought she knew — the same painting Bobby King had told her about — but she wanted to hear it from him.

"Some painting that Thana did. Thana wanted more floor space at the Center. Maria told her no, she was already getting more than anyone else. Maria wanted things to be fair. That is her way, to look after everyone, not just the privileged. Thana got mad. They argued. Thana got Maria in trouble." He scrunched his eyes tighter, then opened them. Their intensity startled Megan. "Thana claimed Maria stole a painting. Ruined it. Had her fired."

"So the detectives think Maria acted in retaliation?" Exactly what King had said.

"According to my wife. Like someone would kill over a job. Like Maria would kill anyone. Me? Someone could believe that I might do such a thing, a crabby old man like me. Maria? No way."

Sitting now, watching her friend literally writhe in anger, Megan thought he had a point. "Surely she had an alibi."

"What alibi? She was supposed to be working, and then she was supposed to be gone. She'd been fired that morning. But she's a perfectionist, so she stayed to get things together, make sure everything was okay for the artists. It wasn't their fault, she said. But how could she prove that she was working if she was alone."

"Computer records?"

"She was organizing her paperwork. Getting things in order."

"We saw her, Alvaro. At lunch later that day." But even as Megan said the words, she realized how lame they sounded. She'd also seen Sylvia. Either could have done the deed and been back in time for lunchtime cocktails.

"It is all that bastard's fault. Elliot. I can't believe he had the nerve to show up here. I should have never trusted him. He's changed, Zaneta said. He's making good now, she said. *Bullshit.*"

"Zaneta?"

"My sister. Elliot is her stepson. A head case. A thief." Alvaro shook his fist in the air. "I should have never listened to Zaneta. She has the judgment of a drunk college student." He swung his head around. "I blame him. I blame me."

From somewhere down toward the house, laughter rang out. Megan heard car engines starting up, the sounds of people leaving. The event was over. She felt torn. No, she thought. She should be here, with Alvaro. She should be helping her friend. It was really Clay and Clover's night — and they could see it to the end.

Megan said, "Elliot was Thana's boyfriend, right? What did he have to do with Maria and the Center?"

But Alvaro was finished speaking about his wife. His expression obstinate, he locked his arms around his knees and rocked back and forth on the small hill. "You should put some benches out here," he said. "Maybe a patio. Facing the hills and that old house. It's calming."

"Alvaro, what did Elliot have to do with Maria's arrest?"

"If I hadn't come out here, I may have hurt him. The fresh air is calming." Alvaro stood. "A patio, some tables. In the fall it will be nice to eat warming pizza on a patio overlooking the hills."

Megan watched Alvaro wander down the hill toward his car. She'd forgotten to ask him if Maria had a lawyer.

"I can't. Work."

"Tomorrow's Sunday. You're done at noon. My appointment is at two."

Clover gave a half-hearted smile. "In that case, let's go." She held out her hands. "You've been working me hard these days. I could really use a manicure. And if I happen to get lost on the grounds?" She placed a hand over her mouth in an "oh, my" gesture. "I'm just not that smart."

Megan laughed. She thought about the card in her pocket. She'd finish her farm chores by ten, then try to find Elliot. Sunday's dance card was quickly loading up.

Clover yawned, and Megan suggested she leave. "Thanks for everything you did today. I can finish up here and lock up."

"Are you sure?"

"Yes. Just be careful going home. You never know."

Megan felt drained. She took a last glance around the barn to make sure everything looked clean and in place, and her gaze locked on Thana's paintings. Denver was right; the face depicted in the portrait echoed her own. Why had Thana used her as a subject? This painting had been done years after she and Thana lost touch. Had Thana simply needed a model and she pulled out some old photo of the two of them to use for inspiration? Had it been an unconscious act on Thana's part? Or was there something more sentimental about the painting's genesis?

She would never know.

Megan took a deep breath, shut the lights, and went outside. The night air felt oppressive against her skin. The sky was clear, a sprinkling of stars like pinpricks overhead. Megan decided to check on the goats before heading back to the house. She could see the kitchen and parlor lights on; Bibi was still up.

As Megan crossed the threshold that led from the barn to the goats' pen, she heard a rustle behind her. The skin on the back of her neck prickled, and she felt goosebumps erupt along the length of her arms despite the heat. She slowed down, her body tense, ready to fight or run.

Another rustle.

Slowly, she gripped the keys in her pocket, and pulled one between two fingers, point out, the way they taught in self-defense at the senior center. She spun around. No one was there.

"Megan?" It was a woman's voice. Tentative. Melodic.

"Charlotte?"

A woman stepped out of the shadows beyond the barn. Megan recognized her from their encounter over Christmas, only this time she was dressed like a Ninja. She wore black pants and a sleeveless black tunic, belted at the waist. Her hair was pulled back and pinned up with a tortoise-shell comb. Her face remained undecipher-able, hidden as it were by the darkness.

"You came," Megan managed. "But why . . . why are you out here?"

"I arrived while things were going on. I didn't want to distract you — you seemed to have your hands full — but I was afraid if you'd spotted me in the crowd and I left, you'd be hurt. So I waited."

"You startled me." So many questions, Megan thought, and that's what comes out of my mouth.

"I'm sorry. I certainly didn't mean to scare you."

"It's okay." Megan looked toward the house. The lights were still on. "Do you want to come down and have some tea? Or a drink? We could steal some of my grand-mother's brandy."

Charlotte smiled. "She still drinks tea with a shot of the hard stuff? Bonnie's done that since I . . . well, you know." She shook her head, as though warding off painful memories. "I don't think that's a good idea right now."

Megan agreed. She wasn't sure she was ready for this. Bibi? She wasn't sure her grandmother would ever be ready.

"I can't stay, Megan. I have to drive back to New Jersey, and I'm sure you've had a long day."

"I was just on my way to check on Heidi and Dimples, our goats. Want to join me?"

"How can I say no to that invitation?"

The girls were curled up in the enclosure, Heidi on the ground with Mutton Chops, the barn cat, and Dimples on a hay bale. Dimples jumped down, stretched, and greeted them at the gate.

Megan watched as her mother knelt down to pet Dimples. The goat rubbed her tiny head against Charlotte's leg, leaving a smear of dirt and hay on her pants.

"Dimples!"

Charlotte smiled. "She's fine. I love animals." She tickled Dimples under the chin, where the skin was soft and punctuated by wiry hairs. Dimples leaned into her harder.

"How did you hear about the dinner?"

"Your Aunt Sarah."

"I thought you . . . had other things going on."

"You mean my new grandchild?" Probably seeing the look of discomfort on Megan's face, Charlotte said, "It's okay, Megan. We obviously have a lot to share and talk about. The child belongs to my late husband's daughter, Kelly. I never had any kids after you."

"But all the pictures at Aunt Sarah's?"

"David's three kids and their families. He and I married about fourteen years ago. He was divorced, but his wife was an addict and not very responsible. I guess I finally settled into some semblance of mother-hood." She looked down at the goat and her face darkened. "David died four years ago. His kids' mother, a year before that. I'm all they have now."

Megan let that sink in. "Sarah never told me."

Charlotte smiled. "You know your aunt. She will not divulge anything she deems not to be her business. Half the time she won't even divulge the things that are hers to tell."

Megan had certainly experienced that. Because she needed something to do with her nervous hands, she sat by Heidi and lifted a reluctant cat onto her lap. "Sarah said she wouldn't tell you about tonight."

"Case in point. Isn't that what you lawyers say?"

They both laughed.

"Actually," Charlotte said, "I saw a flier for the dinner at the café yesterday. I was in town to see Sarah and take care of some business. I asked her about it, and she said you had mentioned it but that I shouldn't go because of Kelly." Charlotte shrugged. "I did what I normally do with Sarah. I thanked her and did what I wanted."

Megan smiled. It sounded like how she handled Sarah. Apparently they shared the stubbornness gene.

"I'm glad you came."

Charlotte swallowed hard, then nodded. She stood abruptly. "I should really go. I just wanted you to know I was thinking about you."

"You haven't seen the pizza restaurant. Would you like to take a quick walk through?"

"Would you mind?"

Megan smiled. "Of course not."

They secured the gate to the goats' pen and walked back across the yard to the public barn entrance. Megan unlocked the doors, flipped on the lights, and motioned for her mother to come inside. The air was still scented by roasting garlic and tomatoes and tinged with the pleasant smell of wood smoke.

Charlotte took a deep breath. "Oh,

Megan, it's lovely." She turned toward Megan and smiled. "I'm sorry I missed the dinner."

Megan didn't say anything. She watched as this woman who'd given birth to her, who walked out of her life without so much as a backwards glance, strolled around the room. She touched the delicate flower petals still in the Mason jars Megan had left on the tables. She looked inside the big stone wood-fired oven. She even glanced in the small kitchen off the rear of the room.

"A law degree. A farm. A café. And now this? Quite an accomplished woman." Charlotte paused by the paintings on the far wall. "Are these by that artist who died?"

"Yes. Thana Moore."

Charlotte didn't say anything for a moment. One slender hand reached out to the portrait and traced the edge of the cheekbone. "It's you."

Megan didn't respond. Her mind had wandered once again to Thana's murder, to Alvaro's anger and Maria's incarceration.

Charlotte spun around. "This is the artist from New Beginnings Ministry. Are you familiar?"

"I think Sarah mentioned it. Thana had done a mural for the mission?"

"Yes, that's right. I know the pastor, Elizabeth Yee. She and I grew up in Winsome together. I ran into her again later in New York, in the art world of all things. I was an editor for *Art* magazine, and Elizabeth was the subject of one of our pieces about art rescuing kids."

Elizabeth Yee. Sarah had mentioned her. "They must be heartbroken at the mission over what happened to Thana."

"I imagine they are. I haven't seen Elizabeth in years. I get the ministry's newsletter. That's how I know about the mural." She turned back to look at the portrait. "It's a swirl of faces and buildings and green pastures. Meant to be Winsome, I think. Or a collage of Winsome impressions. Quite something. You should go see it."

"Do you still have that newsletter?"

"I don't think so. It would have been a year ago, or longer." Charlotte pulled herself away from the paintings and returned to the front door. She shifted her small red bag so that it was held in front of her, like a shield. "Why?"

"Just curious. A friend's wife is being accused of the murder. No one who knows her thinks she's capable."

Charlotte's eyebrows shot up. "Isn't that always the case with murder?"

"Often, yes." Like desertion, Megan

thought. And then pushed the uncharitable notion away. "Oh, well. I was looking for some introduction to Yee."

"How about if I introduce the two of you by email? Then you can go over and talk to Elizabeth. She probably knew Thana fairly well."

Megan thanked her. She could go on her own, but Yee might be more willing to chat candidly if she knew they shared a connection.

They left the barn in silence. Megan felt awkward, unsure what to say next. Suggest a dinner? Ask to meet the baby? Say goodbye and hope for the best? She wasn't even sure what she wanted to happen.

At the parking area, only one car remained — a small, older model BMW. Charlotte glanced at the car, smiled, and then reached out, as though to give Megan a hug. Out of nowhere, a white furry creature ran between them. Gunther. He stood in front of Charlotte, his posture a warning.

"It's okay, boy," Megan said. "Down."

The dog dropped to the ground. His tail wagged, but his eyes remained on the stranger.

Megan said, "Charlotte, meet Gunther." She glanced around. "I wonder who let him out."

She didn't have to wonder long. A few seconds later, her father's form came ambling up the sidewalk. "Your grandmother was worried about you, Megan, and —" He stopped mid-sentence. "Charlotte?"

Eddie Birch said the name with such sadness, that Megan felt tears for her father well up in her eyes.

Charlotte said softly, "Eddie."

Megan backed away. All at once, she saw Charlotte's departure as something more than just her own heartbreaking legacy, the albatross she would forever wear. She saw a young man not much older than Clay left with a future alone, confused, anguished, and forced to parent despite being not much more than a child himself.

Slowly, her anger toward her mother started to roil and burn, pressing against her insides like a noxious substance. "You'd better go," she said to Charlotte.

Charlotte nodded. "Eddie," she whispered again before disappearing into her car. Then more urgently, "Eddie?"

But Eddie was rooted to his spot.

Silently they watched Charlotte drive off until she was a speck in the distant night, father and daughter each lost in their own thoughts.

EIGHTEEN

True to her word, Charlotte had sent an introductory email to Elizabeth Yee later that night. Megan awoke Sunday morning feeling groggy and determined, still nursing an emotional hangover from the night before. When she saw the email, she pushed her own sentiment out of her head and replied by asking Yee if she could stop by to talk with her about the ministry and Thana. Yee suggested she come by that morning, after their nine o'clock service. The small congregation would be sharing baked goods and coffee and planning for the week. They could sneak away for a few minutes.

Megan had wanted to track down Elliot, but she decided to head to New Beginnings first. She was curious about the mural, and even more curious to get a glimpse of who Thana had become through someone else's eyes.

After showering and donning a brown

pencil skirt, wedge sandals, and a favorite patterned vintage blouse, Megan ran down the steps and into the kitchen. She didn't want to talk about the exchange between her mother and her father, if one could call it an exchange, and she preferred to leave the house unnoticed.

No such luck.

Bibi sat at the kitchen table reading a newspaper and munching on scones. She was wearing her pink Sunday-church suit, but had slippers on her feet. She frowned when she saw Megan.

"What happened last night? Your father came in and stormed upstairs."

Megan grabbed her purse off the table. As casually as she could manage, she said, "Charlotte was here."

Bibi was about to take another bite of a scone. She lowered it, mouth opened and eyes wide. "Charlotte as in *Charlotte*?"

"Yes. Charlotte."

"Why in heaven's name was she here?"

Megan took a deep breath. She called on the good lord to give her strength for this conversation. "Because I invited her."

Bibi's put the paper down on the table. "You invited her here? Why would you do that, Megan?"

"Because she's my mother." Megan felt

221

herself getting defensive. She placed her purse back down on the table and took a second to get her feelings under control. It dawned on her that none of this would make sense to Bibi. She didn't know about the hospital or the letter or the nights Megan laid awake, wondering what to do about Charlotte and how to do it. "And because I needed to."

Bibi was about to say something else, and Megan raised a hand to stop her. "Clearly there's a lot I haven't told you that I should have, but I've been turning things over in my mind, trying to decide what matters and what doesn't. Right now I have somewhere I need to be, but we can talk later. Maybe over dinner tonight?"

Again Bibi looked ready to protest. Instead she nodded, although worry was evident on her face.

"Thank you," Megan said. She left, feeling like the world's worst granddaughter.

New Beginnings Mission Church was less traditional church and more storefront. It inhabited the north corner of an older one-story strip mall on the outer edge of Winsome. Next to it was a bakery that advertised organic bread and vegan muffins, and next to the bakery was a camera shop. The parking lot contained about a dozen cars of various makes and models. As Megan pulled beside an older model minivan, she saw Thana's mural. It was hard to miss.

Megan climbed out of the truck and walked to the side of the building, where Thana's mural had been painted over a flat brick wall. It was, indeed, a Winsome collage. She could make out historic Canal Street, the walking trail, Merry's stately foursquare, and what looked like the Washington Acres barn and the shadow of the old Marshall property. She saw Potter Hill and the state park. In the almost dizzying swirl of colors, she also identified faces. Young. Black. White. Some bruised and worn, others with the hopeful glaze of youth.

When standing farther back, the mural had a dream-like quality, the kind of crazy, mixed-up images one might see while trying to awaken from a deep slumber or an anesthesia-induced fugue state. But up close, Megan saw the workmanship that went into every tiny element, every face and building. Thana had talent. She used color in unexpected ways and made her own impression on her subjects. If art was supposed to make a person feel, then this was art. Megan felt shaken. Aware of her town in a way she'd never been before.

"Pretty amazing, isn't it?" Megan turned to see a man standing behind her. He was tall and slender, about her age, and wore jeans and a neatly pressed button-down shirt. Above a trimmed sandy beard was an aquiline nose and a set of intelligent, kind eyes. His head was completely shaved. He held out his hand. "I'm Joseph. Joseph Muller. I work with Elizabeth."

Megan shook his hand and introduced herself. "Elizabeth is expecting me." She turned back toward the painting. "Thana did this? It's . . . awe inspiring."

"Yes. And what's even more amazing is that she did it gratis. Wouldn't take a cent." He walked toward the front of the building and Megan followed. "Come on in. You're just in time for fellowship."

They entered directly into a large reception area. Folding tables stood against two walls and folding chairs had been sprinkled around the room. Each table was covered by a white table cloth and an assortment of breads, cheeses, and baked goods had been displayed on one table. A coffee urn, pitchers of juice, and small paper cups were offered on the other. The paneled walls were bare except for a cross, a Biblical painting, and a poster depicting a teenager panhandling on a street, head in his hands, which read, "Do you need help?" above a phone number.

About thirty people were in the room. Some were standing or sitting alone, eating. Others talked in pairs or small groups. Joseph touched Megan's elbow and nodded toward the back of the room where a sturdy Asian woman in her fifties was talking to a teenage girl. Joseph waved and the woman finished up her conversation before joining them.

"Megan." Elizabeth greeted her with a firm handshake and a warm smile. "It's so nice to meet you. Why don't you come into my office for a few minutes? Joseph, can you hold down the fort?"

"Sure." Joseph clapped his hands, looking eager to be the man in charge.

Megan followed Yee through the reception area, into a small worship room that held little more than a few rows of wooden benches and a podium, and into a back room. Yee flipped on a light and Megan found herself in a simply furnished office space. A large metal desk sat to one side, and three padded armchairs faced it. Bookshelves lined the walls, and Megan made out everything from Bibles, to self-help and pop psychology titles, to Aunt Sarah's mysteries.

Yee must have caught Megan looking at the fiction, because she said, "I'm a huge fan of Sarah Estelle's." She pulled an armchair out into the center of the room for Megan, then positioned another across from it. When they were both settled, she said, "We get runaways sometimes. They call the hotline. I try to make the office as casual and welcoming as I can. So many of these kids are easily spooked."

Megan understood. "Is that what persuaded Thana to do the mural? A desire to help with your ministry?"

Elizabeth stood. She walked to her desk, opened a drawer, and donned a pair of fashionable red glasses. Then she picked up a scheduling book from on top of her blotter.

Sitting back down, she said, "Thana actually approached us. Or, more specifically, approached Joseph. She wanted to give back to the community and thought she could do it by creating a mural, something lasting that would capture the area and what we're doing here. We own the building and so I thought, why not? If it helps bring attention to our cause, then it could be a good thing."

"And what is the cause? I'd love to better understand the mission of New Beginnings."

"We're a church. We have a small but loyal and passionate congregation. We cater to the disenfranchised — families unable to make ends meet, people who have felt the sting of social or racial injustice, runaways and teens who are burdened by drugs or mental illness." She smiled. "Everyone is welcome. Many churches say it, we mean it."

"That's a lofty goal — welcoming everyone. Isn't it sometimes difficult to remain true to those tenants?"

Yee nodded. "Of course. If it were easy, everyone would do it. But we're small so our needs are also small. I have faith, and so far God has provided."

"Did Thana's mural help?"

"It didn't hurt."

"But it didn't get you quite the attention you were hoping for?"

Yee took her time closing her appointment book. "Thana wanted us to call the media, make a show of the mural. She wanted, I think, attention for her charitable act."

"But attention like that would spook the very population you're trying to help," Megan said. "And so you didn't pursue it."

"You are Charlotte's child." As soon as she said it, Yee's face flushed. "I'm sorry. That was insensitive."

So she knows, Megan thought. Megan didn't want to go down that path. She didn't want to think about Charlotte. "Thana, Elizabeth."

"Yes, of course. You're correct. Thana wanted attention, but many of our flock are terrified of the limelight. They want to find peace, find God. They don't want fanfare, no matter how well intentioned."

"Thana went quietly?"

Yee seemed to consider the question. "Thana was a complex young woman. She had skill with the paintbrush, no doubt about that. But she was a chameleon, trying on personalities like other women try on clothes. When she first approached Joseph she was all smiles and good intentions. After the mural was finished, we saw a different side."

Megan thought about what Bobby King had told her — how Thana turned on Maria at the Center when Maria didn't give her more floor space. "Do you think Thana had mental health issues?"

"No, that wasn't it. I said chameleon, but maybe that's the wrong descriptor. She was like Jekyll and Hyde. When she wanted something, she was sweet as Georgia pecan pie. But I sensed that was a façade. Underneath there was something else festering.

An insecurity, a need not met." Yee shook her head. "The woman did us a favor, and here she's been gone only a few days, and I'm talking about her this way. Now tell me, Megan, why do you want to know all this about Thana?"

Megan debated on what to tell her. "A friend's wife has been accused of Thana's murder. I'm trying to understand if it's possible . . . if something could have triggered this murder. I knew Thana once, long ago. It seems she changed."

Elizabeth stood, the conversation over. "Or perhaps she grew into who she'd been all along." Yee held open the door. "I work with teens and young adults all the time. I've learned to love them unconditionally, but love does not demand gullibility. Many of those who need help the most are con artists. They've had to con to survive; it's become second nature."

"You think Thana was a con artist?"

"In a way." Yee started to head back into the worship room. She paused before reentering the front reception area and turned toward Megan. Her voice was low, almost a whisper. "My sense was that Thana had learned to put on the face that got her acceptance. But that mask would fall away

from time to time. And what was underneath wasn't always so pretty."

NINETEEN

The Center seemed back to business as usual. The parking lot was full of high-end vehicles, and live bodies populated the restaurant veranda, mostly couples and a few single ladies lunching. This was Clover's first visit to the new wellness resort, and she walked along the grounds with her mouth open.

"Someone had a lot of money. That building is new."

Megan nodded. "And made to look old and genteel."

Clover pointed to the real stone foundation. "No expense spared?"

"Wait until you see the interior. For a yoga and meditation retreat center, it is not humble."

Megan and Clover entered the Welcome Hall and were greeted by one of the aqua-clad minions. She inquired about the names with friendly reserve.

"The spa, please," Megan said, giving her name.

Clover asked for the restaurant. She'd decided to enjoy a meal on her own and then snoop around the Center while Megan did the same with the spa.

Today's "hostess" — a twenty-something with giraffe legs and a toothy, thin-lipped smile — pointed Megan in the direction of the spa before escorting Clover to the restaurant.

"Catch you later," Clover whispered.

They agreed to be out by the truck in two hours.

Megan followed directions to the spa. She walked through a solarium, past the hall that led to the "guest retreats," and down a glass enclosed walkway that looked out at the pastures, the Center's vegetable gardens, and the hills beyond. Admittedly, whoever designed the spa — presumably Carly Stevenson — knew what they were doing. Despite being less than an hour from Philadelphia and two hours from New York City, this felt like a country oasis, with only the best of rural living highlighted.

The spa was at the end of the glass corridor. An aqua door with the word "Wellness" marked the spot. Megan opened it slowly. She was immediately greeted by cool, moist air and the lingering scents of lavender and tea tree oil.

Spa reception consisted of a series of low teal ottomans spread throughout a dimly lit room. Soft instrumental music played overhead. A mister was the source of the scent, and cool lavender-tinged air sprayed from a Himalayan salt diffuser. A glass counter housed a single hostess. Like her Welcome Hall counterparts, she wore aqua, although hers was a soft aqua dress, not a suit, with the name "Trish" on a tag below her shoulder. She smiled when Megan approached.

"I have a manicure appointment." Megan gave her name.

"Ah, yes. This way, Ms. Sawyer."

Trish led her through yet another aqua door and into a locker room — although it was unlike any locker room Megan had ever been in. The room was open and airy, with off-white walls and dim lighting. The same soft music played overhead, and diffusers sprayed subtly scented cool, moist air. The floor was bamboo. Vanities lined two walls. The other two walls were lined with bamboo lockers. More aqua ottomans joined aqua, yellow, and lavender patterned oversized arm chairs. Three women lounged in armchairs while another was undressing in the corner.

Trish handed Megan a pale aqua robe and matching flat thongs. "The private rain showers and dressing rooms are through there." She pointed to a wall of glass. "If you'd like a sauna or steam room experience after your treatment, they're through there." She pointed to two additional glass doors. "We also have a meditation parlor if you'd prefer that."

With a forced smile, Trish left Megan to get ready for her treatment.

Clover called just as Megan was turning off her phone.

"This place gives me the creeps. Is it just me? Everyone is smiles, smiles, smiles, but I feel like they're holding machetes behind their backs."

Megan laughed. "It is all rather surreal."

"And the food? I want to hate it, I really do, but the Salad Nicoise was a delight." Clover lowered her voice. "I'm going to order dessert. Just as part of the surveillance, mind you, and then I'm going to take a walk around the grounds, maybe talk to some guests."

"Just be careful."

"Of course. You?"

"I'm in the Wellness Spa getting ready for my treatment. My phone will be off. I'll meet you at four like we planned."

Megan hung up. Despite the calming ambience, the muted lights and soft music, she felt knotted up inside. She wasn't sure if her anxiety was in spite of the Center — or because of it. Something just felt off.

"Relax, Ms. Sawyer. Your hands are telegraphing tension." Megan's "hand therapist" was a tall, sloping-shouldered older woman with blunt-cut, shoulder-length gray hair. She introduced herself as Gina. Gina rubbed a rich cream into Megan's hands while commenting on the health of her digits. "Do you work with your hands? They're very . . . sturdy."

Megan stifled a laugh. Hours spent in dirt? Yes, they were . . . sturdy. "I'm a farmer."

"Oh?" Gina gave her a "come now" look. "Like you work at one of these farms as a receptionist or retailer?"

"Like a *farmer.* Dirt. Vegetables. Pitchfork."

Gina returned to her ministrations. "Well that explains your nails."

Gina sat in a chair next to Megan, who was lying in a semi-upright position on a

235

white-towel padded lounge chair. Her hand was extended on a padded table that pulled from the side of the lounge. Like the rest of the Wellness Center, their room was dimly lit and softly scented.

"Do you like working here?" Megan asked off-handedly after a few minutes of small talk.

"The Center is new." She worked cream into the palms of Megan's hands in short, slow strokes. "The spa is beautiful. Have you enjoyed your stay so far?"

Megan had to hand it to her — Gina had a politician's ability to skirt the question. "Yes, it's been lovely. I was thinking of applying for a part-time position. Would you recommend it?"

She bent her head over Megan's hand. "Your cuticles could use some attention."

Megan decided to take a different tact. "I heard about that artist. What was her name?"

"Thana. Thana Moore." Gina said in an offhanded tone. She wiped Megan's hands down with a warm, moist white towel. "Yes, a tragedy."

"Had you met her?"

"Briefly. The staff were invited to see the show before it opened to the public. Maria — the event coordinator — hosted a cocktail party just for us. We got to meet Thana as part of it. Striking woman. Talented."

"What a nice thing to do for staff."

"Yes, Maria is wonderful. Sadly, she's since quit."

"Oh, that's a shame." When Gina didn't say more, Megan asked, "Did you like Thana's work?"

"It's certainly unusual." Gina started in on Megan's cuticles, which were admittedly a mess. "I'm no art expert, but I like the landscape watercolors. I found the portraits disturbing." She dug into a particularly stubborn piece of skin and Megan flinched. "I'm sorry. You should be relaxing and here I am blabbering on."

"No, no. I find conversation restful. Art interests me."

"I'm not sure I understand what constitutes art these days." Gina held up a bottle of pale pink polish. "Color?"

Megan shook her head. "It would just chip. Maybe a clear gloss?"

"That I can do." Gina spun around on her chair and pulled a bottle of polish from a drawer. "Organic," she said.

Megan wasn't sure what made a nail polish organic. It sounded suspicious. Nevertheless, she straightened her fingers so Gina could finish that hand. "So about Thana,

I'm familiar with her work. I heard the police were here asking questions."

"Yes, tragic. She died after leaving the Center. We were all very upset. To meet someone famous like that," she shook her head, "and have them murdered right under our noses. Wrong."

"Do the police know who did it?"

"Not that I know of, but it had nothing to do with the Center. An unfortunate coincidence."

"One big happy family, huh?" Megan kept the sarcasm out of her voice. "It must be nice to work in such a supportive environment."

Gina was slapping polish down on Megan's fingers with more fervor than Megan might have liked. "Would you like a second coat?"

"You're the expert."

Gina frowned. "You need a second coat."

"Well, I'm sorry to hear about Thana," Megan said. "I imagine you're all being extra careful when leaving at night. Given what happened and all."

"I'm sure the killer is long gone," Gina said. "Probably a sick passerby. Or a deranged boyfriend."

Ah, the things we tell ourselves so we can sleep at night, Megan thought. But she put her head back and enjoyed the rest of her treatment, not saying another word.

After using the sauna, Megan was getting dressed when the spa receptionist found her in the locker room. "Ms. Sawyer, can you stop by reception before you leave?"

"Sure. Is everything okay?"

"Everything is fine. I have something for you."

Megan finished getting dressed quickly. She waited while Trish checked in two more guests before approaching the glass counter.

Trish smiled broadly, showing all those white teeth. "Mr. Cruise asked me to give this to you." She held out a certificate for the restaurant. "He will be held up until after four, but he thought you might like a bite to eat and then he would love to speak with you."

How did he know she was here? Megan nodded. She took the certificate — it was for fifty dollars. A lot of food for one person.

"Thank you. Did Mr. Cruise say why he wants to see me?"

"He didn't share that, Ms. Sawyer. But he sounded happy you were here." She smiled again. "I hope you'll see fit to stay. Mr. Cruise is a generous man. You must be special if he's giving you comps."

TWENTY

Megan skipped the restaurant — she wasn't hungry anyway. Instead, she took a walk on the grounds in search of Clover. She'd meet Ray later — she was interested in what he wanted to say — but first some exploring.

Outside, the sun beat down with relentless determination. Despite the humidity, the sky was clear and blue. The grass along the Center's buildings and in the pastures was turning brown, evidence of the drought, and the flowers in the copious beds were wilting in the heat. Megan looked for the walking path Sylvia might have taken on the fateful day Thana died. She spotted an entrance to a paved path past the tennis courts. It snaked around the barns and entered the woods between two large maple trees.

Megan headed in that direction. She walked down the length of the main building, and in an effort to find some shade, ducked under the awning that separated the Meditation Gallery and the guest quarters. She was about to round a corner when voices stopped her. They were women's voices, and their hushed tones and the smell of tobacco smoke said they'd found a private spot to grab an unpermitted cigarette and quiet gripe session.

"I don't get it," one was saying. "Ten days in a row? Is that even allowed?"

"Just try and question it and see how fast you follow in Maria's footsteps."

Someone laughed.

"We all saw that coming," voice number one said. "You just don't challenge her."

There were murmurs of assent. Voice number two said, "I don't get Ray. Why doesn't he do something? First Maria, then Sierra Jo, and now you're on the hook with this schedule." There was a pause. "He's sleeping with her. I just know it."

Megan held her breath, afraid they could hear her. She strained to listen.

"He was sleeping with that artist. At least that's what I heard." This was a new voice — a woman Megan recognized as her "hand therapist," Gina. "Mistake on both their parts, ask me."

"Look where she ended up." Voice number

one chuckled. "Sleep with Ray and you get axed."

Gina said, "We need to get back. I have an appointment in fifteen. Need to rid myself of this smoke smell."

"Yeah," voice one said. "We don't need her coming down on us for that too."

Megan backed up a few feet, as quietly as she could. When she was far enough away, she continued in their direction, trying to make it look as natural as possible. They were heading back to work through a side entrance. Megan saw Gina, the front desk hostess, and someone she didn't recognize. All wore the Center's aqua garb. None seemed to notice her.

Megan mulled over what she'd heard. Ray Cruise, ladies' man. Sleeping with Thana? And who was the woman they were referring to? Whoever it was, they clearly disliked her. Perhaps it was someone else with motive to kill Thana. Her hunch was Carly Stevenson. Maybe she could figure it out later, when she talked to Ray.

A glance at her watch told her she had another forty-five minutes until Ray would be ready. She needed to find Clover, who wasn't answering her phone. She texted her, letting her know there was a delay. They would have to stay at the Center longer than expected.

The wooded path meandered through the forest that surrounded the Center, climbing through the trees to the top of a hill before opening up to a meadow of wildflowers and tall grasses. From this vantage point, Megan could see the Center below, to the south, the stream to the west, and the web of back roads that led to the Center from the north and east. Slightly winded, she sat down and put her head back, wishing for a breeze.

There were multiple spots at which the path broke off and headed downhill, toward the stream or even the roads. She was pretty sure someone could take the path most of the way to the unnamed road where Thana was killed. By the same token, it would have been possible, she figured, to leave the Center with Thana, kill her on that road, and hike back via the trail most of the way. She pulled up Google Maps on her phone. *Most* of the way. Based on the satellite view, it didn't look like any of the small unnamed roads intersected with the trail. So someone would have to hike part of the way in the woods, past the stream until they reached pavement.

Pavement.

Megan thought about Sylvia's shoes. Caked with mud and grass, as though she'd been in a stream bed. A stream that was low and muddy due to the drought. Megan glanced at her own shoes. They were clear of any detritus. Someone who was simply going for a walk would stick to the paved path. Pennsylvania was riddled with poison ivy. Why risk it — or a twisted ankle or tick bites — if you had a level path to use?

Unless you were up to no good.

Sylvia wouldn't tell anyone what she and Thana had been arguing about. Sylvia had insisted she'd simply gone for a walk to clear her mind. Sylvia had several hours unaccounted for. Sylvia had fought with Thana. Sylvia's scarf was the murder weapon. Sylvia wanted money wired from Italy.

Sylvia was her father's wife. How could she be guilty of something so heinous?

Megan stood, her legs suddenly shaky. She didn't particularly care for Sylvia, but she'd been trying hard not to let that cloud her judgment. Trying too hard? Had she refused to see what was before her?

Sylvia as a killer. Admittedly, the woman seemed to have killer business instincts, but that was about it. There had to be another explanation for what were surely coincidences. As Megan made her way back down the path, toward the Center, she racked her brains trying to consider what they may be.

TWENTY-ONE

"Megan, it's always good to see you. You look amazing, by the way. I didn't want to say that last time, in front of your grandmother." Ray Cruise smiled, flashing white teeth and one deep dimple. "Farming agrees with you."

Ray had found her in reception shortly after four and he was leading her back to his office. He wore a gray summer-weight business suit with a pale blue shirt. No tie. His hair was combed back with easy elegance, and his skin glowed with the even tan of someone who worked on it. Megan watched as his aqua minions eyed their boss. She thought of the conversations she'd overheard outside. Eligible, wealthy bachelor? Or womanizer?

Suddenly Ray stopped. "You know what? Let's not go to my office. Let me take you to another of my favorite areas. Come this way."

They walked silently back through the solarium, down the spa corridor, and out a side door. Ray led her through a courtyard. Near the Mediation Gallery he took a hard right and walked around to the back of that building. Megan hadn't noticed it before because it was so well hidden by bushes and flower plantings, but there was another solarium off the back of the Meditation Gallery — only this one housed a pool.

"Come on. This is something to see."

They entered the solarium through a staff door. Inside was a large lap pool. It was divided by a wall in the center so that half was indoors and half was tucked into tropical plantings, in the solarium area. The tropical area boasted a waterfall and a hot tub, along with a view of the outdoor gardens.

"That's not all," Ray said. He led her around the pool, which was currently accommodating a few dozing women on full-length lounge chairs and an older man swimming laps in the more utilitarian indoor portion. "Come with me."

They walked through another spa-like area that offered fluffy white towels, an assortment of cold beverages, and a ready supply of magazines and newspapers. Beyond that were three doors. Ray unlocked one.

This brought them into another solarium-like room. Once Ray turned on the lights, Megan saw it was a small suite. Lined with windows, it contained a chaise lounge, a small ornate desk and chair, and a soaking tub. A door led into a small but elegant bathroom. One long wall was lined with windows that looked out on an enclosed courtyard filled with flowers and bird feeders. Inside the suite, the walls were painted a pale shade of aqua, the linens were buttery yellow, and the furniture was deep brown. No television, no computer. The effect was calming and peaceful and Megan wanted to hunker down and hide away from the world.

"What is this?" she asked. "Clearly it's not a bedroom suite."

"We call them our Escapes. They're booked by writers and artists and business people who need a confined but beautiful space to escape and think and work." He smiled. "Like it?"

"It's different."

"You think it's extravagant?"

"I'm wondering who can afford this."

"It's not as expensive as you might think. We rent it by the day or the hour." Ray walked toward the window and looked outside. "Sometimes people need to disappear for a while. This is a nice place to do that. Meditate. Swim. Soak in a warm tub while watching the hummingbirds. Find yourself in the quiet escape from your hectic life."

"You sound like an infomercial."

"That's me. A walking infomercial. I kind of have to be." Ray sat down on one of the armchairs. He motioned toward the other. Megan accepted the offer.

"We're trying out an experiment here," he said. "There are other centers with top-notch yoga programs or meditation retreats. There are Zen programs and plain old health spas. This center is different. It's part health center, part pamper spa, part yoga retreat, part old-school resort."

"Can you be so many things and do any of them well?"

Ray leaned forward. "You tell me. Are we doing this well?"

Megan sat back, maybe in part to counteract Ray's sudden infringement on her space. "Tell me, how did you know I was here?"

"The security cameras are working now."

"Convenient. Or perhaps you learned your lesson?"

Ray smiled. "I'd say we learned our lesson." His eyes probed hers. "And you? Why three visits in less than a week, Megan? What are you searching for?"

"The truth."

"About?"

"Thana's death."

Ray frowned. "And you think you'll find it here?"

"It was the last place Thana was seen. She had multiple arguments here. Seems like a good place to start."

Ray stood. He walked over to the windows and looked outside, arms crossed over his chest, feet shoulder width apart. "When we first put in these windows, they were mirrored for extra privacy. But the birds kept flying into them. Some were merely stunned; others died."

"That's awful."

He nodded. "And upsetting to our guests. We replaced them with regular windows after that and planted the shrubbery for privacy. Cost us, though. Damn birds and their suicidal tendencies."

"I imagine you have a point with that story."

Ray spun around. "Thana Moore never changed. She was as capricious and unpredictable in adulthood as she was when we were kids. She made reckless choices. She acted against her own self-interest."

"As in?"

"As in dating that loser, Elliot. As in mismanaging her career." He shook his head. "She had a death wish. Courted the wrath of others. Sought attention when she shouldn't have, hid away when it was ill-advised." He pointed to the chaise lounge. "These rooms were her ideas. She suggested artist retreats. A place for an artist to paint or sketch that was removed from the demands of their daily life." He shrugged. "She had a point. In today's world it's hard to be creative. Structure and demands and nonstop streaming may be our collective reality but they are not good for the creative process."

"But real artists can't afford your prices."

"No, they can't. So voila. Her idea, reimagined."

Megan thought about this. "So that means you had contact with Thana over the years."

"We remained friends."

"Not lovers?"

The question came out on impulse and Megan immediately regretted it. Ray's eyes narrowed. He looked angry at first, and then he broke out into a boyish grin. "Are you still angry about what happened, Megan? Me and Thana? That was years ago."

"Hardly."

Ray sat back down. "Thana and I were friends. That was all." His gaze strayed once more toward the picture window. "I always regretted what happened. She played me, convinced me you were using both of us. I was dumb and young and horny. I made a poor choice. But I can't say I regret where life has taken me since."

"I know what you mean."

They remained like that for a few minutes. Megan appreciated the silence and the warmth of the late afternoon sun. The room was charming and comfortable. She could see working here. Escaping to use the pool and sauna. Stopping for an hour of meditation. This, more than the spa, held appeal. Solitude. Silence. Ray was right. It was hard to be creative in a world that always demanded you be "on."

"What do you think happened to Thana?" Megan asked.

"She made someone angry enough to kill her."

"Who? Certainly not Maria."

"No. Not Maria. Maria Hernandez was treated unfairly. By us. By the police."

Megan's eyes widened. "If you know that, why don't you speak up?"

"I'm a more of a silent partner. I handle

finances, deal with our investors. Carly makes the design and personnel decisions. That's our deal." His smile was apologetic. "I shared my opinion with the police. I'm afraid that's all I can do."

"So you let Maria be scapegoated."

Ray shook his head. "Don't fool yourself into thinking Maria was completely innocent. Maria has a temper. Cross her and you'll see. She became belligerent with a guest. She was in the wrong and it was Carly's prerogative to fire her."

"But she didn't kill Thana. And she's being blamed for her death."

Ray hung his head and nodded. When he looked up at her, Megan saw real remorse in his eyes. "That's why I need your help."

"My help?" Megan was surprised. "What can I do?"

"I may be the sole person at the Center to say this, but I think Elliot killed Thana, not Maria. Not Sylvia. Elliot Craddock isn't a nice man. He controlled Thana's career, her finances. He's the real reason Thana and Maria argued. It was Elliot who insisted on more floor space. It was Elliot who became enraged when Maria said no. He pushed Thana into reporting Maria."

"I thought they had broken up?"

"On a personal level, perhaps. But he

remained her manager. Or so he thought."

This time it was Megan who stood and walked to the window. She watched a Robin tug on a worm in the dry courtyard dirt. "Why kill her? If she was his meal ticket, wouldn't he want her alive?"

Ray was silent for what felt like an eternity. Finally he said, "Jealousy. I lied when I said we were just friends."

Megan spun around. "So you were in a relationship with Thana?"

"We slept together. Just once. But it was enough to set Elliot off." Ray crossed his arms over his chest again. "I'm afraid we were careless. He found us here, at the Center."

Megan crossed the room until she was standing near her old friend. Jealousy would indeed be a motive for murder. "Was Elliot here the day Thana died?"

"Yes. He brought more paintings for the extra floor space she was hoping to receive."

"So he had opportunity."

When Ray didn't respond, Megan said, "Did you share this with the police?"

"Of course."

"And?"

Ray shrugged. "They took notes, did their thing. But in the end I guess they blamed Maria."

■ ■ ■ ■

Megan found Clover standing next to the truck, on the phone. She was doing a lot of nodding. When she saw Megan walking toward her, she nodded a few more times, said "Okey doke. Love you." and hung up.

"Hey," Clover said. "Sorry I couldn't answer when you called. I was riding a horse."

"Well, that wasn't what I expected to hear." Megan unlocked the truck doors. "Hop in. You can tell me about it on the way."

"Where are we going?"

"To find Elliot Craddock."

Clover climbed into the passenger seat of the truck, and Megan pulled out of the parking area. She made a right at the bottom of the long, windy drive that led to the Center. At the bottom of the hill, she made another right onto an unnamed stretch of country road. The trees hugged the sides of the narrow roadway, and heavy foliage made a canopy overhead, blocking the sun.

It only took Megan a moment to pick out the spot where Thana had been killed. Deep ruts marked the side of the road, eating into the vegetation and spilling small piles of dirt on dry pavement. Megan pulled over.

"Creepy," Clover said. "This is where it happened?"

"From what I can tell." Megan slipped out of the truck. Feeling like she was walking in a cemetery, she made her way the fifty yards or so to the spot where the tire ruts ate into the earth. "Look at this."

Clover joined her. Megan pointed past the trees, past the small stream, where the land began to climb. She could just make out a blue horizon in the distance. And the outline of a roof.

"That's the Center," Megan said. "I took the walking path earlier. There's a meadow at the top that has a view of the whole valley. Someone could have done the deed here, then easily made their way through the woods and back to the Center."

Clover's gaze followed the imaginary trail. "Someone fairly fit."

"Unfortunately — or fortunately, depending on your perspective — both of our middle-aged ladies are pretty fit."

"Maria spent many hours in the woods on the commune," Clover said. "She used to forage for berries and mushrooms and medicinal plants. She would definitely be up for the hike." Clover put her hands on her hips. She grinned. "Except the police let her go."

Megan turned sharply toward her friend. "And you waited this long to tell me?"

"You were all intent on finding Elliot and seeing this spot. Besides, I just found out. Bobby told me." Her face darkened. "But he's not happy. He feels like they knew they didn't have enough evidence. They were trying to scare Maria."

"He told you that?"

"Confidentially, of course. But he knew I was with you." Her smile was sheepish. "Everyone knows I can't keep a secret."

"Hmmm. They let Maria go." Megan wondered what they were up to — and whether they had more on Sylvia. Her thoughts flashed back to the paved trail and Sylvia's dirty shoes. "Did Bobby say anything else?"

"He wants you to call him later."

Megan nodded. She took another look at the spot where Thana must have died. Hard to believe such an innocuous area could be the site of a hideous murder. How awful to die here, in this isolated place.

Echoing Megan's thoughts, Clover said, "Seen enough? I hate that Thana died here. Let's please go."

Megan called the number Elliot had left for

her the night before. There was no answer, and the voicemail was a generic "leave a message." Disappointed, Megan provided her name and number and hung up.

She continued on toward the café thinking perhaps they could regroup there. After the morning's interaction with Bibi, and the knowledge that Sylvia could be back on the hot seat, she didn't relish going home. She wished Denver were around. Suddenly the wish turned into an ache.

"Did Bobby say how Alvaro was faring?" Megan asked.

"No. He said he told them to ask you for the name of a good lawyer, but Alvaro said he's using someone from Maria's family." Clover shrugged. "You know Alvaro. Cheap as he is ornery."

Megan didn't think he'd be cheap about something like this, so hopefully whomever he'd chosen was good. "Tell me about the horses. The great investigator had enough and decided to play princess?" Megan smiled. "Some sleuth."

Clover laughed. "Actually, I was on the clock. I was hiking around the property after lunch and I found myself up by the main barn. Did you see it?" When Megan shook her head no, Clover said, "It's pretty impressive. State of the art, even. And the horses."

She rolled her eyes in mock ecstasy. "They're all rescues, but absolutely gorgeous."

"And they told you who killed Thana?"

Clover laughed again. "No. They let me pet them, and one particularly sassy lady named Storm let me ride her around the paddocks. Or should I say her handler, Marcy, let me ride her."

Megan waited. She knew besides not being able to keep a secret, Clover wasn't great at telling a story in a linear fashion. She'd get to the point . . . eventually.

"Anyway," Clover continued, "Marcy introduced me to her partner, Mark. Mark and Marcy. They're this hipster couple who live at the Center. She takes care of the horses and runs the stable and he is the head groundskeeper."

"Mark and Marcy, nice. And what did they have to say, aside from letting you ride Storm?"

"I kind of introduced the topic of Thana. They both knew her. They said she was fond of the horses and used to come up and brush them when she was feeling depressed."

Megan pulled out onto the turning lane and made a quick left onto Brindle Lane. "Did they have any idea who might have wanted to harm Thana?"

Clover shook her head. "But they did say a few things that seemed interesting. For one, Thana rarely came to the Center alone. Her boyfriend Elliot was almost always with her. But when she visited the horses, he'd stay down at the Center."

"Not a surprise given what we've heard about Elliot. Controlling. Possessive. But horses probably posed no threat."

"Actually, they said he was a super nice guy but the horses spooked him."

Megan turned onto Meadowland Farm Road and pulled over in an empty parking lot. She wanted to try Elliot again. "Hmm. That's not what I've heard. Most of the people I've spoken with have said he has a temper." She told him about her conversation with Ray Cruise. "Did Mark and Marcy have anything else to add?"

Clover had pulled her phone from her small backpack that doubled as a purse. She was skimming through pictures on Instagram. "Here, these are Mark and Marcy." She showed Megan a photo of a grinning couple in their early thirties. Both blond, both with long hair and deep tans, they were standing outside on a pair of hay bales holding hands across the gap. They could have passed for siblings. "Pretty upbeat people, so maybe they just didn't see that side of Elliot, if you know what I mean.

"Anyway, they mentioned that with all the comings and goings at the Center in the days before it opened, they lost track of who was there when. But once it opened, they noticed a guy who seemed to be following Thana around."

"A guy?"

Clover nodded. "I asked if it could have been Elliot and they said they didn't really know. The guy always wore a baseball cap." Clover held up a hand. "And before you ask me, not something distinctive. Just a blue or black cap. Jeans. Nondescript t-shirt. Based on his gait, they thought he was young — under fifty."

"So it could have been Elliot?"

"Yes, I guess so."

Megan thought about the man she'd seen at the pizza farm opening. Tattoos. Broad shoulders. Pretty identifiable fellow. "No tattoos?"

"Not that they mentioned, but I didn't think to ask. They just said Thana would come up and see the horses and when she left they sometimes caught a glimpse of this guy from afar. He seemed to be watching her."

"But not before the Center opened?"

"They couldn't say. The place was also crowded with people coming and going."

Which made sense, Megan thought. Contractors. New staff. Inspectors. The place would be swamped the days and weeks before it opened. "Did they tell the detectives?"

"They said no one talked with them or they would have. But Marcy — she was my favorite — didn't think it really mattered since they couldn't describe much about this guy."

"Perhaps. But it means someone may have been stalking her. That seems pretty relevant to me." And the fact that the stalker sounded like someone very much *not* female — like Sylvia or Maria — seems especially relevant, Megan thought.

Megan grabbed her phone from the front console and was about to dial Elliot's number again when the mobile started to buzz. The display said the number was restricted.

"Hello?"

"You were looking for me?" Male voice. Gruff. "This is Elliot."

"Yes," Megan said. She motioned at the phone and Clover, understanding, grabbed a pen and pad from the glove compartment. Megan put the phone on speaker. "Thanks for returning my call. I was hoping we could meet. About Thana."

Silence. Then, "I have twenty minutes now, but I need to catch a plane down in the city, so you'll have to hurry."

"Where should I meet you?"

"You know where the old ice cream bar was? The Dairy Cow? On the corner of Broad and Wilson?"

Megan repeated the address and Clover jotted it down. "Okay, I'll be there as soon as I can."

He hung up.

Clover placed the address on the console. "You can't go alone."

"I can and I will. He knows you from the apartment complex. I'll call you and leave my phone on, if you want. Then you can hear if something's going down."

Clover didn't look happy but she nodded. "I don't know what you'll gain from this."

"I'm not sure, either." Megan started the truck. She knew the deserted ice cream stand he was talking about and the café was on the way. She'd drop Clover off on Canal Street beforehand. "But right now we have nothing, so at least I can ask him some questions." Like why Thana was talking with Sylvia, Megan thought. And why she had Maria fired.

Twenty-Two

By the time Megan reached the old ice cream stand, clouds had begun to move in and the blue sky was now an angry pewter. Rain, Megan thought as she parked the truck in the empty lot. *Hallelujah.* She locked the doors, picked up her phone, and dialed Clover's number.

"Is he there?" Clover whispered.

"You don't need to whisper," Megan said. "He wouldn't be able to hear you even if he were here, which he's not."

Megan scanned the area, looking for signs of a car. She remembered coming to this ice cream spot when she was younger. The parking lot would be full, teenagers would be sitting on the picnic tables — gone now — and the woods surrounding the parking lot would provide cover for illicit teen trysts. Now the shop was a burned-down shell and the parking lot pitted and gray.

She heard engine noise, then saw a silver

sedan snaking its way down the road. It pulled into the lot.

"Okay, I'm going to put you in my pocket. I'll keep the sound on."

Megan watched as the driver of the silver sedan parked about ten feet away from her truck. He climbed out of his car and walked over. He was tall and muscular. His hair was black and slightly spiky, with just a few streaks of premature gray that made him look older than he was. He wore a black tank, faded jeans, and checked Vans. Sunglasses hid his eyes.

Megan rolled down the window.

"I'm sorry for the odd location," Elliot said. He glanced around the abandoned lot. "Last time Thana and I were here it was still intact. I guess someone burned it down."

"Looks that way."

"You don't need to get out of your truck. I'm actually heading to Philadelphia, then on to LA. I have some business there, and with Thana gone, well, the distraction will be good."

"I was sorry to hear about Thana."

Elliot nodded. "Look, my friends said you stopped by?"

"I was hoping to get more information." Megan debated how much to say. She decided on, "My father's wife was one of the people who'd argued with Thana the day she died. I don't understand what transpired between them — or why. I thought maybe you could shed some light on what happened."

"I wish I knew." Elliot's jaw clenched. "Thana was a free spirit. If she liked someone, things would be great, but the moment she turned — watch out."

"Thana's father mentioned that she'd had some trouble recently. Maybe financial issues?" Not true, Megan knew, but she wanted to see how Elliot reacted to the mention of Thana's dad.

Elliot laughed. "We're artists. We always have financial troubles. But Thana? She was on the way up, man. Her money woes were behind her. Did her dad tell you she'd been paying his mortgage for the last few months? That's the kind of person she was."

"Very generous.'

"I'll say. Thana had a big heart."

"I knew her a long time ago — back in school."

"I had no idea. Here in Winsome?"

Megan nodded. "We went to junior high and high school together."

"Huh. No, she never mentioned that."

"Ray Cruise went to school with us as well."

Elliot's jaw clenched again. He leaned backwards, as though distancing himself from the name. "You want to talk to someone, it should be that guy. He's bad news." Elliot shook his head vehemently. It was then that Megan noticed his shaking hands, the sweat above his lip, the red bumps on his arms. "Things changed when Ray got back in touch with Thana. *She* changed."

"In what way?"

"She became more demanding. Suddenly our life together wasn't enough. I wasn't enough."

"Because of the Center?"

Elliot took a deep breath. He seemed to will himself to calm down. "The Center offered her the opportunity to get her work in front of some higher class people. You know, the kind of people who'll pay five grand for a painting because they like the color or have heard of the artist. Of course she'd jump at that."

"But it came with strings."

"You could say that."

"Did Ray set the rules?"

Elliot didn't respond, but he wrapped his arms around his chest and rocked forward. Elliot was a handsome man who practically dripped with virility, and Megan could understand the attraction. He and Ray Cruise were night and day. Testosterone and danger versus drive and sophistication. How had Thana ended up in that love triangle?

The same way she ended up in Megan's?

"How did Thana get involved in the Center? Did Ray invite her?"

"Yeah, he reached out, but I was all for it. I have to own that." Elliot looked around the parking lot. "I knew they'd been friends and figured he could give her a leg up, maybe buy some of her art for his project. She wasn't as popular when they first started talking about this."

"And she was open to being part of the Center?"

"Not at first. I had to push her. She told me how Ray used her to get to another woman. How he cheated on her. I figured it was kid stuff, so I kept pushing. Man, I regret it now."

Interesting, Megan thought, how Thana had turned it around when she told the story to Elliot. "So she called Ray back."

"I called Ray back, and he invited her to meet with him and his business partner, Carly Stevenson. Thana brought some work with her. They bought a piece for the spa, but it was Ray's idea to have the art show.

As an added attraction for the opening month."

"A good idea."

"He wanted to look cosmopolitan. He wanted that damn suffocating place to seem hip. Not happening. It's a stuffy resort in the tradition of stuffy resorts."

Overhead, thunder grumbled. In the distance, pewter was turning to black. Elliot looked up. "Oh man, I gotta go. I'm sorry. I can't miss this flight."

"I understand," Megan said. "But just one last thing. Maria Hernandez. She was working at the Center the day Thana left in that van. Did you meet Maria?"

"Yeah, she seemed okay."

"Can you tell me what happened between Thana and Maria?"

Elliot shrugged. "Thana wanted more room for her artwork. Ray had promised her more. Maria couldn't do it. She had other artists to work with too." Elliot shook his head again. "Thana was good people. She could get worked up, though. Hot and cold. I should know."

The rain started, sprinkles at first, then harder.

Elliot ran to his car. Once inside, he rolled down the window. "Look, I don't know what happened, but whoever killed Thana

269

will pay. They should just hope the police get to them first."

Elliot rolled the window back up and sped off.

Megan pulled out her phone. "Well, that was a waste of time," she said to Clover. "Mostly."

"Yeah. He actually sounded like a nice enough guy."

"A little on edge, but more polite than I thought." Megan pictured his posture, the way he fidgeted and rocked. "Maybe more than a little on edge."

"Drugs? It wouldn't surprise me. You should hear him and his buddies when they're drinking," Clover said. "Alvaro's back, by the way. He and I are cleaning up the kitchen." She lowered her voice. "He's so relieved they released Maria that he's actually in a good mood. Want to stop by?"

"I'd love to, Clover, but I'm going to have to beg off — unless you need me. I promised Bibi some girl time tonight."

"Girl time with your grandmother. Bibi's scones dripping with butter, iced tea spiked with honey and brandy, some fresh peach cobbler. Talk about relaxing. I'm jealous."

Megan knew she meant it, but after this morning's conversation, Megan wasn't so sure relaxing was on the menu.

■ ■ ■ ■

Maria Hernandez was home alone — part of the reason for Megan's detour. She knew with Alvaro at the café, his wife might be willing to chat. Maria answered the door with a wide but weary smile. She ushered Megan inside to a kitchen fragrant with the smells of garlic and roasting meat. "Alvaro thinks he's the chef in the family." She winked. "He's wrong."

Megan smiled. "Can I talk to you for a few minutes?"

"Of course. Let me stir the pasta sauce and I'll meet you in the living room. Make yourself at home."

Megan wandered into a cozy living room full of overstuffed furniture, crowded bookshelves, and framed family photos. Maria joined her a few minutes later carrying two glasses of iced tea.

"Would you like some cookies? An apple?"

Megan laughed. Maria could rival Bibi. "No, I'm okay. I was wondering how you are?"

"I'd be better if my husband wasn't such a basket case."

"He's been okay at work."

"Thank God for work. I think it's the only

thing grounding him." She pointed to a plaid couch. "Sit, please. I'm happy for the company."

Megan obliged. "Maria, what happened at the Center? With Thana, I mean?"

"They fired me. The police tried to use that as evidence that I killed Thana as retribution."

"Yes, but why? Why did they fire you?"

"Thana and Elliot, Alvaro's nephew, wanted more real estate during the event. We had committed to a number of artists and I couldn't accommodate that. It was never the agreement."

"And they became angry?"

Maria's eyes narrowed. "It wasn't anger as much as desperation. As though the amount of floor space Thana's work received would somehow make or break them. In retrospect, I should have known something was going on. I think Elliot was using drugs, not thinking straight."

"But the argument wasn't what caused Carly to fire you?"

"No, it was Thana's painting. She'd brought a rather lovely painting of a young girl walking through a meadow. Beautiful colors — a rich palette. Thana had a gift. It's such a shame, a waste." Maria looked pained. "The painting was destroyed and they blamed me."

"Who do you think destroyed it?"

"I've been racking my brains trying to figure that out. My first thought was Thana herself, out of spite. Or Elliot. He got me that job — he and Thana pulled some strings with Carly and another owner, Ray — and I figured they were using the painting to get back at me. Now I question whether that's accurate."

"Could it have been Carly or Ray?"

"It could have been anyone."

"And there was no surveillance." Megan frowned. "Have Jones and Lewis let up at all?"

"They call to check in, always letting me know they're watching me." Maria forced a smile. "It's their job."

"I guess. For what it's worth, they've been doing that with my stepmother, Sylvia, as well."

"Ah, Sylvia." Maria's smile was less benevolent. "She's a handful."

"She had issues with Thana too?"

"She was a guest, so we needed to be accommodating, but never have I met a guest with so many demands. Your father must be a patient man."

"That's one way to describe him."

Maria's laugh was warm and throaty. "We

often choose our opposite, Megan. Alvaro is the sand to my ocean. Perhaps your father has found his forever match, the one who will create balance."

Megan left with that thought in her head. Forever match. She liked the sound of it.

Megan returned home to an empty house. No sign of Bibi's Subaru and no sign of her father's rental car. Even the dogs seemed reluctant to greet her. Gunther's tail thumped from his spot on the kitchen floor, and it took Sadie to come yawning and stretching into the room. Only half amused, Megan dumped her purse on the kitchen table but not before grabbing her cell phone from inside.

Upstairs, she changed into sweatpants and a Penn State t-shirt while dialing Denver's number. It was late in Scotland — too late to be calling him — but he'd called earlier and she didn't want him to worry. Plus, if she was honest with herself, she wanted to hear his voice.

After several rings, she was about to give up when a woman's voice chirped "Daniel's phone."

"Hello?" Megan said, suddenly feeling unsure. "Is Denver there?"

"He's occupied at the moment, love. Can

I take a message?" The voice was young and cheerful — not the voice you want answering your boyfriend's phone late at night.

"Just tell him Megan called."

"Will do, love." No further ado. No questions. And no apparent recognition of the name. Megan felt worse than she had before the call.

She laid on the bed, staring up at the ceiling. She didn't like feeling insecure — who did? — and she especially didn't like the old emotions it brought up.

Mick had been the first real love of her life, but she had been infatuated with Ray once upon a time. The days when she, Thana, and Ray had hung out had been some of the best times of her youth. They'd been inseparable. Until Mick came along.

Megan's friendship with Mick Sawyer had started innocently enough. He'd been on Ray's baseball and basketball teams, and eventually familiarity turned to conversation. He didn't have an interest in Thana despite her persistence, and while Megan had found him attractive, she'd done nothing about it. Until Thana stole her boyfriend Ray. Then she'd turn to Mick for support, and the rest, as they say, was history.

Kids' stuff. But often kids' stuff is the basis for character development, and it always bothered Megan that a ten-year friendship had ended on those terms.

Megan heard Sadie padding down the wood-floored hallway toward her room. She sat up, remembering her grandmother's memory drawer. She wondered if her own childhood treasures were still buried amongst the school photos and math awards.

Megan nearly ran out of her bedroom, almost tripping over Sadie and Gunther in the process. Bibi used to keep her memory drawer in one of her bedroom dressers, but a few years ago she moved it to a cabinet in her sewing room. Megan hoped it remained.

The sewing room was a drafty bedroom next to the guest room. It consisted of a quilting frame, an antique wood cabinet, a sewing machine, and a small chest of drawers. Megan bee-lined for the cabinet. She opened it, but all that was inside were folded remnants of material and quilting and knitting supplies. Disappointed, she looked around the room, her gaze falling on the dresser.

She found what she was looking for in the bottom two drawers: her entire childhood.

Megan closed the door before sitting down, Sadie and Gunther laying behind her. She began digging through old crayon draw-ings, report cards, school pictures, and classroom awards until she spotted the box she was looking for. The top was covered with a collage of photos of her and her friends — mainly Thana and Ray. Smiling faces in awkward states of puberty. Thana had made her the box and given it as a gift when they matriculated from ninth grade. It was big enough to keep the notes they'd passed and the photos they'd saved. As Megan opened it, she realized she'd been holding her breath.

Inside was a handmade scrapbook. Megan removed its yellowing pages and carefully placed it on the floor beside her. Underneath that was a letter. She took this out of the box.

She stared at the scrapbook.

Thana had worked on it all throughout ninth grade and given it to her at the end of the year as a surprise. Painstakingly, she'd cut out Polaroids and snapshots of the three of them and glued them alongside little captions, snippets of notes passed between them, and other memorabilia. Megan paged through it slowly, thinking of the young woman who'd made more of a splash in the newspapers in death than in life. And in these photos were proof that perhaps she'd wanted some form of fame or recognition all along.

In almost every photo, Thana was at front and center. Wedged between Megan and Ray on a park bench. At the Jersey shore. Getting ice cream at the Dairy Cow. Megan on the sidelines looking plain and boyish in her jeans and sweatshirts and oversized sweaters. Ray, handsome back then in a boyish, charming sort of way. Even a few photos of Mick, with his reticent smile and long-lashed eyes. Mick had been more of an afterthought back then, before all the drama. Before he became Megan's life.

Megan realized she was gripping the book so hard her fingers ached. What had she hoped to find in its pages? She wasn't sure. Some inkling, perhaps, of the woman Thana would become. Some proof that none of this was Megan's fault.

But she saw three lives — four lives, really — full of promise. A war on foreign soil had stolen Mick's, and now someone had robbed Thana of hers just when she was finally getting the acclaim she wanted.

Megan placed the scrapbook back in its box and opened the letter. It was from her to Thana, a note she'd never delivered. Megan read the thoughts of a sixteen-year-old Megan, explaining to Thana how she was trustworthy, how she would have never stepped out of line and stolen another girl's boyfriend. So full of angst and remorse — yet it remained in the box, an empty apology.

She tried to remember why she hadn't sent it. Lingering anger, maybe. Thana had stolen her boyfriend, Ray, after all. Back then it had felt like the ultimate betrayal. Or a realization that Thana would not have accepted the apology?

Or maybe, deeper, the understanding that Thana Moore had been looking for an opportunity to go after Ray Cruise. That Mick had been a handy excuse. That Thana had been waiting for the chance to go after what she felt was rightfully hers. Megan glanced back at the pictures. Thana, staring at Ray. Thana, basking in his attention.

Abruptly, Megan put everything back and slammed the box shut. It was bad enough that she and Thana had ended their friendship, but she refused to sully her old friend's memory with such an opportunistic view of her.

They had only been kids, after all.

Megan placed the box back in the drawers. She was returning the rest of the memorabilia to its home when her eye fell on another book, this one thinner, wedged behind a box of artwork. Megan pulled it out. The cover was aged white satin, the pages black. She felt her heart pounding in her chest, and she realized the root of her nervousness was the fact that she'd never seen this book before. Bibi had shared all of their memories.

Megan opened it, her breath catching in her throat. The photographs mounted within the album were of her and her parents. Right after birth, cradled in Charlotte's arms. Her christening, held by a younger Eddie, who sat with a joyful smile between Charlotte and Bibi. Christmastime when she was a toddler, dressed in a pink nightgown and bending before a bedazzled tree, Charlotte by her side. Megan went slowly through the ten or so pages, absorbing the pain, welcoming it. Wondering for the millionth time what made her mother — this mother — leave.

The last picture was like a fast forward in a movie. Megan looked to be seven or eight — pigtails, a missing tooth, wearing bell-bottomed pants and a too-small sweater. Charlotte's sweater was blue and oversized, her hair flat and lifeless against her skull. Megan was grinning, her face captured the moment before she would blow out the candles on a cake, only the side of which was visible. Charlotte looked on, but her gaze seemed faraway.

Adult Megan searched her mother's face for a clue. What had changed in those years?

Megan was still staring at that photo when the door slammed open. Megan tore her attention from the album to the doorway. It took her a moment to register her father and grandmother standing there, looking upset.

"What are you doing?" Bibi asked. She sounded alarmed.

"Didn't you hear anything?" Eddie said.

Megan noticed her father was carrying a phone, that Bibi's alarm seemed focused on something other than the photo albums. She put the book back in the cabinet and closed the door.

"What's the problem? What's wrong?"

Eddie and Bibi looked at one another. Eddie said, "Someone broke into the barn."

"That's impossible." Megan stood. "It was fine when I got home." She glanced at her watch. Had it really been two hours ago?

"Bobby's on his way here." Bibi's voice was a weary reprimand. "Whoever broke in trashed the restaurant."

TWENTY-THREE

"Megan, walk me through your day again."
Chief Bobby King looked down at his pad
of paper. "Just one more time."

Megan recounted her day — the trip to
the Mission, her visit to the Center, her
meet up with Elliot Craddock, and her
return home. "I've been home since about
seven."

King glanced at his watch. "It's after nine.
Your grandmother says she left at four forty-
five, Clay left at three, and your dad and
Sylvia went to dinner at five. You didn't
notice anything out of the ordinary when
you got here?"

Megan shook her head, feeling chagrined.

"So you sat in your room, on the phone
with Denver —"

"I called Denver. He wasn't there."

"And then sat on the floor in the craft
room —"

"Sewing room," Bibi said.

"Got it, ladies. Sewing room. Until your grandmother came and got you."

"Yes, that's right."

Bobby's blond eyebrows arched. "And the dogs? Where were they?"

"Sleeping by me in the sewing room."

King shook his head. "Look at this? How did you not hear it?"

Megan looked around, her head pounding. How had she missed it? The carefully painted door was down — having been literally taken off its hinges. Not something she'd have failed to notice when she arrived back at the farm. Inside, the tables were askew, some of the Mason jars had been smashed, and there were printed menus all over the ground. Thankfully the oven remained intact, but the hostess station Clay and Clover had so painstakingly built was nearly destroyed and the large clock was broken.

"It looks like someone was looking for cash. Drugs are my best guess. With this opioid crisis, it could have been kids looking for easy money."

Megan said, "We don't keep cash in the barn. None whatsoever." She felt Eddie's hand on her back and tried to decide if he was propping her up or looking for support. "This barn has seen its share of troubles."

She didn't need to say more. She knew King was as aware as anyone that the new business was an attempt to wash away the ghosts of nearly two years ago, when a body turned up in the barn. They were standing just inside the restaurant now. Twilight had descended, and the broken door did nothing to keep out the mosquitoes.

King jotted something in his notebook. The corners of his mouth turned down. "They must've gotten frustrated when they couldn't find anything to steal."

"Other than the paintings," Megan said.

"The paintings?"

Bibi nodded. "You're right. They were over there." She pointed to the far wall, now bare white. "Even the hangers are gone."

"They were done by Thana Moore," Megan said. She let the name sink in. When Bobby's eyes widened, Megan said, "Maybe it's time to contact Lewis and Jones."

"Motive for her murder?"

Megan said, "Certainly seems like a connection is likely."

King ran a thick finger down the open page in his notebook. "And you spoke to the boyfriend, Elliot Craddock, today."

Megan nodded. "He was here Saturday. He'd have known about the paintings. According to Thana's father, they'd broken up recently. Maybe he felt like he was entitled to Thana's work."

"Or maybe he needed money," Bibi said. "You mentioned that he seemed shaky when you met."

"Drugs?" King asked. "Did he seem like he was on something?"

"Maybe." Megan thought back to their parking lot conversation. "He seemed nervous. But, to be fair, his girlfriend had just been murdered."

Eddie, who had been quiet up until that point, cleared his throat. "If this Elliot lied to you and came here to steal the paintings, then who knows what else he did." Eddie looked at King for support. "He could have murdered Thana. And if he did, and the police can prove it, then Sylvia will be free to go home."

The tone of her father's voice made it very clear that home is exactly where he wished he was right now.

King gave a noncommittal shake of the head. "None of this is my call, Eddie. My officers will be investigating the theft, and if there's a connection, we'll cooperate, of course. But the murder took place out of our jurisdiction." King turned to Megan. "We'll need a formal statement about the paintings. A description, appraisal, invoice, or even photos if you have them. These paintings could be worth some significant money."

Megan nodded. "Of course."

"And you'll look into Elliot Craddock?" Eddie said to King.

"For the thefts? Yes, as part of a broader inquiry. Anyone looking for cash — drug money or otherwise — would know those paintings had value."

"But they'd have to find a buyer," Megan said. "And that's risky."

Eddie said, "So anyone who came to the opening of the pizza farm kitchen could be a suspect."

"That's right," King said.

"How do you think the thieves got in here without Megan or the dogs hearing them?" Bibi asked.

King walked outside and they followed. He stood on the grassy knoll in front of the old oak. "My guess? The abandoned Marshall place. I wish you'd buy that place already, Megan."

She smiled. "I wish I could buy it."

King regarded her for a moment before saying, "They came through that property and around the back. Why Megan didn't hear the door come down is anyone's guess."

"Professionals?" Eddie said.

"Or Megan was preoccupied," Bibi replied. "By the memory drawers."

Megan thought her grandmother's tone seemed sad rather than annoyed, as Megan had expected her to be. She held no love for Charlotte. There was a reason those photos had been stuffed in the back of a dresser.

King said, "That would explain Megan, but not the dogs. Of course, if the pups were asleep in that sewing room with the door closed, and with all those cabinets and shelves on the walls, maybe they didn't hear anything." King walked down the knoll, past a greenhouse, to the line of tall grass that delineated the abandoned property. He pointed to spots where the meadow had been trampled, just darker shadows now in a sea of shadows. "Someone came through here. So either the dogs didn't react because they thought it was someone they knew — Brian or Clay, perhaps — or the perps were exceptionally quiet."

"Or it was someone they knew," Megan said. She couldn't help it — her mind drifted to Sylvia. All that sneaking around. Her desire to acquire Thana's work.

Megan followed King's footsteps until she was just inches from the Marshall property. Her mind spinning, she recalled the murder in the barn almost two years ago, and the possibility of treasure on one of these properties. Back then, someone had invaded her land — for a very specific purpose. "Do you think the ransacking of the dining area was a decoy? To make it look more random than it was?"

King agreed that was a possibility. "Stranger things have happened. In the art world — and in Winsome."

"For sure," Megan said. "If it was a decoy then what they really wanted were those paintings."

"More reason to assume this is connected to that artist's murder," Eddie said. "And not to my wife."

Megan glanced at her father. She tried not to be annoyed that in the midst of all this he was thinking only of Sylvia. She tried not to consider that just maybe her father's new wife was somehow involved.

"My father has a point, Bobby. I know you say this is a job for the Dartville detectives, but you and I both know things that appear to be coincidental rarely are."

Bobby's back was turned toward them, and seemed to be studying the old Marshall house. The building — another historic Colonial, albeit smaller than Washington Acres, and once part of the Birch land —

stood stately despite years of neglect. Only a set of old easements and a relatively small lot seemed to keep it from being sold at auction to some developer. "That place is an eyesore and a risk. Drug addicts, runaways." King sighed. "Until someone buys it and cleans it up, it's a danger to you and your grandmother. But I know that's a double-edged sword." He spun around. "I'll have my officers check it out. Just in case someone is, or was, hiding over there." He looked at Eddie. "And again, I'll make a report and connect with Lewis and Jones. Until there is evidence that this was connected, it will be treated separately."

"I need to patch up that doorway," Megan said. "A temporary patch will be enough. Otherwise we'll have raccoons nesting in the woodstove."

King nodded. "I'll give you a hand while I wait for the patrol cars."

"Don't you think you should go now? In case someone is still there?" Eddie asked.

Megan and King shared a look of exasperation, but it was Bibi who said, "Eddie, go inside. There's more at stake here than your wife's patience."

Eddie seemed to catch himself. "You're right, of course," he said. "Let me check on Sylvia and then I'll come back and help you with the door."

Megan watched her father recede into the shadows. On one hand, she was impressed that he offered to help. On the other hand, she wasn't holding her breath.

Megan, Bibi, and King had the doorway covered with plywood and the area secured before the patrolmen arrived. Two black and whites pulled onto the Marshall property, and Megan watched as four uniformed male officers climbed out. King excused himself just as Megan was hammering the last nail.

"I'll leave you gentlemen to your investigation," Bibi said. "Megan, shall we head back in? It's been a long day."

Megan nodded. She placed the tools back in the main portion of the barn, checked the goats, and joined her grandmother for the stroll back to the house.

"When your father gets hyper-focused on something, he can't see straight. He's always been like that." Bibi's voice had a slight pleading quality Megan wasn't used to. "He means well. He really does."

Gunther was walking back to the house with them, and Megan appreciated the firm feel of the dog's body against her leg. He was guiding her, she knew, and had probably picked up on the tension and was being especially vigilant.

"A little late, Gunther," Megan mused. She reached down and stroked the dog's nearly white fur. "But you're a good boy."

"Megan?" Bibi stopped walking under the glow of the porch lights. "Before we go inside, do you want to talk? About Charlotte and your father? About Sylvia?"

Bibi's earnestness took Megan aback. Bonnie Birch was a pragmatic woman, given to strong opinions and short on patience when it came to anything she perceived as drama. Megan assumed her grandmother would want her to get over Charlotte and move on. This sudden concern for her feelings was even harder to deal with.

"I found the photo album you keep in the memory drawer."

"It was painful to look at, wasn't it?" Bibi sat on the porch step and Megan settled in next to her. "I kept that for you."

"Why do you hate my mother so much?"

Bibi looked out into the darkness. "She hurt Eddie and you. That's the easy answer. And the mostly true answer."

"But there's more?"

Bibi was quiet for a long time. Megan heard the commotion inside the kitchen give way to silence. Her eyes adjusted and she watched as two bats circled and swooped overhead. Her grandmother was her rock. It was hard to see her so vulnerable. Another reason to resent Charlotte.

When Bibi finally spoke, her reason surprised Megan. "Jealousy. There, I said it." Bibi put her head back and something like a twisted laugh escaped her lips. "I was married to your grandfather from the age of seventeen. He had a cruel streak, Megan. You didn't see much of it, but I can assure you Eddie did. As did Sarah and Charlotte — and me."

"You're jealous that my mother escaped?"

"No. And don't take it that way, please. There's not a day in my life I would trade. Not to be a queen or a lottery winner or even a Bridge champion. But Charlotte did something unspeakable, especially for an old crow like me. She changed course. Most of me hates her for backing out on her commitments. You just don't leave a child. But a tiny part of me wishes I'd had just a few ounces of her courage. Maybe I would have told your grandfather where to put it once in a while."

Megan laughed and Bibi joined her. "I can see that. Whether we agree with my mother's choice or not, she took responsibility for her own life."

Bibi nodded. "In a way that's unimaginable to most of us — especially people from my generation."

The bats swooped close to the porch light and Megan followed their progress. She thought about her mother's letter. "I think Charlotte accepts blame. I think she really does own her decisions."

"She's not a victim of circumstance," Bibi said.

Like my father, Megan thought. She felt Bibi's hand reach for her own. Bibi squeezed and Megan squeezed back. Grandmother, friend, surrogate mother . . . whatever Charlotte had done had led to this — and this was a pretty good place to be.

Twenty-Four

Megan couldn't sleep. While she felt better after her talk with Bibi, what she hadn't told her grandmother was that the call to Denver — having the breathy stranger answer the phone — added to her unsettled feelings. Thana's untimely death. Her father's return. Charlotte's appearance in her life. She was, she thought, in love with the veterinarian, and this was perhaps the first test of that love. Were they failing?

Megan climbed out of bed and flicked on the light. Gunther remained downstairs, guarding the property from his perch in the kitchen, but Sadie was curled up on the foot of the bed, and she stood and stretched, echoing Megan.

"Let's do a little digging, girl, shall we?" Megan turned on her laptop and waited for it boot up. She didn't feel like heading to her home office in case she came across her grandmother or her father — or worse, Sylvia. She'd do her digging from the comfort of her bed.

Legs crisscross on her quilt, Megan typed in her first search — Elliot Craddock. His name pulled up more than two dozen relevant hits. She scrolled through his social media sites, but other than the kind of frat-boy photos she'd expect to see from a twenty-something partier, there was nothing of relevance. His artist website was another story.

Elliot's main website painted a picture of a struggling artist of minimal talent. Megan didn't pretend to have an eye for art, but even based on the little she knew, these were paintings and sculptures of the amateur category. The paintings were basic watercolors, mostly of old cars and garages. Unlike Thana's work, there was nothing differentiating the use of color or subject. Like his paintings, most of the sculptures were of cars or car parts. Elliot had taken everyday household items — cans, hangers, Slinkys, metal bracelets — and fashioned them into vehicles or vehicle parts. They were more interesting than the paintings, but unlikely to warrant the four-figure price tags Thana's work seemed to merit.

Which is probably why the website's last copyright date had been 2014.

Megan clicked on the "All about Elliot" tab. Elliot had laid out his personal story — how he had been born in a poorer section of Northeast Philly to a janitor stepfather and homemaker mother, how he'd lost his older brother to a gang when Elliot was only eleven, and how he'd attended two years of college for business, bucking the family trend. He'd discovered his passion for art during college and never looked back.

Yet for someone so passionate about his artwork, he hadn't done much in several years.

Keeping that tab open, Megan searched for Thana's webpage. This one seemed more professional. Her name was in black lettering across the top, and a menu of items along the left hand advertised her latest works as well as sold items. Megan was startled by the pricing. Some of Thana's paintings had sold for as much as forty-thousand dollars.

Suddenly, the theft of the two paintings seemed even more grave. And the likelihood of a connection to Thana's murder, stronger.

Megan returned to the search results. There was little more she could find about Elliot. He seemed like a pretty average guy, and she had some difficulty reconciling the controlling man Thana's father spoke about and the laid back, grieving man-boy she'd met in that parking lot. Nevertheless, he seemed the most likely suspect when it came to those paintings.

Set his alibi by telling her he was leaving town.

Then break in and steal what he'd probably convinced himself was his for the taking.

But killing Thana? If he was a controlling boyfriend whose career and ego were shattered when Thana left him, then perhaps so. Clearly his own art career had not taken off, and Thana's had become lucrative over time. Losing Thana likely meant losing his income.

Men had killed over less.

Megan's eyelids were feeling heavy, and she found she was having trouble staying awake. She logged off her laptop and placed it on her bureau. She paused by the window, looking out into the yard. Her journey home had been fraught with trials, but she loved it here. The farm. The café. Her grandmother. Denver.

Denver.

Megan closed the curtains, flipped off the lights, and crawled into bed. Denver never called her back. She fell asleep thinking about Scottish women and large, fancy casseroles.

The next morning, Megan had the unpleasant task of telling Clay what had happened to his beloved farm pizza kitchen. They were on the phone and it was five-forty, twenty minutes before Clay was due to arrive, but she wanted him to know before he set foot on the property. His reaction surprised her.

"This gives us a chance to make it even better," he said after a long pause. A very long pause. "Clover and I have a list of things we'd do differently. Some smaller tables inside, for one. And patio seating. That's Alvaro's idea. He likes the woods and says people will enjoy dining outside."

"Yes, we could do those things," Megan said slowly. She was collecting eggs, the phone plastered between her ear and shoulder. "You do understand what I said, Clay. Someone intentionally destroyed this property."

"I understand, but there's nothing either of us can do now except make the best of it. My concern is for you and Bibi. This means someone was on your property. I realize Eddie and Sylvia are there, and you have the dogs, but I can stay with you, Megan. Just say the word."

Megan placed another egg in the basket and stood straight. "You amaze me, you know."

"Because of my stunning wood-fired pizzas?"

"Because you always remind me that there is good in the world."

The morning passed quickly. Today they were harvesting more tomatoes — Roma this time, to sell at the farmers market, to bring to the Philly farm-to-table restaurants, and for Alvaro's rich tomato sauce. Despite the drought, they'd had a good tomato crop, and Megan and Clay worked side-by-side, picking bushels of vine-ripened fruit.

"More rain," Clay said, looking up at a clear lapis lazuli sky. "Think a rain dance would help?"

"My mental state, perhaps," Megan said. "I'll throw in an extra hour of overtime to watch you do it."

Clay smiled. "I don't come that cheaply." He picked up a full bushel and disappeared into the Cool Bot, where they stored produce. A moment later he was back. "Want to bring some veggies to Alvaro for me later this morning, before you head into the city?"

Megan nodded. She had three Philadelphia restaurants buying her produce, and she was careful to provide the white glove touch to each one. This meant driving the produce into the city herself and always making sure she was offering high quality, clean products. One stray grasshopper in a bed of arugula, one batch of mushy tomatoes, and that line of business would dry up. She needed all of the diversity in income she could get right now.

"What does Alvaro need?"

Clay started picking from another tomato plant, his long, slender fingers quickly and carefully plucking fruit from the vine. "Tomatoes, basil, Swiss chard, more lettuce, and broccoli rabe. He says he's making an Italian-themed dinner tonight."

"Sure, I'll stop there. I can bring him some garlic too." Megan placed the two tomatoes she was holding in the basket. She loved the shape and scent of the thick-walled Roma tomatoes. Bibi used them to make her tomato bisque soup, which was on the menu at home tonight. "How did he sound?"

"Back to his grumpy self."

"Any more on Maria?"

Clay stopped working. He wore a babushka over his hair to keep the sweat from dripping in his eyes, and he pulled it off and used it to wipe his face. It was only ten in the morning, but already the temperature outside was near one hundred.

"She's still a person of interest, according to Clover. Bobby doesn't seem to think too highly of the Dartville detectives."

"I share his lack of enthusiasm."

"Their ineptitude is dangerous," Clay said. "Especially if they decide they need to wrap this case up soon."

"It's been all over the papers." Just this morning, Megan saw Thana's death — and the lack of an arrest — splashed on the front page of *The Philadelphia Inquirer.* "That's a real risk."

"Well, it sounds like Maria isn't out of the woods yet. Nor would I assume is Sylvia."

Megan nodded. She was afraid he was right. She glanced around the field, looking at the array of vegetables they had coming up. In every direction she saw the fruits of their labor — and their risk-taking. It amazed her how much could be grown on just a few acres.

"Let me wash up, and then I'll head to the café and into the city."

Clay had resumed picking. Without pausing, he said, "I'll load the truck in the meantime." He met Megan's gaze. "Go easy on Alvaro. I'm afraid this has really shaken his world."

"Yes, I imagine having your beloved stand accused of murder would do that."

"It's not just that." Clay chose another tomato, held it up to the sun, and then tucked it into the basket. "The whole time we were at the commune, when Maria was secretly giving us food, Alvaro never spoke to us. We knew he was complicit. Sometimes he would even bake us special little treats, like mini pies on our birthdays, but he never, ever said anything to us. Not even a real hello. Maria did that. She was the family spokesperson, his connection to the outside world."

Megan thought she understood. "So when he is left to be the advocate, it's hard."

"I think it makes him feel impotent. To not be able to articulate the injustice, to fight for his wife. He only knows one way to fight — with his fists. And it doesn't work for much in the modern justice system."

Megan pictured Alvaro sitting on the grass outside the pizza kitchen. She'd seen that frustration in his posture, in the set of his jaw.

"How can I help him?" Megan asked.

"Unless you can find who actually murdered Thana Moore, I think the only way to help Alvaro is to pray that the police stop focusing on Maria. It's breaking his heart."

"I wanted the Roma tomatoes," Alvaro groused. "And more basil. More." He smelled a bunch of the fragrant green leaves and made a contented growl. "Good, but more."

"I'll tell Clay to drop off Romas and more basil."

"And fresh oregano. I'm making a fresh lasagna. I need oregano and basil. And garlic. No one brought me garlic."

Megan smiled to herself. Alvaro was in fine form today. "It's in the truck, Alvaro."

Her chef grunted. "Okay, well, let's get it. I have work to do."

Megan caught Bibi's eye from across the kitchen. Her grandmother had gone to help out for a few hours, and she was chopping cucumbers for the lunch special — a cold cucumber gazpacho. With Labor Day fast approaching and families preparing for the fall back-to-school rush, they'd seen an uptake in business at the café and the store, and that was Bibi's outward reason for coming. Only Megan knew she really wanted to be there out of concern for Alvaro. Eddie was hiding out in the guest room with Sylvia; there was little Bibi could do for him.

But at least Alvaro was letting her work.

"How's Maria?" Bibi asked casually as Megan trudged back in carrying a basket of garlic.

"She's fine as can be expected." Alvaro brought a cleaver down on a chicken breast. Megan was glad he wasn't angry with her.

"Any more from the police?" Bibi asked.

Alvaro stopped chopping. "No."

Megan and Bibi paused what they were doing to look at the chef. His voice was so full of anguish, of anger. But before they could say anything else, Alvaro was back to cleaving the chicken.

"Basil, Megan. Tell Clay I need it soon. For even a fresh sauce like that, I need to get started early. The dinner rush will be here before we know it."

Megan promised to call Clay immediately. She knew Alvaro would rather cleave chicken than deal with Maria's situation. She'd give him that.

Megan left the kitchen and went out into the café to make her rounds and check on the store. She found Merry Chance sitting at one of the copper-topped tables with Roger Becker and the town librarian. They were deep in conversation but stopped talking when they saw Megan.

"Do you have time to join us?" Merry

asked. She looked guiltily at Roger — or so Megan thought. "We heard what happened at the farm."

Less than twenty-four hours and already the break-in was town gossip. Megan mustered her best fake smile. "I need to get into the city, Merry. Another time."

"But you and Bonnie are okay?" Roger asked.

"We're fine, Roger."

"It's a shame," Merry said. She glanced at the librarian, who gave her a knowing smirk. "It happens in every family."

"What does?" Megan leaned in closer, aware that her nerves were now on edge. "What happens in every family?"

Perhaps realizing she'd gone too far, Merry shrank back against her chair. "Just that we can't always control our loved ones' choices."

Roger nodded. All three were staring at her.

Megan knew exactly what they were insinuating. That Sylvia had something to do with the thefts, and maybe even Thana's demise.

Megan considered calling them on it, since none seemed willing to own it on their own. Instead she walked away, intent on being the bigger person.

Her good intentions didn't last for long. On the way back to the farm to pack for the trip into Philadelphia, Megan called Denver. The call and his lack of response had been plaguing her. Only Denver didn't answer.

"Denver, perhaps your lady friend didn't give you my message from late last night. Call me when you have time." Curt, angry — and instantly regretted. But there was no turning back.

On her way out of Winsome's small downtown, Megan decided to make a stop by Elliot's friends' house. She wanted to see if Bobby was around anyway, and she thought maybe Elliot's friends could shed light on why he'd gone to LA.

King wasn't home, no surprise there, but she found the one who'd been wearing the Drexel t-shirt carrying groceries from his car toward the apartment. When he saw Megan he did a double take and stopped walking.

"Elliot's not here," he said. "That's who you are, right? Thana's friend."

Megan nodded. Drexel seemed friendlier without his posse around him, and she decided to take advantage of the sudden shift in manners.

"Do you have a few minutes?" She pointed to the open trunk of his newer Civic. Two bags remained inside. "I'd be happy to carry these up for you." She knew she was breaking every stranger rule, but she figured he'd say no and that would be her chance to ask a few questions.

To her surprise, Drexel shrugged. "Sure — suit yourself."

Megan grabbed the bags, which were heavier than they appeared, and followed Drexel up the steps to his second floor flat. Like Elliot he was large. Unlike Elliot, he had more fat than muscle, with the firm bulk of someone who had once been athletic but now partied harder than he played. Up close, he had a beak-like nose and small, dark eyes. His shoulders were rounded, hunched — a man who spent his days in front of a computer.

He unlocked the door and kicked it open for Megan. The apartment was a sty. Dirty laundry all over the living room floor, covering a pair of once khaki couches and a plaid chair, circa 1970. A large gaming console sat at one end of the space, a computer desk littered with Styrofoam take-out containers at the other. The kitchen was a dated galley with a stove so covered in empty beer cans as to make it useless, and the sink was full of empty take-out tins and beer mugs.

"Cleaning lady is off today," Drexel said. He shrugged. "Enter at your own risk."

They put the groceries down on a paper-covered portion of orange vinyl countertop. Drexel started putting them away and said. "So shoot. What do you want to ask me?"

Megan made sure she remained between the open front door and Drexel. "Where's Elliot?"

"Hell if I know."

"He lives here, right?"

"He crashes here on occasion."

Megan watched him pull two bottles of Coke out of the bags and place them under the counter. He crumpled the bag up and tossed it on the floor. "When was the last time you saw him?"

"Few days ago. Same as I told the cops."

"They've been here?"

"Twice. Looking for Elliot." Drexel opened the refrigerator and chugged milk right from a half gallon container. He held it out. "Want some?"

"I'll pass, but thanks."

"Suit yourself." Wiping his mouth with the back of his hand, Drexel said, "What's your interest in Elliot?"

"My interest is in Thana. More specifically, why someone wanted to hurt her. I spoke with Elliot yesterday and he was helping me. He and I are on the same side — we both want Thana's killer brought to justice."

Drexel regarded her evenly. "Is that so?"

"Seems to me."

"Huh." He put the last of the groceries into a cupboard and tossed the last bag on the floor, not even bothering to crumple this one. "You sleeping with Elliot?"

"No, of course not." Megan felt her face flush. "Why would you even ask that?"

"Because usually when a woman comes looking it's because she's jealous."

Megan laughed. "I assure you that's not me. Did Elliot often have women come knocking because of jealousy?"

"Just Thana."

"I heard she broke up with him."

"Is that what Thana said?" He smiled. "Maybe it's true, who knows. Elliot keeps to himself and Thana was . . . different."

"Different how?"

He shrugged. "She liked a lot of drama in her life. Attention, especially from men. First with Elliot. Then I heard she was sleeping with some bigwig at the new yoga retreat center."

Ray. "Did Elliot tell you that?"

"Didn't have to. Thana flaunted it. Thought she was hot shit." Drexel reached down under the counter and pulled up a can of Budweiser. "Want one?"

"No thanks. I try not to drink before lunch."

Drexel looked at the clock. "You're in luck. It's lunchtime."

Megan smiled. "Elliot mentioned going to LA. Any idea why?"

"How should I know? I'm not his secretary."

"No, you're not." Megan took a step toward the door. Suddenly the hopelessness of this place was getting to her. "Thanks for your time, Mr. —"

"Stewart. Steve Stewart. And not sure what you're thanking me for. I have nothing to tell you."

At the door, Megan paused. She turned slowly toward Steve and caught him watching her, a blank expression on his bland face. "Was Elliot ever violent with Thana that you're aware of?"

Steve's eyes widened. "Seriously? No. Elliot's not like that." He seemed to understand the reason for the question. "You think *Elliot* could've killed Thana? No way, man. Absolutely not. Just ask his mom. He lives with her when he isn't here or shacking up with Thana. Violent? No way. He would have married that woman if she'd have let him. He was crazy about her."

Megan wasn't naïve enough to think marriage and violence were mutually exclusive. "Where can I find Elliot's mom?"

"Becky? Northeast Philly." His eyes narrowed. "You really going there?"

"Probably not," Megan said. Probably, she thought. After all, that section of the city wasn't far from the restaurants she needed to visit.

TWENTY-FIVE

Megan figured that Becky must be Elliot's birth mother, but she called Clover to confirm.

"Sounds right," Clover said. "I don't know Alvaro's sister Zaneta well. Met her once or twice at Hernandez family functions. Zaneta's new husband is from the city, so Becky must be his former wife and Elliot's mother."

Megan and Clay had just loaded the truck with the fresh vegetable orders for the three city restaurants. She needed to deliver them by early afternoon so the chefs had them for dinner prep. She'd go from the restaurants to Northeast Philly if there was time.

"Bobby said they can't find Elliot," Clover whispered. "He never got on that airplane."

Megan stopped what she was doing. "Had there been a ticket in his name?"

"Yes," Clover said, "He checked in online and then didn't arrive at the gate."

"Another decoy?"

"What do you mean?"

"Hold on." Megan covered the mouthpiece of her phone. "Clay, I'm heading out. You okay here?"

Clay nodded. "I'll be weeding this afternoon. Porter and I may also start to prepare the garlic beds." Gunther barked and Clay patted the dog on the head. "We'll be fine."

Megan climbed in the truck and started the engine. She waited while the phone connected to her vehicle before resuming the conversation with Clover.

"What I mean by a decoy is that maybe all of this — the trip to LA, the robbery — was a decoy. He told me he was leaving so he could break in to my barn without anyone suspecting it was him. He made it look like a random robbery even though the paintings were the target to try and shift suspicion. He never got on that flight, but by the time the authorities figure that out he's driven half way to Mexico."

Clover said, "Pretty smart."

"Or desperate."

Clover snorted. "Desperate people do desperate things. This should help allay suspicions against Maria and Sylvia."

"I hope so."

Elliot did seem the most likely candidate

for murder, but as Megan clicked off the phone, she couldn't shake a nagging suspicion that this was a little too neat, a little too convenient.

Fiddlehead, a farm-to-table restaurant near the University of Pennsylvania, was Megan's last stop. She dropped off the restaurant's order of Yukon Gold potatoes, garlic, arugula, and baby lettuces, and met briefly with the chef while the woman inspected the produce. Happy that every restaurant seemed satisfied, Megan drove north, out of the city. Using the magic of the internet, she'd managed to find an address for Elliot's mother on Crescent Avenue, and she decided to stop by before going home. If his parents wouldn't talk with her, so be it, but maybe they could shed some light on his current whereabouts and his relationship with Thana.

Becky and Leroy Smith lived in a brick rowhome in a neighborhood of other rowhomes bookended by a check cashing business and a Dollar Store. Litter blew across a wide street and under cars parked on either side of Crescent Avenue. Some of those cars looked like they hadn't been moved in years. The Smith home was distinguishable only by its updates — new windows, fresh white trim, pristine white wicker furniture on the front porch, on which a fifty-something woman relaxed now.

Megan turned off the engine and took a deep breath, bracing herself to face a stranger. She considered herself fundamentally an introvert, and these sorts of things never seemed to get any easier.

The woman watched Megan walk up to the house. Megan's first estimation of her age seemed off. Up close, she seemed older — maybe early sixties. She had a wedge of gray-streaked straight, black hair that framed a round, sweet face. She held an orange tabby on her lap and stroked the cat with short, nervous strokes.

"He's not here," she said before Megan could utter a word.

"I'm looking for Elliot, Mrs. Smith."

"I know, and he ain't here."

"He does live here, though?"

"When he feels like it." She tilted her head at an angle, studying Megan. "You one of his girlfriends?"

One of his girlfriends? Megan shook her head. "I knew Thana Moore."

"Oh, the artist." She seemed to relax a little. "Shame about Thana. People these days. No one seems to know right from wrong. I had high hopes for Elliot and

315

Thana. Wasn't meant to be."

"Mrs. Smith, I talked to Elliot two days ago and he mentioned flying to Los Angeles. Do you know anything about that trip?"

"He doesn't tell me where he's going. Maybe ask his father." She frowned. "Why do you want to know anyway?"

"I'm trying to locate him. I have some things of Thana's he might want."

"Things like what? Paintings?"

"Yes." Megan hated to lie and the words stuck there in her throat. "Do you know how I might contact him?"

Becky shrugged. "Call him. Text him. You have his number?"

"He's not answering."

"I don't know what to tell you." Becky looked up and the smile she gave was sad. "Elliot's been gone to us for a long time."

"I'm afraid I don't understand."

"Do you have kids?"

"No."

They both watched a young boy soar down the sidewalk on a bicycle, no helmet.

"Some kids leave you physically," Becky said. "They fly away, make lives for themselves, and fly home on occasion as full adults. I think, as a parent, that's what you want. Other kids? They stick around but they're not connected. See you only for what you can give them. Leroy calls it parasitic behavior." She shrugged. "Maybe he's right." She seemed to remember she was talking to a stranger. "Try Elliot's dad, Oliver Craddock. He may know where Elliot is. Elliot lives here when it suits him, but mostly he treats his room like a hotel suite. Always has."

Megan left Elliot's family home feeling off-centered and melancholy. Once she'd navigated back onto a main road, she dialed Clover's cell number.

"Can you tell me where Zaneta and her new husband live?"

"I don't know offhand, but I can get the address for you. Why?"

"I just visited Elliot's mom. Another dead end. She doesn't know where he is either."

"Doesn't know or won't tell?"

Megan sped around yet another car going under the speed limit in the left lane. "Unless she's an amazing actress I'd say the former, but either way it doesn't matter. Dead end."

"Okay, hold on. Here's Zaneta's address." She rattled off a place just a few miles from Winsome. "She's local."

"Thanks. Did you get it from Alvaro?"

Clover laughed. "Are you kidding? I know

better. I went to his better half, Maria."

"How's she doing?"

"Sounds okay, but she'd never admit to anything else."

Megan pictured Alvaro and Maria the day Lewis and Jones took Maria away. Alvaro with his visage of outrage, Maria in a state of calm. She understood what Clover meant. "I'm going to swing by Zaneta's house and then I'll head home. I have some evening chores to do tonight, and I want to help Clay with the barn door."

"Be safe, Megan."

Megan laughed, but the sound seemed forced even to her. "Tell Bobby to call me tonight. I want to know where things are with the theft."

"I'll tell him. He's out on a call now. I don't expect him back until late." Clover sighed. "The life of a cop. There are much easier professions out there. Why did he pick this one?"

"Protect and serve," Megan said. "And the good ones do."

"He's a keeper," Clover said. "Ugh, Merry's here picking up eggs. I have to go."

Merry Chance and her eggs. Megan needed an entire brood just for her neighbor. "Bobby, don't forget to tell him," Megan repeated. "I'll have my cell on."

■ ■ ■ ■

The Craddock home was a far cry from Elliot's mother's place — in distance and in
style. A sprawling seventies-type ranch on
several acres, it boasted an in-ground pool
and a tennis court. Megan pulled into the
driveway behind a Mercedes and killed the
engine. The door swung open before she
had a chance to ring the bell.

An attractive older woman wearing a black
swim cover-up and flip flops stared out at
her. "Yes?"

"Zaneta Craddock?"

"I'm Zaneta. Zaneta Hernandez." She had
a soft Spanish accent and a high-pitched
voice. "And you are?"

"Megan Sawyer. I work with Alvaro."

"Ah, yes, your name is familiar." The
corners of her mouth turned up in a faint
smile before alarm colored her complexion.
"Is Alvaro alright?"

"He's fine, Ms. Hernandez. It's really Elliot I came to talk about. Is Elliot's father
here?"

Zaneta regarded her coolly. "Did my
brother send you?"

"No, I'm here on my own."

"Does my brother even know you're here?"

"No, Ms. Hernandez. I met with Elliot two days ago. He told me he was leaving for LA. I need to reach him, but he hasn't returned my calls. I spoke with his mother, Becky, and she suggested I reach out to Oliver."

Zaneta looked like she was debating whether or not to let Megan in. Manners eventually won out over suspicion and she pushed the door open farther to allow entry. "Please, come in. Oliver is at a meeting for a nonprofit board he's on, but he should be here soon."

"Thank you."

Megan followed Zaneta through a dark hallway and into a large, open family room-kitchen combination that looked out over the backyard and the pool. The floors were hardwood, the walls white-painted paneling, and the furniture beach chic. Zaneta pointed to the patio and pool outside. "Let's go out there and wait. Would you like a drink?"

"I don't want to be any trouble."

"No trouble whatsoever. Go on out and I'll join you in a minute."

True to her word, Zaneta came outside almost immediately carrying two glasses of iced tea. She took a seat under a large blue striped umbrella and offered the other chair to Megan. The pool was hour-glass shaped and inviting. Megan couldn't remember the last time she'd gone swimming for fun. That she'd done anything for pure fun.

"Elliot is special," Zaneta was saying. "My brother never liked him. Never trusted him. But that's Alvaro — a bit of a misanthrope. A lovable misanthrope." She smiled. "You of all people probably understand."

Megan returned the smile. "Do you know where Elliot might be?"

"I'm afraid I don't, but Oliver might." Zaneta took a sip of iced tea. "He and Elliot are close. At least they have been in recent years."

"Zaneta, I was friends with Thana, Elliot's girlfriend. Did you ever meet her?"

"A few times. Elliot likes to keep his personal life personal, even with family. She seemed like a nice young woman, though. What happened to her was atrocious."

"They'd broken up recently?"

"Had they? Oliver never mentioned anything."

"Does that surprise you?"

"That they broke up?" Zaneta seemed to take the question seriously. "No, I suppose not. Thana was on an upward trajectory

321

with her art. Elliot just doesn't have the talent for a career in art."

"You told Alvaro he had gotten his life together?"

Zaneta rolled her eyes. "My brother can be so dramatic. He thinks he's Mr. Practical, but he's the opposite at times. I told Alvaro that Elliot was a good businessman, and he is. He's a good businessman and a good craftsman. Have you seen those frames he made for Thana's work? Marvelous. Come here, I'll show you one."

They reentered the house and walked through the family room, past the galley kitchen, and into a room decorated completely in white. White rugs, white furniture, white pillows. The only color was a painting of a young girl holding the hand of an older woman in the midst of a snowstorm. The painting was poignant and colorful and a perfect focal point for the room. The frame was also a work of art. The cherry wood was carved and sanded until it shone, a rich counterpoint to the painting.

"This is Elliot's gift. This, and running the business. He's done well for himself. He did well by Thana. I wanted my brother to give him a chance."

"And yet something happened between him and Maria."

"Alvaro blames Elliot for Maria's firing. He thinks Elliot and Thana set her up." Zaneta shook her head vehemently. "That's why I wanted you to see this. Elliot has talent. He seems to finally be figuring out what he's capable of. I don't want Thana's murder to undo everything that's happening for him."

Megan stared at the painting. Like the portrait she had hanging in her pizza farm restaurant, the faces consisted of tiny strokes of color, color that up close seemed abstract, but as the beholder moved backward, the faces — in all of their glorious individuality — became clear.

"Thana definitely had talent, and this frame is gorgeous. But something happened, Zaneta. A young woman was murdered in her van, and the police seem to be looking at two middle-age women whose connections seem tenuous at best. Your sister-in-law and my father's wife."

"Sylvia Altamura is your stepmother?" Zaneta looked surprised.

"My father's wife. Do you know her?"

"I know of her. Through Maria. Sylvia was at the spa during the opening."

Before Megan could ask additional questions, Zaneta's cell phone chimed. She pulled it from her cover-up and answered with a crisp hello. When she hung up, she looked troubled.

"I'm afraid Oliver is delayed. He didn't say why, but he sounded stressed. I don't think it's a good idea for you to wait for him." Zaneta put a hand on Megan's arm. "My brother is a good person, Megan. Don't let his crust fool you. He's soft underneath. Too soft, perhaps."

"I know, Zaneta. Which is why I hope the police get to the bottom of this, and soon."

Zaneta's eyebrows shot up in alarm, realization dawning on her face. "You think Elliot is somehow involved?"

"I don't know what to think."

Zaneta moved toward the front door, Megan trailing behind. "My stepson had a tough life. His mother is flighty — you said you talked to her, so perhaps you understand — and she struggled with relationship problems. Men in and out of the home, Elliot on his own half the time until eventually he ran away. My husband Oliver holds a lot of guilt, feels like he should have gotten involved sooner. I think that's why he's so involved with charities. It's his way of giving back."

"Someone told me Elliot could be controlling with Thana. Violent, even."

"Was that someone Thana's father?"

When Megan didn't respond, Zaneta

snorted derisively. "You don't need to say. Wesley called here making the same claims. Elliot is many things but violent isn't one of them."

They had moved to the front door, and Zaneta opened it. The contrast between the heavily air conditioned house and the heat and humidity outside tightened Megan's chest and made the very act of breathing hard.

"If you see Elliot, please ask him to call me." Megan removed a card from her purse and handed it to Zaneta. "My cell number is on there."

Zaneta nodded. "I'll talk to Oliver when he gets home. Putting this murder to rest will be good for my brother, and good for Elliot."

TWENTY-SIX

Within a half a block from Washington Acres, Megan knew her productive evening was not to be. She still wanted to help Clay with the damaged restaurant, and even with two detours, she still had a few hours of daylight, but King's car and a black and white sat in the driveway, and King and Bibi were standing outside. King's hands waved in an animated fashion; Bibi looked upset.

"What's going on?" Megan asked as she jogged up the driveway. "Did you find out who broke in to the barn?"

King and Bibi exchanged a look. "Can we go into the house?" King asked.

"Of course."

King followed Megan into the house while Bibi remained outside. Once settled in the relative privacy of the parlor, King cut right to the chase. "Elliot is dead."

Megan put her hand over her mouth. "Elliot Craddock? But —" Realizing she was about to say "but I thought he was the murderer," she stopped talking. "How? When?"

"When he didn't show up for his flight, we started looking for him. Found his car in the long-term parking lot at the Winsome train station. Found Elliot in the trunk."

"Strangled?"

"Shot. Small caliber pistol."

Megan let that sink in. "I don't know what to say."

"From what we can piece together, he left the parking lot of the old Dairy Cow and that was the last anyone saw him."

"So his conversation with me —"

"Seems to have been his last." King was sitting on the couch. He leaned forward, studying Megan's face. He looked large amidst Bibi's needlework pillows and dainty doilies. "The coroner's working on a time of death, but preliminary reports indicate he died between nine and midnight that night."

"So he could have broken into the barn."

"Could have, yes, but we didn't find any evidence to support that it was him."

"So if not Elliot, then who?"

"The million dollar question, Megan."

Megan heard noises coming from outside. She walked to the window and saw two uniformed officers talking to Clay in the yard. "Did you have any luck with the old Marshall property?" Megan asked.

"Trampled vegetation, some tire tracks that appeared to have been gone over with a rake or other tool."

"Careful thief."

"Not your average teenager looking to score some petty cash, that's for sure."

Megan sat down in Bibi's recliner. Her hands hurt suddenly and she realized she was gripping them together until her knuckles were sore. "Do Elliot's parents know?"

"Yes. We contacted them a short while ago."

Megan shared her conversation with both Becky and Zaneta. "Little did I know that he was dead. I feel awful."

King didn't say anything. She'd seen the flash of disapproval on his face when Megan mentioned visiting Elliot's parents, but they both knew she'd been instrumental in solving several crimes. They had an unspoken agreement. She tried not to cross any legal lines, and he tried not to become territorial. It was an uneasy truce and Megan hoped it held.

"Megan, I'd like to say this absolves Sylvia, but I'm afraid that's not the case. Syl-

via, Maria, you . . . we will need statements."

"Me?"

"You saw Elliot last."

Megan nodded. She knew the routine all
too well. Clover could back up Megan's
story, though — she'd heard the entire
conversation with Elliot.

King peered at her. "Are you okay?"

Megan smiled at Bobby's sincerity. She
had to remind herself how young he was. It
had been baptism by fire for Chief King.

"I'm okay. You? Somehow I didn't see us
doing this again quite so soon."

"Keeps things interesting, I guess."

Megan listened to the chatter outside.
Through the open window, she heard Bibi
calling Gunther, heard the start of a car
engine. A lot of commotion for a weeknight.
A lot of drama. What had Elliot's friend
Steve Stewart said? Thana was dramatic.
Craved attention. Just as she had when they
were teens.

"Bobby, everything seems linked to
Thana's paintings. Maria was fired for arguing over the amount of Thana's floor space
at the Center, and for destroying one of her
paintings. Sylvia argued with Thana over
lord knows what related to Thana's art. She
died in her van, a traveling art studio.

329

Someone stole two of her paintings from me — and nothing else. And now Elliot, her boyfriend but also her manager, dead. What if this is some kind of art ring."

King smirked. "An art ring?"

"People dealing in stolen art. Trafficking artwork. I read that some of Thana's work was getting twenty-five, even forty thousand dollars. That's the kind of money people scheme and kill for."

"People scheme and kill for far less. Nevertheless, I agree with you. Her art seems to be part of the equation. But why was it so expensive? And what pieces sparked the killings?"

"I wish I understood what goes into pricing art."

King shrugged. "Certainly not my area of expertise."

Megan couldn't argue. She just didn't know enough about art to say what made it valuable. But she knew someone who did.

King rose. "Let's get your statement. I need to talk with Sylvia too. Find out where she was Sunday night."

"I know. Tread gently, okay? For my father."

"For your father, Megan?" King shook his head. "When are you and your grandmother going to stop protecting him?"

Megan felt her face flush. "Bibi *and* me? My grandmother, perhaps, but not me."

"Really? You moved here from Chicago so he could go to Italy. You cleaned up the farm he'd driven into the ground. And the café? It was an abandoned eyesore for years before you came along. You're a bigger savior than Bonnie." Despite his harsh words, King's tone was kind. "Maybe it's time Eddie Birch grew up."

Megan stared King down. His words stung, and not just because they weren't for him to say, but because they resonated with truth. Despite her talk of tough love and setting boundaries and her unending frustration toward her grandmother for always providing her father with an excuse, Megan had been complicit. But Bibi had been right . . . the right choice wasn't always obvious at the time you were forced to make it. Life got complicated.

"I'm ready to give you my statement," Megan said, her tone curt.

King rubbed his temples. "Come on, Megan, don't get like that. I said that as a friend who cares about you. You work hard for this farm. I don't know Sylvia, but ever since they got here things have been weird. You need to step back and be objective. Maybe Sylvia is somehow involved. Maybe your father has blinders on."

He was giving voice to doubts that had been plaguing Megan too. But she didn't want to go there. Her father had never been the most reliable man, but he was her father and she loved him. She couldn't believe he'd marry someone who'd kill someone else.

At least, she chose not to believe it.

Megan got home from the station after nine. By then, Clay had already fixed the barn door and cleaned up the mess in the pizza restaurant. Megan found him in the kitchen talking with Bibi. He was drinking a beer and Bibi had her customary chamomile tea and whiskey — on ice. The window air conditioners in the old farmhouse were no match for the stifling heat, and Bibi was fanning herself with a brochure.

Megan dropped into a chair, exhausted.

Clay slid a cold beer across the table. "You look like you could use one of these."

"That bad, huh?"

"Pretty bad."

"I saw you fixed the door. Thank you. I'm sorry I wasn't here to help."

"You had bigger things brewing. How did it go in Philly?"

Megan told him about her meetings with

the chefs, relishing the farm talk — it was nice to get back to basics. "If we keep this up, we may turn a profit by 2050."

Clay laughed, Bibi did not.

"Expand the farm kitchen," Bibi said.

"Expand it?" Megan said, surprised. "We already have the café. I'm not sure wood-fired pizza is our ticket to prosperity."

"No, but the nice thing about the pizza kitchen is that it's self-sustaining, and you can open it when you want. We already have most of the ingredients right here on the farm." Bibi looked at Clay. "Did the first night turn a profit?"

"Not when you add in the cost for the renovations and the oven itself."

"You'll recoup those over time. When you look just at revenue from that night, was it profitable?"

"Very."

Bibi took a long sip of her tea. She was wearing pink curlers in her hair and a light weight mint green housecoat over a floral nightgown. Despite the bedclothes, she looked bright-eyed and wide awake.

"I've been eyeing up that Marshall property," Bibi said. "We could get it for a steal."

Megan was wondering just how many iced teas her grandmother had drunk. "We don't have a steal."

Bibi waved her hand. "Clay and I were just talking about it. Imagine if we bought the Marshall property. We could turn it into a bed and breakfast, but not just any bed and breakfast — one that served food right from the farm. We could offer organic gardening classes, canning classes, we could work with local elementary schools, and the inn could be a source of patronage for the pizza kitchen."

Bibi was describing exactly what Megan had wanted to do with the Marshall property. Sure, she wanted to grab it before someone else did, but even beyond that she envisioned one large farm and learning center. Cooking classes by Alvaro, seasonal breakfast dishes featuring only foods fresh from the fields, nighttime bonfires and holiday wreath-making classes. All the things she loved as a kid, but packaged for people who've never experienced those pleasures, or who want to re-experience them for a short while.

She loved the idea so much that she couldn't respond. There was just no money for it, and selling arugula to Fiddlehead wasn't going to make it happen.

"We'll start with the pizza farm," Clay said. "Clover told me that despite the scene at the end, it was a huge hit. Café customers have been asking about the next dinner. They love the pizza, they love the farm." His eyes held hers. "Let me put in the patio, make a few touches, and we'll reopen."

Megan opened a beer. She was no match for Bonnie Birch and Clay Hand together. "Sure. Go for it." What did she have to lose?

Before she could go to bed, Megan had two tasks to take care of. First, she needed to call her mother. Charlotte picked up right away.

"Megan, I'm so glad you called. How are you?"

Megan exchanged niceties for a few minutes before getting to the point. "Do you think you could meet with me this week? I have some questions about art valuations I'd like to run by you."

"Of course. How about tomorrow? Lunch?"

"Can we meet at the Center? It's more central for both of us." And it gives me an excuse to see Ray, Megan thought.

"Sure, that sounds good. The Center at noon." Her mother paused. "I'm glad you called, Megan."

"I am too." And she meant it.

Her second piece of business was an internet search on Sylvia Adriana Altamura. It was something she should have done long ago. King had been right; Megan was as much an enabler of her father as Bibi was. That in and of itself was one thing, but what if they'd looked the other way while he formed a relationship with a dishonest woman? Megan could never forgive herself.

A search on Sylvia turned up very little of interest. No social media. No news articles. Only a brief mention of her business dealings in her home town and in nearby Milan. Relieved, Megan was about to shut down her computer when something caught her eye. One of the recommended search terms at the bottom of the page was Chiara Altamura. Megan recognized the name as the aunt Sylvia had asked her to call. More specifically, she wanted Megan to tell this woman to send money for lord knew what purpose.

Megan followed the thread. She searched for anything about Chiara. After a few minutes, she sat back, stunned. Sylvia's aunt was a loan shark. Arrested multiple times, with connections to unsavory factions within Italy, Chiara Altamura was a household name in certain circles. Not the circles Megan generally moved in.

What the hell to do with *that* information?

■ ■ ■ ■

The relentless sound of her cell phone ringing woke Megan from a deep sleep.

"I'm sorry for waking ye, Megs," Denver said, "but I couldn't stand the thought of you worrying or thinking I wasn't being true."

It took Megan a moment to wake up, and as she swam through the haze of REM sleep, she latched on to Denver's voice. She was happy to hear from him.

"Denver?" was all she managed. "Are you okay?"

"Aye, I'm fine. It's my sister. She had some complications and had to go back in hospital."

"I'm sorry."

"Not as sorry as she. She hates the food, hates the nurses, and I despise the chairs they give family members. My back's as twisted as a Dali painting."

"Will she be in long?"

"No, I don't think so. The worst seems to have passed. I expect they'll send her home tomorrow, which is good because I think her pets are tired of the litany of sitters who've been caring for them these past few days."

"Sitters?"

"The same bunch who bake casseroles and send cookies."

"Your phone. I tried calling you but I think one of them had your phone."

"Yeah, that — I'm sorry, Megs. That was Dolores MacNamara. She can be a bit exuberant. Left my phone at my sister's flat and Dolores took it upon herself to answer. Anyway, I didn't want you worrying. I miss you something awful."

That was all she needed to hear. Megan put her head back on the pillow and closed her eyes. "I miss you too."

"If you're not too tired, tell me what's going on. I feel removed from home and from you."

Megan filled him in as best she could, struggling to remember the details. She ended with her conversation with King about enabling her father and after some hesitation, added her findings about Chiara. "So you see, a lot's at stake here. My father's wife. Alvaro and Maria. I wish I had a better sense of what Chiara's occupation means — if anything."

"None of this is great news, Megs."

"Tell me about it."

"You're dealing with a lot."

"Nothing I can't handle."

Denver didn't respond right away. Megan heard hospital noises coming through the phone. The click of heels on tile, a request coming over a loudspeaker. Finally Denver said, "Before you tell the police about Sylvia and Chiara, I would talk to Sylvia. Ask her to explain."

"What's the likelihood she'll tell me the truth?"

"As I see it, that's a risk you need to take. Like it or not, she's important to your father. This aunt of hers may mean nothing. If you go to the authorities and cast more suspicion her way, she and your father will never forgive you."

"What if she's the murderer, Denver? What if I wait and she strikes again?"

"Nothing you've told me necessarily adds up to murder. Talk to her. See what she has to say for herself."

Megan agreed. For now. "Thanks," she said. "When are you coming home?"

"Not soon enough," Denver replied. "Not soon enough."

Twenty-Seven

Wednesday brought record temperatures and suffocating humidity. With each humid day, Megan was sure more rain would come, but other than a brief downpour here or there, nothing. She watched as her flower beds slowly withered in the heat, only the hardiest of plants surviving the unrelenting sun and lack of water. Despite the two days of storms, drought measures had been imposed, and while Megan could use water for her crops, she didn't use it for the ornamentals. She hated to see anything die, yet she felt grateful they were still getting a decent bounty — even if some of the vegetables were faring better than others.

Clay had arrived by eight that morning and was hurrying through the morning routine so he could get to the pizza kitchen changes.

"Porter and I have things covered here," he told Megan after she'd finished her morning chores. "You collected eggs for the store, and Porter and I already have the vegetables Alvaro requested for today's menu." He hauled a basket of Brussels sprouts, small cabbage heads still attached to their stalks, onto his shoulder. "He's making a shaved Brussels sprout Caesar salad. Sounds pretty good."

"It really does," Megan said. She watched clay add the basket to the already full truck. He added a basket of leeks for Alvaro's cold leek and potato soup before stepping back and wiping his hands on the small hand towel attached to his jeans.

"We're going to work on the garlic beds and weed and water the tomatoes. Porter has watering duty later today, once the sun starts going down. If we do it now, everything will just evaporate."

"It's too hot to do much of anything," Megan said. She thought of Zaneta's in-ground pool. What she wouldn't give for a dip right about now. "Maybe you and Porter should take the afternoon off."

"We have a date with a pair of shovels." Clay grinned. "Patio time."

Megan shook her head. He really was something. "Well I'll head to the café, but then I'm meeting my mother for lunch at the Center."

"Fancy Schmancy."

"A little side investigating. I've been so obsessed with Elliot that I failed to consider other sides of a triangle."

"A triangle?"

"A love triangle." Megan swung one leg into the truck. "Or two love triangles, depending on how you look at it."

The café smelled heavenly. Megan arrived by nine thirty. After putting away the produce and eggs she'd brought with her, she checked on the stock in the store, making notes on what needed to be ordered. Clover was already there manning the cash register, and Emily had joined them to help out at the café. All of the café's tables were filled, and even the Breakfast Club, the group of men who came to eat foods their wives forbid and to argue politics and sports, had returned. The café was blessedly cool, and customers seemed reluctant to head back outside.

"How about the heat?" Phil Dour said as Megan poured coffee refills. He was a mechanic who owned the town's only auto shop, so everyone had needed to rely on Phil at one point or another. "Haven't seen anything like this in years, if ever."

"It's brutal," Megan said. "You should be

drinking water, Phil, not caffeinated coffee."

"Ah, coffee is a liquid. I'll be fine."

Megan smiled. He probably would be fine. A lot of these Winsome old timers had lived through tougher times.

"How's your father?" he asked. "Heard he was in town but I haven't seen him."

"He's been keeping a low profile. Newly married and all."

"I heard." Phil raised his coffee cup in a mock toast. "Italian bride."

"Sylvia Adriana Altamura," Roger Becker said. "Lovely lady. I met her at the Center. We took the same yoga class."

Megan tried to picture six-foot-two Roger doing yoga. "The Center, huh? Like it?"

Roger waved his hand. "Plastic food, too much aqua, and more expensive than my mortgage. Here I can get coffee and Alvaro's blue plate special for less than the Center's valet parking fee."

That started the men in a whole discussion about the Center's valet parking and other fees, and while Megan felt somewhat vindicated while listening, she had too much to do to yap with them all morning.

"They must be doing something right," Megan said to Alvaro back in the kitchen. "That Center is expensive."

"They cater to the rich and spoiled,"

Alvaro said. The twist of his mouth made his disdain apparent. "Don't let the trappings fool you, Megan. Put lipstick on a pig, it's still a pig."

Megan found Charlotte waiting for her in the Center's Welcome Hall. She wore a heather brown sheath dress and matching pumps, and she carried a flat, brown handbag. Megan, who had traded in her t-shirt for a silk tank, still had on jeans. She glanced down. At least they were clean.

Charlotte's hug was warm. "It's so good to see you, Megan."

"Thank you for meeting me on such short notice."

"Are you kidding? I was happy you called."

They followed a hostess to their inside table nestled next to a window — too hot for outside dining, even with fans blowing — and waited while the waitress poured them ice water.

"This is my first time here," Charlotte admitted. "It's quite something. I guess I was expecting more yoga meditation center, less Hamptons resort."

"It's a little over the top."

Charlotte smiled. "Someone had vision."

"I actually know one of the owners. He and I were friends a long time ago. I'm hoping to meet with him after our lunch."

"Oh? Someone from Winsome."

"He used to be from Winsome. He brought the artist here, Thana Moore. The woman who was killed. Thana, Ray, and I were inseparable once." Megan instantly regretted the statement. When she talked about her childhood, she felt like every utterance was an unintended rebuke.

Charlotte placed her linen napkin on her lap and took a sip of water. Megan appreciated her mother's elegance, the way she made even simple acts seem graceful. "Did you meet with Elizabeth Yee at the Mission?" When Megan nodded, Charlotte said, "I hope she was able to give you some insight into what you were looking for."

"She presented another side of Thana, for sure. A woman who wanted to give back — but was also looking for recognition and attention."

"Aren't many who make grand gestures? She was an artist. It's a tough field."

"True. And that's why I wanted to talk with you. You mentioned editing *Art* magazine, and Sarah told me that you're background is in art. I'm curious about how art is priced. Some of Thana's work was going for tens of thousands of dollars. Isn't that high for someone relatively new to the scene?"

"Not necessarily. Art has no intrinsic value. If you think about it, it's just canvas and paint, or whatever the medium. The value comes in the form of people's perception about the work — and their estimation of its future value. Perhaps Thana's reputation was such that she could demand a higher price for her work."

The waitress returned to take their order. Charlotte selected the quiche and salad special, and Megan asked for the salad with grilled chicken. When the waitress was gone, Megan said, "Mick, my late husband, bought me two of Thana's paintings — the two you saw — for less than a hundred dollars at a craft fair less than ten years ago. Now her paintings are getting thousands. Does that seem odd?"

"It's just hard to say. People pay millions for artwork, Megan. If she established a track record of sales, that would build her brand and make her work more desirable."

"Her work *is* good. To my untrained eye? Really good. Critics pan it, though."

"Lots of artists do good work; that's not enough. Her work is unique and pleasing to the eye, but even that isn't often enough. Somehow things came together for her. She became trendy. It's kind of like acting or writing. You have to have talent, you need to be persistent, and then there's that something extra — luck, fate, marketing savvy, networking, call it what you want — that generally comes into play." Charlotte turned around so she was facing the door. "I saw a brochure advertising the art show for the opening weeks of the Center. Is her exhibit still here?"

"I don't think so."

Charlotte turned back around. She met Megan's gaze with a ferocity that surprised her. "Don't let the pretty pictures fool you. The art world is a cutthroat business. If this woman was murdered because of her art, whoever did it won't stop there. If they think you're on to them, you could be in danger too."

"I understand," Megan said.

Charlotte's touch against Megan's hand was electric. "Do you? I hope so."

There would be irony in finding you only to lose you so soon, was the message broadcast by her mother's eyes. Charlotte didn't say it, though. She didn't need to.

"Megan, what brings you back to the Center?" Ray Cruise met her back in the Welcome Center. He looked a little tired today.

Fine lines around his eyes and mouth seemed to age him, and Megan wondered whether he'd heard about Elliot's death. "I have a meeting in thirty, but I'm always happy to see you."

Megan followed him back to his office. The offices around his had been fleshed out since she was last here. Windowed cubicles sported family photos and landscape paintings. His office had not changed.

When Megan sat, she said, "Tell me, Ray, now that Elliot is dead, who do you think killed Thana?"

"Right to the chase?" Ray smiled. "You've changed over the years."

"Grief changes a person."

Ray's face darkened. "Indeed."

Megan took a closer look at her companion. "You loved her. After all these years, you were in love with Thana."

Ray smiled again, the smile of a man coming to terms with the unfairness of life. "It took me years to figure that out, but yes. I loved her."

"Enough to kill her?"

"What a twisted thing to ask." Ray stood. He walked slowly to a cabinet on the wall, opened it, and removed two glasses and a decanter of Scotch. He poured them both two fingers without asking Megan if she wanted any. She accepted the offering. "And no, I didn't kill Thana. Nor did I kill that brute of a boyfriend, Elliot. Though I might have enjoyed doing so."

Ray sat back down. "The Center is already under water. We didn't expect to turn a profit this year, but we have investors watching our every move, and being associated with a murder doesn't help the bottom line. You saw the restaurant. When we opened, I had waiting lists for tables. Now? Empty real estate." He shook his head. "I lost a friend *and* I lost a business edge last week. You'll have to forgive me for drinking so early in the day."

Megan watched her old friend swirl the amber liquid around in his glass and swallow it down in one gulp. "That's a lot to lose, Ray," she said softly. "What are you doing about the business?"

"Damage control. Carly's in major damage control mode. We're going to do a fundraiser for a local charity, try to drum up some good will with the locals."

"What charity?"

"Some mission church that helps runaways. Carly's idea." There was a sharp knock at the door and Ray said, "Speak of the devil. Come on in."

Megan had seen pictures of Carly Stevenson online, but she wasn't prepared for the woman in person. Tall — perhaps six feet or more — and slender, with a thick, glossy mop of cascading blonde curls and the kind of complexion you see on super models. She wore a body-hugging light gray suit with a deep teal blouse that brought out her blue eyes. Megan understood why this beacon of health and privilege was the face of the Center. Looking at Carly made her want to take up the lifestyle as well.

"New friend Carly meet old friend Megan Sawyer." Ray didn't bother to stand. "What do you want, Carly?"

"For you to do your job."

Ray's eyebrows shot up along with the corners of his mouth. "Pot, kettle."

Megan wasn't sure if they were teasing each other or serious. She stood. "I can let you two get back to business." But Ray motioned for her to sit back down. "My lovely partner was just leaving."

Carly pulled a chair up to Ray's desk. "I'm not going anywhere, Ray. We need to talk." She glanced at Megan. "I'm sorry to interrupt, I really am, but things are happening and I need Ray to focus."

Megan nodded. "No problem. Do you mind if I take a walk on the grounds? I'd like to see the horses."

"Suit yourself," Carly said. "They're all rescues. Spread that around."

"Carly the opportunist. I think we donated to Sierra Club, want Megan to shout that from the rooftops as well?"

"If it helps, absolutely."

Megan left, feeling like she was in the midst of a sparring match no one was going to win.

With the extreme heat pounding down on the Delaware Valley, Megan wasn't surprised to find the horses inside the barn, where at least the sun couldn't find them. She was pleased because it was really their handlers, Mark and Marcy, who she wanted. She found Marcy in a stall with one of the horses. She was cleaning its shoe with a metal gouge.

Without looking up, she said, "No rides until tonight. It's too hot for the horses."

"I'm not here for a ride," Megan said. She stroked the head of a stately mare. The horse leaned into the affection. "I was wondering if I could talk to you about Thana Moore."

"The artist?"

"Yes. She was a friend of mine."

Marcy finished her chore and left the stall. She wiped her hands on a damp towel before walking toward Megan. "And you are?"

Megan introduced herself. "I was just meeting with Carly and Ray. They said I could wander up."

That seemed to put Marcy at ease. She was as cute as the Instagram photos Megan had seen, with long blonde hair pulled into a ponytail and jeans tight enough to be second skin, but worry lines marred her face.

"Thana was a regular up here. The horses will miss her."

"You were talking with my friend, Clover, on Sunday. She said you mentioned a man following Thana when she was here."

Marcy's worry lines deepened.

"I thought maybe you'd recalled more details about him. Height. Build."

Marcy shook her head. She seemed in a sudden rush to end this conversation. "Nothing I didn't share with the cops."

Megan persisted. "Look, two people have died. I have a contact at the Winsome PD who is investigating Elliot's death. If you can help in any way, it could save more lives."

"Are you a cop?"

"No, just a friend to some people whose lives are being impacted by this. And a friend to Thana — once."

Marcy opened the gate to a small quarter horse with a white star on her head. She stroked the horse's neck absentmindedly, clearly thinking about what to say next. Finally, she said, "Carly, she's our boss, is trying to limit information sharing. She doesn't want the Center associated in any way with these murders. You can't tell anyone you even talked to me, or Mark and I will be out of a job. Please."

Megan nodded. "Of course."

The horse nudged Marcy's side and Marcy resumed her stroking. "I did see a man following Thana. On more than one occasion. It wasn't Elliot. I know, because once I saw Elliot watching the man who was watching Thana."

"What did Elliot do?"

"Nothing. I got Mark so he could see too. Thana was heading down the path toward the Center. The guy stepped out of the trees and followed her. I thought maybe it was Elliot keeping an eye on her — really sweet guy, but he had a possessive streak — only it wasn't because there was Elliot at the bottom of the hill watching Thana descend."

"Did you see his face?"

"Yeah, I did. We keep binoculars in the barn in case we see a predator. Once in a while you get a bear or a coyote, or even a hunter with bad eyesight who thinks a horse is a deer." Marcy scrunched her face up in a look of disgust. "So Mark grabbed the binoculars, but we couldn't make out anything about the guy other than his height. Fairly tall and thin — nothing distinguishable. He disappeared back into the woods, just like he'd appeared. Elliot, though? He had this look of utter sadness on his face. Not anger, not surprise. Just sadness."

"What did you make of that?"

"At the time, I thought maybe the guy following her was a lover, someone she was seeing on the side, and Elliot was confirming his suspicions. But Thana talked about personal stuff when she was with the horses and the only guy Thana was seeing on the side — and it wasn't really the side because by then she and Elliot had broken up — was Ray."

"Did Thana seem conflicted? Distraught?"

"Not really. Her paintings were starting to sell well, she'd done that mural for the church. She had the show here. She was never really satisfied — that was the kind of person she was, always restless — but I think she was looking forward to her future."

"How about when it came to Ray?"

"They were hiding their affair, so she

didn't say much."

"I don't think it was a well-kept secret. I heard staff talking about it earlier this week."

Marcy shrugged. "Gossips. We have lots of those here, which is why I prefer working with the horses. Anyway, I don't think Ray would follow Thana around in the woods. It just doesn't seem his style."

No, Megan had to agree, it didn't. But love could bring out the best in people, and the worst. What was the saying? There was a fine line between love and hate. But why would Ray Cruise kill Thana? It was her death that caused the Center financial issues, not her life.

Megan wasn't sure what the connection was, but she was determined to find out.

Twenty-Eight

Megan left the Center feeling more confused than ever. So many potential leads; she wasn't sure how the police managed — although they had surveillance and tools at their disposal. She decided to call King to let him know about her discussion with Marcy, but she realized she had very little to go by other than a hunch interpreting Elliot's expression and the fact that a man was following Thana, which the Dartville police already knew.

She rolled down the truck window in an attempt to wake herself up, but the hot, soupy air felt suffocating, so she closed the window and opted for the air conditioner. While she drove back to the farm, she considered what she knew. Thana's career was just taking off. She'd gone from starving artist selling paintings from a craft fair table to local sweetheart whose work was selling for thousands. A relationship with an old flame brought her to the Center, where she got even more exposure. She broke up with her boyfriend, a wannabe artist with a penchant for woodworking and business who seemed to see himself as her protector and her manager. She was having an affair with Ray Cruise, the Center owner who brought her in, possibly sparking jealousy by the ex-boyfriend. She had an unknown stalker. After arguments with several people at the Center, she was murdered in her own van.

Strangled with Sylvia's scarf.

Sylvia. What did she have to do with any of this? Now seemed like as good a time as any to find out.

Megan's tank was low so she pulled into the nearest station, a Wawa off Route 611. She was pumping gas when she spied two people who looked vaguely familiar. She was putting garbage in a receptacle and he was filling the car's tank with gas.

Megan squinted in their direction, blocking the blinding sun. The woman had medium-length steel gray hair tied in pigtails on either side of her head. She wore patterned purple pants that looked like pajamas and a Native American print t-shirt. One headphone dangled down the left side of her neck. Her companion was a handsome bald man with a sandy beard. A glance at the car triggered her memory. A New Beginnings bumper sticker had been plastered to the rear end of the old Toyota Camry.

Joseph Muller. From the Mission. Perhaps the woman was one of the congregants Megan had seen when she visited. The pair got in the car and pulled out, deep in conversation. Off to do their charity work, perhaps. They seemed to be gaining some traction in the community.

Megan grabbed a bag of pretzels and climbed back in her truck. She was a quarter mile from Washington Acres when her phone rang. She didn't recognize the number but she answered anyway.

"Megan Sawyer?"

"This is she."

"Dr. Oliver Craddock. You were looking for me yesterday? About my son, Elliot."

He didn't sound like someone who had just lost a son, and Megan wondered whether King's officers had talked with him.

But then he said, "My son was killed, Ms. Sawyer. I don't know if you knew that, but I have to wonder why you were at my house, asking about Elliot in the midst of all this."

"I'm so sorry for your loss, Dr. Craddock."

"Can you explain the connection?"

Megan pulled over to the side of the road. She gave Elliot's father a brief summary of her dealings with Elliot. "Thana was my friend, and now several people I care about have been implicated in her murder. I was hoping, had been hoping, that Elliot could shed some light on what happened."

"Whatever scum took Thana, took my son." Oliver's voice was a Long Island accented low growl. "Look, I don't know how he could have helped, but I'm going to do everything I can to find out who took his life and bring the bastard to justice."

"I can understand that, Dr. Craddock."

"Are you near Winsome?"

"Yes. I'm on my way there now."

"Meet me at 1212 Juniper Lane. Across from the old bowling alley. That's where Elliot's shop is. I need to go now and pack up some of his stuff; I want to get there before his partners do and clean everything out."

"Couldn't that be evidence?"

"The police are meeting me there as well. Look, if you want to talk, that's where I'll be."

Megan thanked him and hung up. It seemed Sylvia would have to wait while she headed to Juniper Street and the good Dr. Craddock.

Megan placed a quick phone call to Clover. She told her where she'd be and with whom — just in case. "I'm driving and can't use my phone. Can you look up Dr. Craddock and let me know what kind of doctor I'm dealing with?"

"I don't need to do that." Clover was at the café and Megan could hear the muffle of voices behind her. "He's a psychiatrist. I remember Alvaro rolling his eyes when his sister announced she was marrying a doctor."

"A psychiatrist, huh?"

"Yeah. I think he's partially retired. Hold on, I'll check." She returned a moment later. "Board certified. Specializes in childhood and adolescent anxiety disorders. Works a part-time schedule out of New Hope." Clover made an "hmm" sound. "So Elliot's dad is a shrink. Go figure."

"Go figure is right. That explains the fancy house and expensive pool."

"Wasn't he an absentee dad?"

"Until recently. They found each other later in life, at least according to Alvaro's sister." Megan pulled up in front of a signless storefront, behind a brand new Infinity.

No sign of police cars. "Okay, Clover, I'm here. I'll call you in two hours. If you don't hear from me, call Bobby. In the meantime, maybe Dr. Craddock can use his knowledge of human behavior to shed some light on what's going on."

Oliver Craddock was still sitting in his car. When Megan slid out of the truck, he got out as well, locking the door with a quick grasp of the handle.

"You're late."

"It took me a few minutes to get here."

"Nevertheless." Oliver glanced at his watch. "I'd like a chance to go through this before Chief King gets here. I checked you out, you know. Through my wife, but also online. I know you were instrumental in solving a string of crimes in Winsome last year."

"I worked closely with the police."

"False modesty becomes no one."

Megan gave Oliver a bemused smile. For a psychiatrist who worked with kids, his bedside manner was severely lacking. He was of moderate height for a man, with a neat, closely cropped salt and pepper beard. His clothes were expensive but casual: pink Polo shirt, pressed summer weight flannel pants, an argyle vest. Shoes were shined until they mirrored the blue sky above them. She tried to match this man and his tattooed son. It was difficult.

"You wanted to talk with Elliot. Why?"

Megan opted for candor. "I think Elliot may have stolen two paintings from my farm."

"Why would he have done that?"

"Because they were Thana's early work and likely worth something."

Oliver stroked his beard with the thumb and pointer finger of his left hand. "My initial reaction is to deny it, of course. As any parent would want to do. But I'm afraid you might be right."

Not the answer Megan was expecting. She waited for Oliver to say more, but he was removing a key from his pants pocket. They reached the front door of the unmarked building and he paused.

"You see, Elliot confided in me that he'd been having some issues with his business associates — art dealers, I presume. They were pressuring him to give them more of Thana's work. He was pushing Thana because the demand was there, but she was an artist." He slid the key in and turned his wrist while giving Megan a raised eyebrow look that said *you know artists.* "Thana worked when inspiration hit her. Elliot

362

didn't tell me he was leveraged, but I suspect he owed some of these people money by the way he was acting." Oliver shook his head. "I wish he could have just asked me for money, if that was all he needed."

"Sometimes it's hard for kids to admit when they need help."

"True. And he could be stubborn. So I called the police out of concern for this place. It was his haven. Zaneta said she showed you Elliot's work. Gorgeous, right? So his workshop is all I have of my son, really —"

Oliver pushed open the door and immediately stopped talking. His skin under the beard was bright red.

"Oliver?"

He kicked the door so that it opened the rest of the way. Other than a small pile of wood scraps and some old beer bottles, the workshop was empty.

"What the hell?"

He took a step forward and Megan's arm shot out, blocking him. "You said the police are meeting you here?"

Oliver nodded.

"Then wait for them. Either Elliot cleared this place out," — which was Megan's gut based on the cleanliness of the room — "or he was robbed. Either way, the police should be the first ones in here."

"Nonsense. I'm his father."

Megan interrupted him. "As a man of reason, you see the folly in messing with evidence. Footprints, fingerprints, who knows. You want Elliot's murderer caught, don't you?"

Oliver's face seemed to cave in on itself, and Megan saw the first hint of true grief. Oliver hung his head, but he backed out of the doorway and closed the door. Sinking down on the front stoop, he placed his face in his hands. Megan called King to be sure he was on his way, then sat on the far side of the entrance, giving Oliver his space.

It was after supper time when Megan finally returned home. The oppressive heat from earlier in the day had given way to angry skies and a hot breeze, but still no rain. Megan sat in her truck for a few minutes watching Clay as he and Porter dug beside the old barn. It was too hot to stretch much less dig. But there they were.

As she opened the truck door, Gunther and Sadie tore down the courtyard toward her, tails wagging furiously. It would be an idyllic scene had it not been for the murder just a few miles away.

Megan placed her purse in the enclosed porch and traded her sandals for muckers before heading up toward the barn. If they were going to withstand this heat to improve the property, the least she could do was help them.

In the barn, she grabbed a shovel and met the men outside. The sun was just starting to set and the sky glowed orange and pink. While still hot, the space was shaded by the old oak and the barn and so the evening was more pleasant than it could have been. They worked silently for a while. Clay and Porter were drenched in sweat and streaked with dirt, but their occasional grunts seemed born of contentment rather than pain. After about twenty minutes, Clay stopped. Megan, now also drenched in sweat, was glad for the reprieve.

"What do you think?" Clay asked. He took a long swig of water from a jug by the tree. "This will be the main outdoor eating area."

"I can't believe how much you got done. And on a day like today."

"It's too small," Porter said. He was drinking Gatorade and he swallowed the blue stuff in three swigs. It wasn't long ago that Brian Porter had been battling his own demons in the form of alcohol addiction. As a veteran suffering from PTSD, Megan knew this job and Denver's friendship were sometimes the only things that kept Porter on track.

"What do you mean?" Megan asked. "It looked pretty large to me."

Porter pointed to the dirt they'd dug up outside of the barn. "Not enough space for more than two or three bistro tables. For this to really work, you need more space so you can get five or six tables and still have room for the wait staff to walk around comfortably."

Megan saw what he meant. Right now, the patio would be fine as a household space, but tight for a commercial operation.

"We need to contain it near the restaurant," Clay said. "It's part of the permit. So we can't go too far toward the greenhouses or the neighboring property."

Megan leaned on her shovel and looked out over the farm property and the Marshall house beyond. "So you want to take down the tree?" she asked. She kept her voice steady, but that tree was special to her. She and Mick had sat under it as teens. Before that, she and Thana had planned for high school by its shady limbs. It always reminded her of childhood, when her grandmother would tell her to go up to "the big Oak" to get some fresh air and pack her sandwiches and small containers of fruit. It was as much a part of her youth as the house.

But chopping down the tree was not what Clay wanted. "Just the knoll. If we flatten that area, we'll have enough space, and some of the tables will be shaded by the tree."

The small grassy knoll was part and parcel with the tree. "This means a lot to you, doesn't it?" she asked Clay.

Clay didn't respond, but Porter caught her gaze and nodded slightly. Of course it meant a lot to him. The vision of the farm he and Bibi had shared — with the inn and the teaching programs and the restaurant — wasn't that a dream they all shared?

"Sure," Megan said. "Just watch for the tree roots, okay? I don't want to lose her." She patted the great trunk.

"Absolutely." Clay picked the shovel back up and they worked for another hour, until the bats flew overhead and the mosquitoes had determined they were supper.

By the time Megan went inside, she was achy and worn, but it was the best she had felt in days. Honest labor. She understood its draw and its ability to provide perspective.

A sandwich and a bath later, she was in bed, down for the night.

TWENTY-NINE

Megan's alarm went off at four forty-five, but she'd been awake for fifteen minutes. Her hands had gone numb during the wee morning hours, a product of sleeping with her arm under her head so as not to disturb Sadie. Thinking about her numb hands made her think about her manicure, and that's when she remembered where she'd seen the woman pumping gas at Wawa. Gina, her Center spa therapist.

Megan hadn't recognized her in that odd outfit. Quite the departure from the sedate-looking woman at the Center.

So why was Gina with Joseph Muller from New Beginnings Mission Church?

Megan recalled Ray telling her that the Center was doing a fundraiser to increase its good will with the community. Was that it? But why would they send a therapist from the spa to coordinate a major event with the Mission? They wouldn't.

Probably a logical explanation, Megan thought. *She belongs to that church, or she volunteers with New Beginnings.*

Still, the image of the two of them stayed with her while she showered and dressed. It seemed like such a random connection.

Downstairs, Bibi was already up. She greeted Megan and sliced off two thick pieces of pumpkin bread. After toasting them in the oven for a few minutes, she spread softened butter over the top and slid the plate to Megan along with a steaming cup of coffee.

"Another hot one today," Bibi said. "Drink lots of water."

Megan nodded. "Where's my father?"

"They're still sleeping. I heard that woman get up a while ago, but haven't seen them yet. Sylvia's on princess time."

"Is that so?" Sylvia walked in the kitchen just then. Her hair was held up in silver clips, and she wore a long, white dressing gown. The irony was not lost on Megan or Bibi, who gave her granddaughter a surreptitious smile.

"Good morning," Bibi said without missing a beat. "Pumpkin bread?"

"Such an American thing. No thank you. Do you have sweet rolls? Or maybe just some tea biscuits?"

"I'm sure the bakery in town does," Bibi murmured, and Megan gave her a look.

"Have you heard any more from Detectives Jones and Lewis?" Megan asked. "With everything happening, I thought maybe they'd give you the green light that you're clear."

Sylvia smiled. "No, not yet. They're clowns, those two. Making me wait. They call every day or so, and I send them to my lawyer. Thank you for that."

Megan knew she needed to talk with Sylvia about Chiara, but she dreaded that conversation. With a glance at her grandmother, she decided to head out on a high note — and she'd take the thank you as a high note. She drained the remainder of her coffee and grabbed another slice of pumpkin bread to go.

"I'll be in the greenhouses," she told her grandmother. "I have to transplant the lettuce and I want to do it before it gets too hot outside."

"Good idea." Bibi handed her a sandwich she'd wrapped in wax paper. Then she handed her another. And another. "For you, Clay, and Brian. You never eat enough while you're working."

Sylvia, who had poured herself a cup of coffee, said, "She doesn't look like she's

371

starving."

Megan left before Bibi, whose face was turning as pink as her "Winsome Cares" t-shirt, could respond.

Oh, Dad, she thought as she headed toward the barn, what were you thinking? All the women in the world and you chose her?

Sylvia found Megan in the fields later that morning. In a nod to the Birch family vocation, she'd donned sneakers with her long linen skirt, matching blouse, and wide-brimmed hat, and as she picked her way across the field, she held the soft beige skirt material up to keep it clean.

Megan didn't want to tell her it was a losing proposition.

"Good morning," Megan said. "It's nice to see you up and around."

"I've been up every day," Sylvia replied. "I just needed to get some things in order. That takes time." She glanced toward Clay, who was still working on digging the foundation for the new patio. "Can I talk to you for a few moments in private? Perhaps somewhere out of the sun?"

Megan was weeding the Swiss chard. She nodded and pulled off her gloves. "Let's go in the barn."

Sylvia followed her inside the pizza restaurant, and they sat at one of the tables that Clay had repaired. The air conditioner wasn't on, but at least the air was cooler inside with the lights off.

"Did you call my aunt?" Sylvia asked without pretense. "Chiara is waiting to hear from me."

"Then you should contact her."

"You have not?" Sylvia looked stunned. "But I asked you to."

"In the midst of a murder investigation."

"This again?" Sylvia slammed a hand down on the table. "You don't trust me?"

"I didn't say that, but I'm an attorney. I'm not in the habit of calling strangers to make statements about money when there's an active investigation going on and the person making the request won't give me any information."

They stared at each other. Megan refused to back down. Days of stress and missing Denver topped by the nagging heat had her on edge. Sylvia jutted a jaw forward, clearly not used to being challenged.

The door swung open. Eddie stood there looking dapper in straight-legged checked trousers and a slim-fitted button-down shirt. Both women said, "Please leave" at the same time. Eddie glanced at each in turn, shook his head, and backed out.

When the door was closed, Megan said, "Why didn't you tell me your Aunt Chiara is a loan shark?"

"Why does it matter?"

"Because my integrity matters to me. What's the deal, Sylvia? Why do you need money from a loan shark? And while I'm at it, why were you arguing with Thana Moore?" Megan realized she was practically shouting. She made a conscious effort to lower her voice. "You're not telling me anything, yet you expect me to trust you."

Sylvia glanced at the door through which Eddie had just left. And that's when Megan understood.

"This is for my father."

Sylvia pursed her mouth, nodded.

"But for what? I don't understand." And then suddenly she did. The clothes. The new look. The money. "You're setting him up in business."

Sylvia stood. Her small frame paced across the room. She stopped where Thana's paintings had been. "It was a simple plan. Convince Thana to let me introduce her work to Europe. A dealer keeps significant profits. She was getting enough for her paintings to bring in twenty, thirty thousand euros a painting. Maybe more. I needed to raise only another thirty thousand euros to buy into the men's clothing store Eddie so wants to run."

"And he would never know you paid to get him the position."

Sylvia turned to face Megan, hands on hips. "That's not true — I would tell him. Eventually, once he built his confidence. He's a smart man, your father. Sensitive in a way few men are. He has a gift for clothes, but also for people. This would give him direction. Energy."

"And when Thana refused, you argued. You went off in the woods to calm down."

"Your father cannot know. It would break his heart."

"But a loan shark?"

Sylvia shrugged. "I'll find a way to pay her back."

Megan felt breathless. She hadn't expected an act of such selflessness from this self-centered woman. "So the phone calls. The secrecy — all for this?"

Sylvia nodded.

Reluctantly, Megan asked, "Do you still want me to call Chiara? I will."

"And you won't tell your father?"

"I think he should know. But no, I'll leave it up to you to make that decision."

Sylvia's curt nod was one of thanks. At

least that's how Megan took it. She watched her stepmother leave and felt at least some of the weight coming off her shoulders.

Chiara didn't answer on the first or second try. Her voicemail had no message, just a beep, so Megan said exactly what Sylvia asked her to say — no more, no less. Let the chips fall where they may.

THIRTY

Megan spent the remainder of Thursday on the farm. She finished weeding, played with the goats, and helped Clay and Porter with the patio. Despite the heat, she relished the time on the farm and tried not to think about Thana or Elliot or anything beyond the borders of Washington Acres. But the outside world caught up with her in the form of a visit from Bobby King. He stopped by a little after three to ask Megan some questions and show her a picture.

"Let's go in the house," Megan said. "I need some water, and I bet Bibi has some freshly baked cookies in there. She's been talking about making them all week."

"I'll have to pass on the cookies," King said.

"Got it."

Inside, she poured them each lemon water and put a plate of Bibi's oatmeal raisin cookies on the table. King took a handful and stuffed them in his mouth, one at a time. Megan simply looked at him, amused.

"You can't put them near me, Megan. You know I eat when I'm stressed." He put a file on the kitchen table and grabbed two more cookies. "Bonnie sure can bake."

"So what's going on, Bobby?"

He stopped chewing long enough to say, "Coroner found drugs in Elliot's system. Heroin."

"Not really surprising."

"Tell that to his father. Swore up and down that Elliot didn't take drugs. Not since he'd gotten clean a few years ago."

"Parents are often the last to know."

"Maybe." King opened the file and slid a picture across the table. "Recognize this guy?"

Megan pulled the picture closer, but more out of habit than need. She knew who he was immediately. "Yeah, and so do you. That's one of the guys who lives near you and Clover. Elliot's sometimes roommate." She snapped her fingers. Drexel came to mind. "Steve something or other."

"Steve Stewart." He slid the photo back into his file.

"Why are you asking about Stewart?"

"Because an eye witness saw Elliot and Steve emptying the workshop the day before

Elliot was murdered."

"Together?"

King nodded. "I was wondering if Elliot had mentioned this guy to you, or maybe he was in the car with Elliot when you met."

Megan shook her head. She told King about her trip to the Center and her conversation with Marcy the horse handler. "A stalker? Detectives Jones and Lewis didn't have that in the chart."

"Think it could have been Steve?"

"Based on Marcy's description — 'a tall male' — it could have been me." King had been staring at the remaining cookies and he snatched one, looking angry at the cookie as though his lack of will power was its fault. "But I suppose it could have been, I just don't know why. We questioned Steve and he denies having anything to do with Thana and her artwork. Says that was Elliot's thing and he was just helping out."

"Did you believe him?"

"No reason not to." Although King looked troubled. "I spoke with Maria to see what she had to say about Elliot since she saw him at the Center. She said he was chummy with the head honcho, Carly Stevenson, and that he and Thana helped Maria get that job. And then they turned on her."

"How so?"

"By becoming irate when she wouldn't give Thana more floor space — that we knew — and by blaming her for the ruined painting."

Megan told King about her conversation with an art expert, leaving out the small fact that the expert in question was her mother. "So with paintings going for that much money, I can see why they'd be upset."

"Maria said it was ridiculous to think she would have destroyed a painting. And it was Elliot more so than Thana blaming her."

"His own relative, sort of. That's not quite how Elliot portrayed it to me, Bobby. He made it sound like Thana was the temperamental one."

"And we can't question either of them." King drained the last of the water and stood up. "Did you meet this Carly Stevenson?"

"Briefly."

"She's what my mother would call a piece of work. Smart, driven, but a little loco."

And beautiful, Megan thought — which King wouldn't mention. "So?"

"So, it bothers me that Jones and Lewis barely interviewed her. She's the one who brought Thana in to begin with."

Megan looked at him sharply. "Ray Cruise brought her in."

"That's not what Carly told me. It was

her idea." He shrugged. "Anyway, I think the detectives should have spoken to her. Gotten her perspective."

"So you interviewed Carly, then?" Megan asked.

King nodded. "Related to the break-in. Given everything that happened, it feels like there could be a connection." He paused. "Interesting woman."

"Did she tell you the Center's having problems making ends meet since Thana's murder?"

"She told me business has been so-so."

"I think it's worse than that." Megan shared what she witnessed between Carly and Ray. "Carly seems desperate to keep their investors happy."

"Hmm. Anger at poor business dealings could be a motive for murder."

"Are you thinking perhaps Carly blamed Elliot? Took care of him in her own way?"

"Maybe. The murder weapon was never found, but I think Carly deserves an extra look." King frowned. "It became apparent to me in talking to Carly and Ray that these people have no lives other than the Center. No family, no hobbies. And when business goes south, well, what else is there?" He brightened. "I, for one, am going to go home to Clover. She should be off work soon, and I'll let her make me her absolutely awful meatloaf and pretend to like it."

"Made easier by the fact that you ate a dozen cookies."

King laughed. "There is that."

Megan walked King out. As unhappy as she was that another murder had taken place in Winsome, she welcomed the comradery. King was only here on an unofficial basis, but she was glad he valued her opinion, and she in turn admired his willingness to be open minded. In her years in law, she realized that the best cops were those who knew they didn't know everything.

After King left, Megan went back inside to shower and call Denver. Her head hurt, her back ached, and she had a splinter in her left hand that was driving her crazy, but she felt grateful for the people in her life.

When she rang Denver, he didn't answer. On impulse, King's words echoing in her head, she pulled up a search engine and looked for flights to Scotland. She found a reasonably priced one that left a week from Saturday and booked it. She'd surprise him. After all, life was short.

In her excitement, Megan couldn't sleep. She tried to ring Sylvia's Aunt Chiara again with no luck. She returned to her computer and made some half-hearted searches into Steve Stewart. His name was so common that she had trouble finding him on social media. She searched for Elliot again, and once again she saw the same collage of party pictures: a sea of mostly male faces drinking and playing games late into the night.

Had heroin been on the menu?

Before she logged off, Megan turned her search to Carly Stevenson. Lots of stuff about her speaking engagements, business ventures, and high profile design projects. And a wedding announcement from four years ago in the Philly papers. Followed by a few pieces that mentioned her "imminent divorce" and then her "recent divorce."

Based on what Megan could piece together, they'd been married for three years. Nothing in the papers said whether or not the divorce was amicable.

Megan let that sink in: Carly Stevenson had been married to Ray Cruise.

Carly and Ray as an item. The scene she'd witnessed — the passion poorly disguised as anger — made more sense. As did the conversation Megan had overheard between the staff near the spa. Ray and Carly weren't simply business partners; they had been life partners. And from what Megan saw, there could still be feelings there. A person scorned could be a killer. Perhaps she'd visit Carly again tomorrow. Not to ask the official sorts of questions King would ask, but to get to the heart of Carly's heart.

Would she kill to get back a man?

THIRTY-ONE

Megan slipped out of the house early, before anyone could ask where she was going. She grabbed Bibi's mail off the table — the post office was as good an excuse as any — and made it to the Center shortly after dawn — early enough to watch the sun make the rest of its appearance over the hills. The Center was beautiful this time of day. A moist dew reflected the sun's rays in a million tiny shards of glass, forming baby rainbows promising a brighter tomorrow.

The parking lot was only partially full, but a line of yoga-pants-clad women were run-walking from the main building toward the pool house. Early morning workouts.

Megan took a deep breath and settled into her truck. She was waiting on one person in particular and would stay put until she arrived. In the meantime, she thought about haggis and casseroles and telling a bubbly blonde named Dolores where to stick it.

The phone rang at seven. Denver. She welcomed his call but kept her eyes on the "reserved" parking spots — in particular, the one marked "C. Stevenson." Both that one and the one for "R. Cruise" were empty.

"Hey," Megan said. "How's your sister?"

"Better, thank you. She's home again and complaining up a storm."

"I'm glad to hear it. The home part anyway."

"With her, feeling better and mouthing off go hand in hand." Denver's voice softened. "How are you? I spoke with my aunt earlier and she told me there's been more happenings in Winsome."

"Yeah, not good." Megan shared the news about Elliot's death. "This is a weird one."

"Is his death connected to the break-in?"

"We think so, but until we know more it's all speculation."

Denver became quiet. Megan watched a small Miata wind its way up the driveway toward the Center, holding her breath.

"I don't like it, Megs. It's bad enough when I'm there, but from here I feel like I can't be any help at all."

"I'm fine, Denver." Megan watched the Miata pull into "C. Stevenson." "Although I need to get off the phone. Can I call you later?"

"Megan, I —"

"I love you."

"I love you too, Megan, but —"

Megan clicked off. She watched as Carly's long, bare legs appeared from the passenger seat, one at a time, before another figure emerged from the driver's side. Ray Cruise. Before going into the Center, they paused for a deep kiss. Carly went toward the front entrance, and Ray walked around the side, toward the Meditation Gallery.

Megan hurried out of the truck. She arrived in the Center just as Carly was getting ready to walk through the doors that led to the offices.

"Ms. Stevenson?"

Carly stopped walking. She turned around slowly, her face registering surprise. When she saw Megan she let out a sigh of annoyance.

"You sounded like Thana for a moment. Nothing like being visited by a ghost to get your heart pumping."

"I'm sorry to bother you, but I was hoping we could talk for a few minutes."

"I have a meeting —"

"I checked with your assistant and she said you were free this early. I'd like to discuss the fundraiser you're holding with New Beginnings Mission." The lies were flying now. Megan didn't know whether to feel pride or shame.

Carly seemed to be making up her mind. She made a show of looking at her watch-less wrist before giving a curt nod. "Ten minutes."

She led Megan to her office, which was much larger and more posh than Ray's. Glass walls with inset privacy screens. A large glass desk. Original artwork. A Tiffany lamp. A beautiful handwoven rug that incorporated the aqua the Center held so sacred. No skimping for this woman.

"Sit, please." Carly moved around the desk until her tiny butt was perched in its edge, just a few feet from Megan. A power move Megan recognized from her law firm days.

"The fundraiser you're having with New Beginnings, when will that be?"

"Three weeks from Saturday. Why? Are you with the press?"

"No, but I have connections at New Beginnings. I thought perhaps I could try and help. It's for a good cause, after all."

"Indeed. That's very generous of you." Carly leaned slightly forward. "So why are you *really* here?"

"To ask you about Thana."

"I thought so." Carly stood and walked to

the glass walls. She hit a button and the privacy screens turned the walls opaque. "What about Thana Moore? Between the press inquiries and news coverage, our nervous investors, and the staff's questions, she's done more harm in death than any single person could do." Carly spun around. "Marcy told me you were up there asking questions. We don't have secrets at the Center."

"You make it sound like a cult."

"More like a family."

"Is that what you and Ray are? Family?"

Carly's pretty face darkened. "None of your business. Next question."

"Did Thana know you two were married?"

"Divorced."

"Only recently."

"You did your homework." Carly smiled. "Ray and I are best when we're not committed to one another. His little tryst with Thana made me remember how cute he is in bed. I call, he comes." She laughed at her own pun. "But I don't see how any of this is relevant."

"Just following the trail, Carly. And it just keeps leading back to the Center." Before Carly could respond, Megan said, "Whose idea was it to bring Thana in for opening week?"

"The art show was my idea. Actually, one of my staff made an off-hand suggestion and I ran with it. A poor choice in hindsight."

"Ray said it was his idea to bring Thana in."

Carly dismissed this with a wave of her hand. "I asked Ray to contact her once I found out they'd been friends."

Megan thought about that. "Did Ray tell you they knew each other?"

"No. I don't recall how I found out, a staff member perhaps, but Ray confirmed it and was only too happy to rekindle that friendship." She put air quotes around the word friendship. "I understand you had a friendship with Ray once as well." More air quotes. "He gets around."

Annoyed, Megan had the urge to ask Carly where she was the day Thana died, but she knew King would have already asked that question. Instead she asked how well Carly knew Elliot.

"Her manager? He's the main person I dealt with. Scrappy. I like that."

"And when your employee Maria got into an argument with Elliot and Thana, you took their side."

This time Carly looked troubled. "That was a hard decision. Maria was a good worker, but the destroyed painting was worth eight thousand dollars. I couldn't tolerate that."

"How do you know she destroyed it?"

"It was locked away from the public. Who else would have done it?"

"Did you investigate?"

"As best we could. That said, Maria had access and reason. Common sense."

"If it were so common, more people would display it." She held Carly's gaze until the other woman opened the door.

Megan nodded. She'd outworn her welcome, she was sure. She tried to picture Carly as the killer. She had the ambition, but doing it herself seemed too messy, too personal. Megan rose to leave.

"Megan?"

"Yes?"

"Please don't come back to the Center. You're not welcome here anymore."

"What happened to your open, inclusive policy?"

Carly's smile sent a chill up Megan's spine. "It's exclusive of you."

THIRTY-TWO

The café was quiet, so Megan took the pile of mail and walked to the post office. The skies were overcast and darkening rapidly, so she hurried her gait. When she reached the small stucco building, she heard the crack of thunder. She ducked inside.

Bibi had placed stamps on all of the mail, but still Megan slid them in the slot one by one. She got to the end of the pile and realized two thick brochures had made their way in. She recognized one as the paper Bibi had used to fan herself. She was about to toss it in the recycling bin when the front caught her eye. It was a brochure for New Beginnings. She took it and left.

Outside the sky had darkened to the color of overripe plums. Megan stuck the brochure in her bag and sprinted back to the truck, arriving just as the sky opened up and rain poured down. She looked up at the drenching sheets of precipitation, grateful, and let it pelt her face for a moment before seeking the safety of the car. Thunder boomed followed by a bright flash of lightening.

Megan opened the brochure. Elizabeth Yee's face was inside, next to a Letter to Those Who Care. Megan skimmed the parts about the church, focusing in on the mission. Helping runaways. Getting kids off drugs and off the streets. Offering a caring environment to those with nowhere else to go. Such noble quests. The back of the brochure listed the nonprofit status and the names of the board members.

Megan called home, and Bibi answered on the fourth ring. "Megan, Clay's been looking for you."

"The New Beginnings brochure — where did you get that?"

"It was at the café. I grabbed it because it made a fine fan. Did you take it? I hope you didn't throw it away. It was just the right thickness —"

"Why was it at the café?"

"I think Alvaro brought a stack in. Something about his brother-in-law."

Megan stared at the board members' names. Dr. J. Oliver Craddock. "Thanks, Bibi. I'll call Clay later." She hung up, another memory niggling at the corners of her mind, one she couldn't quite catch.

This time, the New Beginnings Mission Church was empty. Megan found the front door open. She walked through, calling "hello" as she went. Elizabeth Yee met her in the worship room. The pastor wore a long, gray skirt made of sweatshirt material, flat sandals, and a thin, black, short-sleeved shirt. A silver cross hung around her neck. She looked as though she'd been reading — her eyes were red, her forehead creased, and glasses hung from a lanyard around her neck.

"Megan," she said, her smile warm but worn, "what brings you back?"

"I was wondering if you had a few minutes to talk about Elliot Craddock."

"Elliot!" Yee's face lit up and then quickly fell. "Dr. Craddock's son. Of course, come in."

In Yee's office, Megan found herself once again sitting in the chair across from Elizabeth. She reminded herself that Yee had known her mother, that the pastor had been a lay person before finding this calling.

"What do you want to know about Elliot? I can't believe he's gone. Poor man. Poor Oliver."

"It's awful," Megan agreed. "I spoke with his father. I know he's looking for answers."

"He won't find them out there." Yee's tone was firm but kind.

"Was Elliot someone the Mission helped?"

"I can't really talk about that, Megan. I will say that Elliot has a long history here. It's why his father supports our program."

"Was that why Thana agreed to do the mural?"

"Part of the reason, I'm sure."

Megan regarded the other woman. "Did Elliot visit regularly? Have any special connections?"

"He knew most everyone. We're having a special service for him next Sunday if you'd like to come."

"I'll be out of the country, but thank you."

The front door opened and closed, and Yee stood up to see who'd come in. "Joseph, we're back here. I'll be out in a few minutes." To Megan, Yee said, "Joseph and I are going into Allentown tonight to look for homeless kids. We try to go into the same city every week for two months. We hand out pillows, water, toiletries, and snacks. Eventually they come to trust us and we can help them." She smiled. "We're always looking for volunteers if the spirit moves you."

"Maybe one day. Is anyone else going with you tonight? I think I saw Joseph and another volunteer recently. They were getting gas. I didn't have a chance to say hello, but I assumed they were on their way to do work for the Mission. Such zeal." Megan wasn't actually sure they were doing mission work, but she hoped Yee would confirm the identity of the woman Joseph was with.

Yee smiled. "All the volunteers are passionate. Tonight it's just us, but sometimes other alumni or members join us, or occasionally ministers from other churches."

"This was an older woman. She works at the new yoga center. Graying hair, interesting dresser."

Yee smiled. "That would be Gina. She's not a volunteer, she's Joseph's mother." Yee glanced at the doorway, toward where Joseph was waiting. "He's been trying to get her to join us for years. I don't see it happening. Frustrating when one of your own doesn't share your beliefs. Now if you'll excuse me, we need to get packed for this evening." Yee stood.

Megan thanked her for her time. On the way out, she ran into Joseph, who was stuffing quart-sized baggies with travel-sized toothpaste, mouthwash, shampoo, soap, and granola bars. He smiled as Megan passed.

She stopped short, trying not to stare. Her mind flashed to a series of photos on Elliot's social media sites. Men partying. Drexel — a.k.a Steve Stewart — was there. And so was Joseph Muller. Megan was sure of it.

She said a quick good-bye and ran back into the rain.

THIRTY-THREE

In the truck, Megan tried to process what this meant, if anything. Elliot knew Steve — that Megan already knew. Elliot was connected to the Mission — that she hadn't known. The Mission and the Center were connected through Joseph and his mother — that she hadn't known. And Elliot, Joseph, and Steve all knew each other — that she hadn't known, either.

But what did it all mean?

Megan closed her eyes, listening to the patter of the rain and sifting through the random bits of information in her mind, looking for connections.

Two things stuck with her: the painting destroyed at the Center, and the image Marcy had painted of Elliot's face when he saw someone stalking Thana. Sadness, not fear or anger or surprise. As though he knew the stalker.

Megan dialed the Center. She tried Carly,

but Carly didn't answer. Not a surprise. She'd asked her not to return to the Center. Forbidden it, in fact. Why would she take her calls? So Megan tried Ray's numbers. He didn't answer his office phone. He picked up his cell.

"Megan, I can't talk now." He sounded out of it, depressed.

"I need to meet with you."

"I'm busy."

"Where are you?"

"You know where I am."

Megan fought to keep her voice calm. "Ray, stop being coy. Where are you?"

"Pretty birds. We should have taken care of the windows sooner."

The rain had stopped. Worms washed onto pavement during heavy rains. Worms attracted birds.

Megan hung up. She knew where Ray was.

The Center was hardly Fort Knox. Megan decided not to risk parking in the lot. She'd seen the path from the road to the walking trail when she had hiked up to the meadow, so she parked along the same unnamed road where Thana had died and climbed her way through the thicket and toward the Center. Thorns grabbed her ankles, tree branches snapped in her face, but she made her way across the stream at its narrowest point, sorry the day's storms had come when they did. She was a muddy mess.

She found the walking trail twenty minutes later and followed it toward the Center, staying under the tree line and out of site. Once the Center was in full view, she stayed under cover of the trees until she got close to the tennis courts, then she hustled to the backside of the fitness center. It took her a moment to identify the small retreats Ray had shown her, but once she figured out where they were, she found Ray's quickly. The lights were on, and Ray was standing in his tiny courtyard, staring at the ground.

Megan climbed over the fence. She knew she was a sight — between the muddy, bleeding legs, wet hair, and snagged clothing, she probably looked deranged. She took Ray's hand and led him back into the retreat room. He followed like a child.

She sat him on the chaise lounge, then used the bathroom to wash her face and clean up her legs. She kept the door open, watching her charge. Satisfied that she wasn't bleeding on the pristine décor, Megan sat next to Ray and took his hand.

"You knew all along, didn't you?"

"No. Only recently."

"You knew Maria had nothing to do with

Thana's death."

"I knew it was Elliot's fault."

"Elliot's dead."

Ray turned to her. His smile was ghostly. "Doesn't mean he wasn't to blame."

"It wasn't Thana's paintings they were after, was it?"

"She had such talent. We didn't see that when we were young because we were too caught up in ourselves, in each other. Thana was always the third wheel, the one who had to fight for attention. I don't know why I didn't see it back then. I was a fool. I think it made her who she was. That need to be noticed, to have someone love her."

"Perhaps." Megan knew memory was a dangerous thing, and revisionist history was common, but the final portrait of Thana, with all her conflicting dimensions, was coming clear.

Ray said, "Elliot used her."

Megan nodded. "Her paintings were used to transport drugs."

Ray smiled. "The paintings were mules. When she found out, she went crazy. Told Elliot to stop."

That day at her father's. He'd heard something smash, Thana claimed they'd been fighting about sales. "So she didn't know."

"No, that's why they broke up. Elliot tried to convince her he'd done them a favor, made her famous. She was aghast."

Yes — the night at Thana's father's. The timing fit.

Megan said, "He designed the frames to hold drugs between the backing and the painting." When Ray nodded, she said, "Pretty clever."

"He didn't count on Thana's art taking off. They priced the paintings in accordance with the value of the drugs, but to the outside world — and the IRS — it was her paintings fetching that kind of money. The prices her work acquired got noticed, and she started trending."

Just as her mother had explained. The high prices signaled value, and people started wanting Thana's work because they believed it had worth. "Eventually Elliot didn't need the drug money," Megan said. "The paintings were enough."

Ray stood and paced, his agitation evident. "It was too late. The pressure was on for him to continue. Thana was threatened, he was threatened."

"And the Center? It was a way to attract high-end customers, perhaps even users willing to pay the prices her art was now earning."

Ray hung his head.

"You didn't think of inviting Thana to be part of the Center's opening, did you? That's how I put it together, Ray. It was Carly who convinced you to call Thana, only it wasn't Carly either, was it? It was Gina Muller from the spa. Because her son Joseph was Elliot's partner in the drug trade, and he knew Thana was your friend. Carly didn't know that — it had to come from someone else."

Ray nodded. "Elliot and Joseph met at the Mission. They concocted this plan back when Thana's paintings were worth nothing. It grew, and Joseph became greedy. They wanted Thana planted here to attract rich people, to expand their clientele. Gina saw the opportunity and ran with it."

"Gina ruined the painting."

"She was looking for drugs. By then they knew Elliot was squirrely. He wanted out, Thana wanted out. Thana could compete as an artist — the drugs were no longer needed. But Joseph and his mother weren't going to let things end that easily."

The man following Thana had been Joseph. Elliot's sadness at seeing him was spawned by a realization that they couldn't simply walk away. Everything became clearer. Oliver Craddock's insistence that

Elliot owed money. Elliot's drug use. Elliot knew they were in too deep. That it was too late.

Megan said, "So Joseph killed them?"

Ray shrugged. "I honestly don't know who killed them. I thought it was Elliot. Now I'm not so sure."

"How did you find out about everything?"

"I grew suspicious over time, watching Elliot and Thana. Then she told me when we were together. I didn't say anything about the drugs because I didn't want to implicate the Center any more than it was already implicated. I figured Elliot would get busted for Thana's murder and that would be the end of it." He dug his fingers into his eyes and rubbed. "I was clearly wrong."

A crow swooped in front of the picture window and took off again, soaring high into the gray sky. "This really is a special place," Megan said. "These rooms, the thought that went into the Center. You did well, Ray."

"It's over. Our investors are closing in and Carly wants me out."

"Just this morning I saw the two of you together."

"A last ditch fling. I mean nothing to her. She only wants whatever she can't have."

They sat in silence for a few minutes while

outside the birds reclaimed the airways after the storm.

"Your leg is bleeding onto the chaise lounge," Ray said.

"I'd reimburse the Center, but I've been banned by Carly."

They both laughed.

"So we're no closer to the killer," Ray said.

"I think we are."

Ray looked at her sideways. "Who?"

"Not ready to say yet. Think you can drive me to my truck? I had to come here incognito." She pointed to her bleeding leg. "It's a killer of a hike."

"Sure. Until she bans me, too, I'm still a boss."

THIRTY-FOUR

Once back on the road, Megan called King on his cell phone. When he didn't answer, she tried Clover. It was Clover's day off and she answered immediately.

Clover said, "Clay's trying to reach you."

"Clover, I need you to get a hold of Bobby. Tell him to meet me at your house."

"My house? Why? What's wrong?"

"Just trust me, okay?

"Megan."

Megan sighed. "Fine. Keep an eye on your neighbors' house — the one with all the parties."

"Elliot's place."

"That's the one."

"Are his friends involved?"

"I think so. But whatever you do, don't go over. Just keep an eye on the house and get Bobby to meet me."

Megan hung up feeling jumpy, a lead weight in the pit of her stomach. She dialed

411 and asked to be connected to the Dart-ville Police Department. If she couldn't reach Bobby King, Jones and Lewis would have to do.

The house Clover shared with Bobby was empty. Megan cursed under her breath. She shouldn't have said anything; it was just like Clover to go over there.

Megan walked around back but didn't see Clover there, either. It was only midday, and all Megan heard was the hum of air condi-tioners and the slam of a car door. She rushed around front, forcing herself to walk slowly when she saw Steve Stewart in his driveway, loading a duffle bag into his car.

"Hey," Megan called. "How are you?"

Steve smiled and tipped his baseball cap in her direction. "Megan, right?"

"Right."

Steve ran up the steps to his apartment and pulled the door shut. He checked the lock before descending the steps again. His smile was relaxed, his gait easygoing, and Megan found self-doubt eating at the edges of her mind.

She recalled the pictures of Steve and El-liot and Joseph.

It had been Steve who helped Elliot empty the workshop. Elliot thought Steve was his friend. He was wary of Joseph, but Steve he trusted. Roommate, pal, business partner. Murderer.

Megan pictured the snarl on Steve's face when they discussed Thana. At the time she thought it was Thana being Thana, causing trouble, but now she saw a different image. Steve upset that Thana had broken up the party — their little money making business ruined because of her. He couldn't tell Elliot that, but he'd taken things into his own hands. Attending the Center grand opening, following Thana into her van, strangling her with the scarf Sylvia had dropped when she stormed off into the woods. Elliot didn't know. He thought Joseph — the Center stalker — was the bad guy. He trusted pal Steve.

Trusted him enough to tell him where he'd seen more paintings — at Washington Acres. So Steve had the paintings and the equipment. With Thana dead, her paintings were worth even more, so two or three good scores and he could stop working for a while. His needs were simple. Beer. A small apartment. Maybe a beach.

Bastard.

Steve smiled. The perennial frat boy looking to have a good time.

"Have you seen your neighbor?" Megan asked.

Steve opened his car door. "That really narrows it down."

"Five-five, thin, long dark hair. She was supposed to meet me here."

"Sorry." He squatted to get into the car. "I really need to leave."

Bile rose in Megan's throat. She couldn't let him go. And where the hell was Clover? Her car was here. Suddenly movement caught Megan's attention. One of the taillights was wobbling back and forth. Keep him talking, Megan thought.

Steve put the key into the ignition. "Look, I need to go. My parents are expecting me." He slammed the door shut. The engine roared. Megan choked down panic. *Think.* She saw the taillight fall and a sneaker wiggle through the opening. If she rushed the car, he'd take off, so Megan gave him a casual wave, trying not to look in the direction of Clover's foot. She got into the truck, which was between him and the street. She started the truck, a vapid smile plastered purposefully on her face.

"I totally understand. I'm sorry about Elliot," she yelled through the truck window.

"Thanks." Only Steve didn't look thankful. His face was flushed, his hands gripped the wheel. Where were the cops?

Steve peeled forward. Megan floored the gas pedal and slammed into the passenger side of his car, spinning the vehicle. It was a calculated risk but it worked. Steve started screaming at her. She ignored him, backed up, and came at the car again, careful to avoid the back end. Clover was contained. She'd be okay. The important thing was not to let him leave with her in that car.

That would be a death sentence for her friend.

Megan slammed into the car again, this time clipping the left front panel. She saw Steve trying to open the door, heard the wail of sirens. Megan pulled the truck up against his driver side, blocking his escape. She knew he owned a gun because that's how Elliot died. She just hoped to hell it wasn't within reach.

Steve pushed at the driver's side door, his face a mask of rage. When it wouldn't budge, he turned in his seat and used his feet to kick open the passenger door. Once, twice — the third kick a charm. He crawled out. Megan started her engine.

"Crazy bitch, stay back!" Steve pulled a gun from his waistband. He waved it in her direction. "Stay back or I will shoot. I've done it before. Don't push me!"

Megan threw the truck in reverse. She slammed down on the gas, aiming the truck in Steve's general direction. He pointed the gun at her windshield and she ducked, at the same time lunging the truck right at him. She heard a shot and a scream. She risked a look over the dash and saw him running out into the street, the gun still in his hand. She followed.

He took aim again. She could run him over or let him go. He wouldn't go far — he was too out of shape. But he'd been to her house when he and Elliot had broken into the barn. She couldn't risk him getting away.

"Stop!" she screamed.

He kept running.

She gunned the engine. He waved his arm and she sped up again, no hesitation. She clipped his outstretched arm with the right front side of the truck. Going fast enough to knock him down but not fast enough to kill him. The gun clattered to the ground. Megan shifted into park and hopped out of the truck. She dove for the gun just as he did, only his arm was broken.

"Crazy bitch," he said again.

Megan's lungs were heaving. She aimed the gun at Steve's chest. "Didn't your mother teach you any manners? It's *Ms.* Crazy Bitch."

Moments later two cop cars pulled into the lot. Megan had never been so happy to see Lewis and Jones. She put her hands in the air, dropping the gun, and said a prayer of gratitude.

THIRTY-FIVE

"You are one crazy lady." King hugged her close and whispered "thank you." He looked at Clover. "And where did you learn to kick out the taillights?"

"The senior center. I did a self-defense course with Bonnie."

"Well, I guess I'm glad my girlfriend hangs out with octogenarians."

"I just wish I had used some of the other moves before he threw me in the trunk." She shook her head. "I saw him leaving and wanted to stall him. I tried to talk to him, but he must have suspected something." Clover closed her eyes. "I never saw it coming."

"You should have stayed out of it," King growled.

Megan touched her friend's hand. She knew that had Clover stayed out of it, they might not have caught Thana's killer. Clover was unscathed — physically, at least — but

Megan knew the trauma of being kidnapped, even for such a short time, would play over and over in Clover's head like an unwanted movie.

King closed the door to the interrogation room. Statements had been taken and Megan and Clover were getting ready to leave.

"You okay to drive your truck?" King asked. "I can give you a ride."

Megan nodded. Her truck was barely drivable, but she'd get it home. One way or another, she wanted to go home. She'd had enough of the police for one day.

"It took courage to slam into the car that way, to chase him down," King said. "He may sue you for assault with a vehicle, but it's a suit you can defend."

Megan understood she might have some legal battles on her hands, but what else was she going to do? Let him take her friend? Let him come after her and Bibi? Not after what he'd done to Thana and Elliot.

Megan said, "Did you find Elliot's stuff in Steve's vehicle?"

"We found drugs and paintings in the car, some of which are now ruined. The Dartville PD picked up the Mullers and they had some of Elliot's things too. Your paintings weren't in the lot, Megan. They may have been sold. You can make an insurance claim. They should be worth some good money."

Megan thought of the portrait, of her face on that older woman's body. Had Thana wished things would have turned out differently? That the two of them could have accepted each other's foibles and remained friends? Perhaps. That's what she'd choose to believe.

On the way out, Clover asked her if she'd ever spoken to Clay. Megan sighed. "No, I never called him back. Been kind of busy."

"He found something in your yard."

That startled her. "What did he find?" *Please don't let it be a body.*

"Under that small hill by the big oak. A trunk of some sort. I think he wants to explain himself."

"Well, I'll be." Megan knew what that probably was. She stepped on the gas, pushing her wounded beast of a truck as fast as it would go.

By the time Megan and Clover reached Washington Acres, news of their exploits had spread. Besides the usual crowd — Bibi, Eddie, Sylvia, Clay, and Porter — Megan found Merry Chance, Roger Becker,

415

her Aunt Sarah, and Alvaro and Maria at the house. Emily was holding down things at the store, and Alvaro had made the executive decision to close the café for the remainder of the day.

Alvaro was the first to greet her. He pulled her close, hugged her tight, and then let go. No words. Over his shoulder, Megan saw Maria smile.

Bibi had reacted to the situation as Bibi always did — with food. The kitchen and dining rooms were loud and crowded, with platters of lunch meat, rolls, and baked goods on every flat surface not reachable by the dogs.

Clay accosted her in the dining room. "You need to come up to the barn."

"Not now, Clay," Megan glanced around. "Not with everyone here?"

"Why?"

"I want this to be private."

Almost two years ago, Megan found the historical letter that mentioned treasure on the property. She hadn't looked for it, hadn't really believed it was real. Now that it was, she wanted to savor the moment. She wanted to share it with Bibi and Clay and Porter and her family, no one else.

"Let's toast, then," Clay said. "To feisty

chicks who drive trucks and to senior centers."

Megan laughed. They clinked juice glasses. "And to friendships that come in all shapes and sizes."

THIRTY-SIX

Clay lifted the chest from the ground and placed it on the white sheet. It was rusty and disintegrating, the lock just a flimsy remnant of its former self. Clay clipped the lock with wire cutters and looked around at the small crowd that had gathered. Gray skies remained, and Megan was hoping for more rain that evening. For now, though, the earlier storms had broken the humidity and the evening air was pleasant.

"Do it," Bibi said. "I'll be in my grave by the time we see what's in there."

Megan lifted the lid. She stared, disbelieving, and saw similar looks of awe on the faces around her.

"Go ahead, run your hands through it."

Megan did. The gold coins felt cool and grimy and substantial.

"There could be six figures in there," Clay said.

"Maybe not that much, but a small fortune." Sylvia's eyes were wide. "Enough to help you with this farm."

"And to think, all those times I sent you to play at the old oak, you were playing on gold. This would have made your grandfather's life much different." Bibi paused. "Different, but not necessarily better."

Megan was thinking of the original owners of this gold, Paul and Elizabeth Caldbeck. Of the woman who buried it hoping her husband would return. Clearly it never happened. Did the family ever reunite? She supposed she'd never know.

"Can you help me bring it inside?" Megan asked Clay.

"Sure."

They took pictures, then stored the chest in Megan's closet. Megan tossed and turned that night, thinking about the gold and friendship, and the vagaries of fate.

When she woke, she knew what to do with the money.

"We need to get it appraised, of course, but there should be more than enough for the business," Megan said. "I did some research and under Pennsylvania law, we're the rightful owners. I'll verify that with a local lawyer. Assuming I'm right, I want to make a donation to New Beginnings, to help them continue the work that they do. But other than that, it's yours. Well, it's my father's."

Sylvia regarded her with a mixture of awe and disbelief. "You would do this for him?"

"Yes."

"He will never know. You understand that?" Sylvia leaned toward her, her gaze piercing. "He will have no idea of the sacrifice you are making for him."

"I understand."

They were sitting in the sewing room, looking at old photos of Eddie and Charlotte and young Megan. Sylvia held a photo of Eddie in her hand. He wore pleated brown trousers and a plaid shirt. A hat fell over one eye. "He was dapper even then."

Megan smiled. "He was, wasn't he?"

Sylvia was difficult and demanding and petty, but she clearly loved Eddie — and saw something in him no one else had. Perhaps her father had found his forever match after all.

Eddie and Sylvia left that evening, after a Bibi-style bonfire celebration. Megan retired for the night at nine, tired and oddly content. It'd been an eventful three weeks, but she was going to Scotland soon and she'd see Denver. Something to look forward to.

Her phone buzzed at four, waking her up.

Megan glanced at the screen expecting to see Denver's number. He'd texted her, all right: *I'M HERE. LET ME IN.*

She ran down the steps two at a time. Denver stood in the doorway wearing a dimpled grin, his arms outstretched. Megan flew into his embrace.

"I was going to surprise you," she said, elated. "I purchased a ticket to Scotland."

"Oh, yeah? How about that?" Denver kissed her. He picked her up and carried her up the stairs, toward her room. "I missed you. And when I heard what was happening back here, I knew I needed to come."

"I'm fine. But I'm so happy to see you." Megan kissed him, long and hard.

Denver paused at the top of the stairs. "We can still go to Scotland," he whispered. "Perhaps Bonnie would like to join us."

"You just want her to cook," Megan said, laughing. She kissed him again. His face was scruffy and warm and smelled like home.

"No more haggis for this Scotsman. Bonnie Birch is crossing the Atlantic. Dolores and Bonnie can fight it out."

THIRTY-SEVEN

The letter came two months later, after the gold had been counted and appraised and given away.

Megan had taken the taxes from the bounty, sent a piece of the treasure to New Beginnings to start a scholarship fund, and with Bibi's blessing, had wired the remainder to Sylvia for her father's business. The letter that arrived not long after the wire was sent was from her father. Megan opened it in the privacy of her bedroom.

The note was short. Sylvia had told Eddie about the payment to the clothing boutique. She'd confessed that the money had come from selling the treasure on the farm. He appreciated the gesture by both of them, but the money was for Megan. He was wiring it back.

Buy the Marshall House, Megan, he wrote. *You should have enough. Next time we visit, we want to stay in the new inn.*

Megan saved the letter.

Later that night, she reopened it, thinking of Maria and Alvaro and Ray and Thana and Denver and her. Perhaps each person did have someone out there who could balance their weaknesses and buoy their strengths. A significant other. A friend. A grandmother. Did it matter who the person was? She didn't think so.

Buy the Marshall House, Megan.

Perhaps she would.

ABOUT THE AUTHOR

Wendy Tyson's background in law and psychology has provided inspiration for her mysteries and thrillers. Originally from the Philadelphia area, Wendy has returned to her roots and lives there again on a micro-farm with her husband, three sons and three dogs. Wendy's short fiction has appeared in literary journals, and she's a contributing editor and columnist for *The Big Thrill* and *The Thrill Begins,* International Thriller Writers' online magazines. Wendy is the author of the Allison Campbell Mystery Series and the Greenhouse Mystery Series.

The employees of Thorndike Press hope you have enjoyed this Large Print book. All our Thorndike, Wheeler, and Kennebec Large Print titles are designed for easy reading, and all our books are made to last. Other Thorndike Press Large Print books are available at your library, through selected bookstores, or directly from us.

For information about titles, please call:
  (800) 223-1244

or visit our website at:
  gale.com/thorndike

To share your comments, please write:
  Publisher
  Thorndike Press
  10 Water St., Suite 310
  Waterville, ME 04901